Gallica's Thorns

I0777848

Derek Smith

Cushing Publishing
www.cushingpublishing.com

Chapter 1

Emily dreamed of roses.

Even as she dabbed at her bloodied lip with a Burger King napkin, she thought how glorious it would be for a florist's van to pull up in front of the trailer, a spiffy delivery boy knocking on the door, barely able to balance a magnificent arrangement.

It would be like a kind of double paycheck and a day with Lyle not hitting her, all rolled into one.

The lush blossoms would be huge and crimson and sweet scented, and no one would yell at her about how much they cost and how that money would have been better spent on baby food.

For a brief moment she would savor their aromatic ecstasy, the nausea of a soiled baby diaper wrapped around her face lost in a good time of smiles, hugs, and flowered fragrance.

Lyle had never bought her flowers; his weekly beer and cigarette budget didn't allow such extravagance. Jupiter and Pluto both would likely plummet from the heavens and whack her on the head before her husband ever dialed a florist. Toss in the cash he spent on nudie magazines, shotgun shells, and reefer and they had nothing.

Emily had rarely known better times, especially in her five-plus years of marriage to Lyle.

Any talk of prosperity in Pierpont, Georgia, in 1997 withered like burned kudzu stemming from the Hercules Tire factory's closing in 1980. About two hundred people had lost their jobs that day and the town had been on life support ever since.

She and Lyle were barely staying afloat, and her waitress' job was anything but secure. She had picked up a few extra dollars by babysitting, but that had led to trouble with Lyle, and she had been forced to stop it.

Emily clipped coupons from the newspaper inserts like it was a new religion based on two-for-one canned corn.

She always had a handful of them ready for the cashier at the Winn-Dixie. In a New York minute she would have bought cat food and passed it off for Star Kist if she thought she could fool Lyle at supper time and avoid a beating.

The muddy boots always set her to trembling. His hunting brogans perched on the back steps were like a burning bush sign that he was home and angrily drunk, seething with cheap vodka as he waited for her. A beating, or dose of "tough love," as Lyle called it, was usually imminent.

She would see the boots when she pulled into their driveway after work, the sight of them making her narrow fingers drum softly on the steering wheel. The scenario varied only with the punishment he inflicted. When she came in, he was usually half-dozing, stretched out in his smelly recliner with a tall can of malt liquor balanced on his belly, the television blaring near maximum volume.

Just seeing her walk in the house lit his fuse and torched him out of his stupor.

It had not always been like this, even though her five-year marriage to Lyle had never been anything remotely wonderful.

She had been two classes behind him at Pierpont High School, and they had started dating a few weeks into her sophomore year in the fall of 1989. Lyle was an end and defensive back on the football team - strictly second string - but that had not mattered to Emily, who was smitten by the Marlon Brando broodiness of her wavy-haired upperclassman.

Lyle wasn't bad looking and Emily always remembered how she would lie on her bed listening to CDs and looking at his photos in the school yearbooks while daydreaming of someday spending her life with him. The brown-eyed boy in the pictures had a shy but nice smile and auburn hair parted at a cowlick. He was slightly heavy and with only a few friends was not among the popular elite of his class, but Emily fell hard for him. There was an intriguing mystery behind this teenager of few words and she was enthralled.

An only child, she didn't have to worry about approving parents. Her father had walked out on her and her mother when Emily was five. Her mother had never been a well woman and already was battling a cancer that would kill her.

The PHS Class of `90 couldn't hold Lyle. He dropped out of Pierpont High two months into his senior year and got a job as a mechanic for a used car dealer just north of town. He did not tell Emily until after he left school, but it made no difference to her. Emily had never dated anyone else and convincing her heart that Lyle was her first and only love meant that she supported any decision he made.

She recalled the first time she met his parents. They walked up to the front porch of their home and there was a sound as if someone had thrown a piece of ham against a wall, punctuated by a pain-laced scream.

They had entered the house, the slam of the screen door announcing their arrival. She followed Lyle into a well-appointed den where his mother and father were suddenly frozen like mannequins in a department store window. Perry Como crooned from a massive stereo and Emily saw a half-empty bottle of bourbon on a bar in the corner. She wondered why Lyle's parents were both breathing like they had run a mile race and Mrs. Gillon was crying, mascara trickling down her cheeks as she massaged her jaw.

Her innocence at the time had prevented her from being warned, but she knew now that Lyle had inherited his violent ways from his father.

When they decided to get married, Emily sifted through bridal magazines and catalogs, imagining the elegance of their wedding despite their poorness. Emily had saved little money from her job at the Portly Pig Diner where she had worked for a couple of years. What she had, however, she gave to Lyle to help with a down payment on a used mobile home.

They were married the following summer, but there was no minister, no lacy gown or maid of honor. A county magistrate performed the ceremony in his closet-like office, substituting a Farmer's Almanac for the Bible since he had misplaced his copy of the Good Book the week before. Lyle and the judge had guffawed over the lapse, but Emily had sniffed back tears. August 5, 1992, would be an anniversary of misery.

The newlyweds had their honeymoon supper at a Pizza Hut on U.S. 63 and settled in to the Harbor Sunset Motel next door to consummate their love. Emily remembered how they joked about the name of the place since they were about three hundred miles from the ocean, the nearest water being Harry Martin's trout farm just down the road.

This was the first time Lyle hit her. It was as if the signing of the wedding papers had made her his property and suddenly, he could do with her as he pleased. He had been pounding down whiskey shots since noon and the 100 proof finally kicked in, Lyle's temperament changing as if a fuse overloaded in his brain.

One minute they were laughing and the next he had backhanded her across the face, sending her sprawling across the bed and onto the floor. In pain and shock she had staggered to her feet, staring at him with tear-drowned eyes. Before she could move, he was on her, forcing her down on the bed and ripping at her clothes. She tried to squirm from under him, but he was too strong, pinning her and threatening to hit her again if she resisted. His fist wrapped in her hair, she flashed back to how these same fingers had caressed and fondled her at the Plantation Drive-In while they were dating.

Now he took her virginity as she sobbed silently.

In the beginning Emily tried to convince herself that Lyle wasn't a bad man, but that alcohol fueled his abuse of her. There was not a mean bone in her body and this made it doubly hard for her to endure, much less understand, his attacks. Sunglasses and heavy makeup to help hide her bruises became part of her daily routine.

On one of the rare occasions when she was alone with Sarah Gillon, Emily tried to talk to her about her son. But Sarah had cut her off abruptly, telling her that she didn't want to discuss the matter. As they looked at each other through their sunglasses, Emily knew that Sarah had her own torment to endure.

The thought of calling the police briefly crossed Emily's

mind, but she quickly abandoned the idea. If Lyle spent a night or two in jail, then he'd be back and there would be hell to pay. He had two shotguns and a hunting rifle and might even use one of them on her in his fury.

Emily had given birth to Brandon the following year - in the last week of July 1993 - and it had been God's gift to all as the Gillon family's first grandchild. But the soul-searing pain of his emergence only intensified the memory of his conception. While the first cries of her son were the madrigals of angels, his creation had been a horror tale for Emily. There was no doubt in her mind when it happened, just under three months after their wedding.

It was a late October night, two days before Halloween, and the crinkled yellow, brown and orange leaves were dancing in the crisp wind coming through the mountain hollows. Emily had always loved autumn in northern Georgia, the first frost silently coating the mountain valleys in mercury. It was a time when summer finally died in a last hot flash of sweat while the foreplay of winter's first soothing temperatures sliced the heat like iced tea after torrid sex. The change of seasons had always been magical for Emily. When she was a child, her mother had told her that elves who lived deep in the forests emerged on one special night to sprinkle sugar over the farm fields and tin-roofed barns.

She would hate it after that night.

Emily was carving a small pumpkin to put on their tiny front porch when the whining tires of Lyle's pickup announced his arrival. He was roaring drunk, and Emily knew that meant a major problem for her. Lyle was a TV wrestling fan and this night he cracked a beer, stomped the pumpkin and grabbed Emily to practice wrestling moves on her.

In their brief marriage she had learned not to fight back when he beat her; to do so only agitated him more. After batting her around for about thirty minutes, he was ready for sex and forced her into the bedroom. Her innards seared as Lyle entered her, the dryness as if the devil's own pitchfork had been driven home. The reek of his whiskey breath, sweat and the grunts of his thrusting overwhelmed her.

Brandon's seed was planted amid her agony.

Their son's life journey was brief as he succumbed to myriad ailments in his sixth month. Emily had gone alone to the funeral parlor and selected the tiny casket with its light-blue lining that was to hold her baby for eternity. Her grief blurred all, the funeral, grave side service and condolences from friends and family whirling around her lost son and the part of her life he had taken with him with his final breath.

In her early years, long before this heartache, Emily had wandered through cemeteries and been especially affected by the graves of children, some who had died centuries earlier. Now she placed a rose on the freshly mounded dirt of her firstborn's last resting place.

Emily could only guess as to what thoughts floated in Lyle's head at the death of his son. He had cried mightily when the hospital doctor broke the news, but a few hours later had gone hunting and come home soused as usual. Emily had handled the funeral arrangements just as she took care of the day-to-day chores of their household. Lyle had the responsibility of a jackass who couldn't even take out the garbage, much less make plans for his baby's burial.

In the weeks that followed, Emily and Lyle rarely spoke to each other. Despite her deep sadness, Emily had hoped Brandon's death would draw them closer together, but Lyle was more distant than ever. His violence too was unabated. The hospital bills shoved them deeper into a financial hole to which Lyle seemed oblivious, refusing even to ask his parents for help.

He had always been more of a hunter than a husband and after Brandon's loss spent even more time in the woods. This was his first love regardless of the season, stalking deer, boar, wild turkey and other game birds, all abundant in the Georgia wilds. He hunted alone, most of his buddies long ago scared off by his heavy drinking and carelessness in the field. During a dove shoot the previous fall, he had nearly killed Sam Schaffer, Lyle's 12-gauge discharging as he knelt to fish his thirteenth beer of the day out of his cooler. The blast of birdshot just missed Sam's face.

Nothing like that fazed Lyle. He felt that if he worked hard, which he did, repairing and patching up lemons at "Honest Pete" Stuart's used car lot, he earned the right to play hard, which meant drinking, smoking some Mexican dirt weed and shooting at anything that moved. His hunting prowess occasionally put some venison and other game on their table, but he was never consistent.

His most precious possessions were his guns, especially a 16-gauge Remington shotgun he called "Old Lucy." Lyle had dropped an eleven-point buck with it and his dad had had a silver plate inscribed and attached to the stock to commemorate the event. Even though Lyle treasured this gun he had stumbled out of the woods in a drunken stupor on two occasions and left it behind. Fortunately for him, other hunters who knew him had found it and seeing his name on the plate, returned it.

Emily knew all about "Old Lucy" and planned to kill him with it. The beatings had become more severe, as was the look in Lyle's eyes as he whaled at her, petrifying her. She had no more love for Lyle; he had slapped that out of her long ago. In fact, her being had hardened to the point that he was an enemy who had to be eliminated.

A demonic junta seemed to possess him, and Emily felt that if she was to survive, Lyle had to die. She had no one to turn to and in the desperation of her mind there was no other way out.

Such a mindset was totally foreign to Emily. She had grown up basically fatherless but with a feeble mother who dearly loved her daughter. They baked pecan pies and watched soap operas together when they could. Her government disability checks, and Emily's job helped keep a roof over their heads and enough food to get by.

Leona Tillman was a small, feisty woman, gnarled by arthritis, but alert to the end and Emily was glad that her mother had not lived to see what a nightmare her marriage had become. Leona had met Lyle while he was dating Emily and did not mince words in her condemnation of him.

"Em, that boy will end up wiping his feet on you like a back doormat," Emily recalled of Leona's reaction. She had brushed off the bad feelings, convincing herself that her mother would eventually come to love Lyle as much as she did. Leona had not lived to see them wed and, thankfully, to Emily was not around to experience the dread and shame that Emily's drastic plan entailed.

Lyle's last dawn on Earth was the raw and cheerlessly gray Saturday after Thanksgiving, 1997. For weeks Emily had pieced together her plot, often lying awake in the dark with Lyle snoring at her side as she concentrated on how best to kill him.

Handling the gun wouldn't be a problem; her Uncle Seth on her mother's side had taken her out shooting many times when she was young. They had plinked cans off fence posts and taken pot shots at snakes curling through the waters of swampy backwaters. She learned to handle everything from a .22 rifle to the various gauges of shotguns. Uncle Seth had taught her well.

She decided to make Lyle's death look like a suicide, using Old Lucy for the deed. Deer season was in and, as usual, Lyle planned to hit the woods alone. He would hole up in his deer stand, which he had nicknamed "The Hootch," which was little more than a plywood tree house he'd built about twenty feet up in a gargantuan oak tree. The stand was in a thick brace of oak and pine on land owned by Pete Stuart, Lyle's boss.

Emily had been to The Hootch twice. She knew where Lyle parked his pickup and was familiar with the meandering path that twisted about a hundred yards to the stand. She suspected that he sometimes shacked up there with Nell Windom, a curvy bitch who had briefly worked with Emily at the Portly Pig. She and Nell had never gotten along, but the few times Lyle had been in the diner he was taken in by the depth of Nell's cleavage as she bent over to take his order. Emily guessed that she might have shared Lyle's sleeping bag in The Hootch.

Two days before Lyle was to die, Emily hid Old Lucy, removing it from the gun rack in their bedroom and hiding it in the trunk of her car. She gambled that he would not notice its absence until the morning he got up for the hunt and this proved to be the case. Lyle's drunkenness allowed only so much awareness of what was going on around him and much of that was focused on beating Emily.

Lyle smacked her across the head about 5 a.m. that Saturday and she curled into a ball under the blankets to avoid any more blows.

"Where's Old Lucy?" he stormed in the dimness of the bedroom.

"Huh? What are you talking about?"

Emily tried to sound as if she had just woken up, although she had been awake for hours, tingling with nervousness about this moment and the event to come.

"She's not in the gun rack. Where is she?"

"Well if she's not there and not in your truck, I guess you must have left her in your deer stand or out in the woods somewhere last weekend, don't you think?"

Like a scared turtle, Emily had poked her head halfway out from the covers. In the semi-darkness, she could see Lyle, clad all in camouflage, standing beside the bed. She watched him raise a canteen to his lips. A few bolts of Jack Daniels always got rid of the chill for him on these cold early mornings and were a good hair of the dog.

"She ain't in the truck. I already checked."

"One of the boys will find her and bring her home. They might even find you out there this morning and hand her right back to you."

Lyle took another pull from the canteen and seemed to ponder her words for a few seconds.

"Guess you're right." He snickered to himself. "I knew there was some reason I kept you around. Be seeing you."

Emily did not answer and was trembling as she watched him take another shotgun out of the rack. For all she knew he had discovered her plan and was toying with her before blasting her as she lay helpless. Instead, he shoved a box of shotgun shells into the pocket of his jacket and lumbered out the bedroom door. Shortly afterward she heard his truck leaving the yard and she relaxed in temporary relief.

Five minutes after Lyle's departure, she arose and showered, the hot water pulsing over her body calming and warming her in primal luxuriance. The respite was short with her mind soon whirling again with the lethal plot she had hatched.

Her mother had raised her to believe the taking of a human life was one of the most horrible acts anyone could commit. A criminal's execution was one thing, but the murder of an innocent person was extreme evil. Lyle's innocence, however, had been destroyed long ago, replaced by rabidity spawned by his father or someone else in the Gillons' ancestral chain. To her, he himself was a murderer, having killed her soul and sentenced her to a life in hell.

With this mindset, Emily believed she would have no trouble pulling the trigger, Old Lucy serving as the exorcist.

Emily waited until the sun's gray light was clawing through the trees atop Tatum's Mountain before she headed out. She wasn't trying to sneak up on Lyle; to the contrary, she wanted him to know she was coming so that he wouldn't mistake her for a deer and open fire from his stand.

The air was frosty and the white grass crunched under her old cowboy boots as she locked the trailer and walked out to her car, a mole-brown Ford Escort that Pete Stuart had given Lyle for little or nothing. It needed an engine overhaul, brakes, tires and new radiator but it still got her around.

Pierpont seemed to be sleeping in this cold Saturday, and there were few other cars or people to be seen as she drove down Main Street. The town, county seat of Bratton County, had a population of about 2,000, two stoplights, six churches and three funeral homes, counting the two for whites and the one for the few blacks who lived there. Pierpont was named for a local patriot who had been killed in a skirmish with the British in the American Revolution and whose family had remained in the area, running a ferry over the Hookachee River.

With the Hercules plant gone there was little industry,

and the population that had topped out around 5,000 in the mid-1960s, was continuing to plummet as the young people left for jobs elsewhere, especially in nearby Atlanta and Chattanooga.

Farmers grew corn and wheat in the postcard-perfect sloping fields sliced by bastions of pine, oak, elm and sweet gum. Reigning over all was Tatum's Mountain and surrounding lesser peaks and ridges, nature's kings mutely surveying the countless human dramas played out below them.

None of this clouded Emily's brain this morning.

As the Escort scuttled into the countryside, she thought of buckshot and revenge.

Lyle rubbed his hands over his hissing Coleman lantern and squinted to see any movement in the trees or in the sallow farm field within his shotgun range from The Hootch. The whiskey coursing in his veins kept him warm, but the sight of a fine buck with a big-ass rack would make him sizzle like a July Fourth sparkler.

He was steamed about Old Lucy and could have sworn that he put her back in his pickup after last weekend's hunt but, like everything else, life was blurred in an alcohol semi-coma. And Em would have to pay as she did almost nightly. With no deer in sight, he looked around his 8x8-foot stand. He'd tried to spruce up The Hootch with a few girlie magazine photos stapled to the plywood walls, a small radio, candle and the sleeping bag that he opened and spread on the floor.

Nell the waitress had liked that touch, even though she hadn't been keen on climbing the wood slats up the tree. They had smoked a couple of joints and screwed on two different weekends at The Hootch, but it was likely over. Lyle had accused her of stealing reefer from his stash and slapped her when she sassed him in response. She had spit in his face and left, and while she was a good lay, he wouldn't miss her as long as he had his Hootch and his liquid courage.

Other than the marijuana, his daddy had made it through life this way and Lyle figured it was good enough for him too.

Thirty minutes or so after leaving home, Emily parked beside Lyle's pickup and pulled Old Lucy from the trunk. The shotgun was loaded with three shells of .16-gauge buckshot she had taken from a box in Lyle's closet. Her stomach roiled, but there was no turning back now, not that she had any intention of doing so. Dark clouds still shrouded the sky, fittingly somber for the deed before her.

She heard pops of gunfire somewhere in the distance. Bratton County teemed with deer and hunters were plentiful as well during the season. It seemed like everyone had a freezer full of venison steaks and many a living room or den had a nice trophy rack of antlers cut from the head of some luckless buck.

The local newspaper frequently had photos of proud sportsmen posing with their dead prey. Emily believed most of them were gutless yahoos like Lyle although she never voiced her thoughts to him. The gunshots she heard, however, were a blessing for her, meaning that the blast that killed Lyle would be lost among many. She had considered faking a suicide note, but abandoned the idea as too risky.

With the Remington cradled in her arms, she leaned against the car, closed her eyes and took a deep breath. The temperature had not budged above freezing since dawn and the cold air poured into her lungs as if she had inhaled a milk shake.

Now she started through the trees and down a leaf-carpeted trail, which was no wider than a hunting dog. She guessed The Hootch was about one hundred yards from where they parked, and with the shotgun slung over her shoulder, she trudged along the path, intentionally cracking twigs and branches to announce her approach.

If Lyle wanted to kill her, this would be his time to do it. He could splatter her all over the forest and claim it was an accident, believing she was a deer. How did he know she would be traipsing around out there?

Hunting mishaps and tragedies were commonplace in Bratton County. Hunters fell out of deer stands or mishandled guns or simply fired at a swaying bush or sharp sound, not waiting to see if it was man or game. The careless, or those like Lyle who drank to excess, had done in more than a few buddies.

Emily recalled the handsome but pimply-faced teenager at the Winn-Dixie who bagged her groceries with one hand after losing most of the other one. He had been dove hunting with friends, one of whom was horsing around with his shotgun. The boy had yanked the trigger, thinking the gun was unloaded, and an iron snowball of birdshot had ripped off three of the bag boy's fingers.

Emily brushed aside a pine branch and saw The Hootch perched in the trees ahead. She whispered a quick prayer that Lyle was up there alone. If Nell was with him, she would probably shoot them both; the plot would be over and Georgia's Death Row would be her new address.

She reached the base of the big oak, not hearing or seeing anything above her.

Lyle had heard her coming and had playfully drawn a bead on her as she wended her way among the trees. "Pow," he whispered to himself, pretending that his gun recoiled into his shoulder as he dropped her like a prize buck.

Below, Emily peered up and saw the lantern's glow through the stand's entrance. To her relief, she sensed that Lyle was alone.

"Lyle, it's Em. I'm coming up," she called in a low voice. There was no response, but she knew that he'd heard her.

Tomboyish all her life, she gripped the first slat and climbed the tree, Old Lucy dangling heavily on her shoulder.

The smell of Slim Jim farts, cigarettes, and burnt kerosene assailed her nostrils as her head poked up through the hole cut in the Hootch floor. Lyle was hunched on a plastic milk crate in a corner, the lantern beside him and his other shotgun resting across his lap. "So what in the hell are you doing here?" he muttered, taking a long draw on his Winston.

"One of the boys brought Old Lucy by the house. Said

you'd left her out in the woods again and they were good enough to return her." She forced a smile as she climbed into the stand and faced him. "Just like we figured, right?"

"You ain't answered my question, woman. Why the fuck did you come out here?"

"Lyle, no need to get bent out of shape. I just thought you might want Old Lucy with you, she being your best gun and all."

To her surprise, Lyle seemed to relax. He sagged on his seat and wearily rubbed his face.

"That was real sweet of you, Em. I ain't the best husband in the world and you sure know that. Why the hell you've stayed with me I sure don't know."

Emily melted like ice in a Dixie August. Lyle seemed vulnerable and innocent and grateful and suddenly there was hope for them to regain their marriage and make it work.

She began to cry, pent-up emotions flooding the words to her mouth, and she listened almost as a third person as she blurted out her plan. She spoke from the heart even while her brain told her she was signing her death warrant.

Emily poured out her being and stood sobbing, leaning on Old Lucy for support. For a few tense seconds the deer stand and clutching woods were quiet. Lyle rose from the milk crate, his face darkening as if eclipsed by the sun, and the familiar glower that preceded his "rough love" savagery contorted his features. This time, however, his eyes spat hatred like overflowing lava.

"So you came out here to kill me, is that what I'm hearing, Em? You think I abuse you and you're just going to blow me away with my own gun, is that it?"

He reached out and hit her across the face, Emily yelping in pain and staggering backwards.

"No, Lyle, don't"

"You ain't seen nothing yet, woman." He drew a hunting knife from his vest. "In fact, I believe I'll just carve up your ungrateful ass right now."

Lyle's slap, however, had reawakened Emily to her original intent. Always, she had resisted primeval urges to resist, believing it would worsen the beating. Now it meant her survival.

She sidestepped as Lyle lunged at her with the knife, the whiskey slowing his reflexes even in the Hootch's close confines.

"I'm gonna slice your throat, whore," he seethed through gritted teeth, Emily blocking the blade's thrust with Old Lucy's barrel. She was done begging now and the rage from hundreds of nights of battering consumed her.

Lyle stumbled over the milk crate, momentarily losing his balance and Emily had her opening. She kneed him as he tried to regain his footing, the blow catching him in the throat.

Coughing and gasping for breath, Lyle sank to the floor on his back, his face turning pink. His eyes, flashing a twisted arrogance moments before, now betrayed helpless fear when Emily stepped over him and chambered a round in Old Lucy. There was no pity, hesitation or second-guessing as she bent over him and placed the gun barrel in his mouth.

Wild-eyed now, Lyle raised his head, Old Lucy's maw bulging in his cheek. She studied him for a few seconds before her years of suffering pulled the trigger.

Emily cringed, eyes closed, as the shotgun deafened her. With the roar's echo dying an instant later she beheld her carnage.

A grotesque bouquet of red now garnished the Hootch's back wall, dark blood, bits of skull and brain matter streaming slowly toward the floor. Beneath her, Lyle had been transformed into a hideous, headless corpse.

Emily dropped Old Lucy, the gun plopping softly between Lyle's spread-eagled legs. Choking back the vomit that burned her throat, she climbed out of the deer stand and, seeing no one else around, staggered back to her car.

In an instant The Hootch had become a mosaic of desperate murder. Two lives had finally been flung apart, one cast into death's abyss, the other to resume her existence with bloodied hands.

Chapter 2

"**H**oney, you are cuter than a mess of newborn puppies."

Emily squirmed on her chair and mustered a faint smile for the man and his pickup attempt.

That line might work on some fresh-off-the-farm bimbo, buddy, but you're playing with more than you can handle.

"Why don't you let me freshen up that drink of yours?"

The Cotton Boll Lounge was one of Savannah's most popular watering holes, and was crowded with happy hour patrons this late afternoon.

Almost a year had passed since she killed Lyle. After six months of feigned mourning and recovery, she had left Pierpont and moved to Savannah, about three hundred miles away on the Georgia coast. She had played the part of a grieving widow, even though her life had brightened considerably without Lyle. Emily had killed to live, and while her last vision of Lyle's body in the Hootch would endure forever, she was much better off because she had pulled the trigger.

Pierpont had been shocked by Lyle's suicide, but those who knew of his around-the-clock drinking were not especially surprised that his life had ended that way. His parents, however, refused to believe that Lyle would turn a gun on himself.

Treat Gillon in particular wouldn't budge from his contention that his son was murdered. The county sheriff and his chief deputy talked to Emily about Lyle's death, but their questions were more about his state of mind than of a suspicious nature. Despite no suicide note, the case was ruled a suicide, by the county coroner and the investigation was closed, at least as far as the authorities were concerned.

Treat was another matter altogether. He swore to find his son's killer if it took to the end of his days to do it, and Emily knew that he was looking squarely at her.

The afternoon of Lyle's funeral was as overcast as his death day, a distant, low rumble of rare winter thunder offering a fitting dirge for the occasion. It had been a closed casket ceremony, obviously, since Lyle did not have a head or face to gaze upon. The funeral home limousines had reminded Emily of sluggish black eels as they inched away from the church and out to the cemetery.

She had not ridden in the limo with the immediate family, instead, sharing a seat with Lyle's senile great-aunt Shirley, who was absorbed in a crossword puzzle book, and assorted cousins in the second car. At the graveside, Treat had stared at her over the casket before it was lowered. His eyes offered no anguish or grief - it was a glare of accusation and betrayal - betrayal of a hushed-up, behind-the-blinds lifestyle that he felt she had violated by killing his son.

Treat's lack of remorse and acceptance made it even easier for Emily on her return trip to the cemetery that night. As she hiked her skirt and shimmied out of her pantyhose, she thought of Treat and his shotgun-beheaded son and the myriad tortures that Lyle had inflicted upon her.

She closed her eyes and relaxed, her water spattering over the lavish flowers adorning her husband's grave.

Unexpectedly, Emily had come into some money from an insurance policy that Lyle had bought from a pretty insurance agent who had dropped by Pete Stuart's dealership. Through the grapevine, Emily had learned that Lyle had listed her as his beneficiary but also told the agent that his marriage was on the rocks. Even though he had committed suicide, enough time had passed so that Emily received a check for $20,000. The money had spurred her to make a fresh start in Savannah.

Nothing held her to Bratton County other than the graves of her mother and baby, and she decided to leave. There wasn't anything about Pierpont that she liked, and if it was swallowed into the Earth's deepest depths tomorrow she wouldn't bat an eye. Savannah was a city and was far enough away that she would never have to see or hear about Pierpont ever again.

Without telling Lyle's parents, she rented a U-Haul trailer, packed her few belongings and drove herself to Savannah. With no place to stay, she spent eight nights at a rundown motel on Ogeechee Road, watching pencil-thin hookers, reeking of rot-gut whiskey, trying to flag down truckers from the roadside.

Savannah itself was a city of majesty and history, having survived hurricanes, fires and war. English soldier and adventurer James Oglethorpe had established a settlement here in 1733 and laid out a grid of city squares south from the Savannah River bluffs where he landed. Now each of the squares was an oasis of azalea bushes, burbling fountains and kingly oaks whose twisted branches were lavished with necklaces of Spanish moss. British troops held the city for most of the American Revolution and a 1779 siege had resulted in one of the bloodiest battles of the conflict. In the Civil War, General William Sherman had ended his epic "March to the Sea" by occupying Savannah and spared it the torch that had devastated Atlanta at the beginning of his trek.

The shady downtown avenues were guarded by grand-pillared mansions and townhouses, many with historic pedigrees, everything capturing Emily's fascination as she explored her new home.

She found a furnished, one-bedroom apartment in the newspaper classifieds and, after seeing the place with the landlord, decided to rent it. The apartment was in east Savannah, on a dirt lane just off Bryan Street and she loved it from the moment she stepped through the front door. The landlord, who introduced herself only as "Miss Alma," was a tough-edged woman who looked like she had been "rode hard and put up wet," as the Southern saying went.

With an economy of words she bluntly told Emily that her monthly rent was non-negotiable and had best be paid on time. Two gay men had lived there for a number of years and when one of them died, his heartbroken mate had decided to return North, leaving behind Savannah and its memories. The lovers had taken great pride in their home, covering one of the living room walls with a wondrous painting of a garden, with elaborate trellises, bird baths with cardinals and bluebirds sweeping down, and luxurious banks of the pink azaleas for which Savannah was noted.

They had painted the scene themselves and Emily saw that Miss Alma had taken great pains to overcoat two cupids screwing near a waterfall. The cover-up had not worked and the fornicating cherubs were still visible through several coats of whitewash, making it appear that they were making out in a fog.

"I liked those boys, even though they were fags," Miss Alma sighed. "They were always on time with the rent, but I declare why they had to desecrate my wall like that I just don't know. Valentine's Day ain't never the same now."

After moving in, Emily pushed a high-back chair against the wall to further block her view of the cupids.

The insurance check had given her a bit of a financial cushion, but Emily still had to find a job pretty quickly after getting her apartment. It was not long in coming.

She was a good waitress and a walk down Broughton Street in the heart of Savannah's business district, soon brought her to the Zackias Deli, a shoebox Greek eatery with four small tables on the sidewalk. The "Help Wanted" sign in the front window nudged her inside, where she met the owner, Nick Mastapoulos, a swarthy, second-generation Greek immigrant in his upper forties, Emily guessed.

In none-too-perfect English fragmented like fine china, he asked her several questions about her background, but she already knew she had the job, their eye contact cementing the deal. There was nothing romantic about it, but each instantly liked and trusted the other and Emily went to work at the Zackias Deli the next day.

"Haven't I seen you in here before?"

Her would-be suitor was not giving up despite her lack of interest. "You staring off into space like that makes me think you don't like me, sugar lips."

Emily swiveled on her seat and looked at him, her left eyebrow arched. Even as a child, when she scrunched her features into this look her mother had told others to back off, rather than endure her daughter's ire. Lyle had beaten the spirit out of her over the years, but now it was gradually returning.

Emily had endured dozens of come-ons in the bars, no one enticing her into a one-night screw. This faceless loser would be no different. Lyle's fists had also hammered away any flirtatious notions she had ever known, no man she had met in widowhood being able to even begin to unlace her mental chastity belt.

"Name's Ed Browling, Southeastern Frame Metal Interiors, Inc."

Emily stared at him wordlessly, twisting a red cocktail straw around her fingers as she had done in a hundred other similar encounters. Something was different this time, however.

Something about Browling conjured deeply buried recollections of her father. Her memories of him were of a fuzzy, yellowed snapshot variety since he left while she was still in kindergarten. The Thanksgiving pageant was most vivid to her. Emily and her classmates had made costumes with construction paper and white glue, the pre-schoolers divided equally as Pilgrims, Indians and turkeys.

The kindergarten's small assembly room had been packed with parents, many squatting uncomfortably on the children's little chairs, and the radiator was throbbing on high, making everyone unseasonably warm despite an icy November wind groaning outside the frosted windows.

Emily had been a squaw, with a crayon-decorated headband and feather that flopped over her head, refusing to remain upright. Her mother had bought a plain brown dress especially for her to wear in the play, despite the fact that she had no lines other than to shout, "Welcome to our Pilgrim friends!" in chorus with some of the other Indians.

As she had stood rigidly around the feast table on stage that day, she had glanced out into the audience, vainly trying to find her parents. Not until the kindergartners had bunched together for the grand-finale singing of God Bless America had she spotted them near the middle of the room, her sudden exhilaration resulting in a little squeal that drew a quick glare from the teacher.

Her father had never been home much, long-distance truckers never were, but on this Monday before Thanksgiving, her dad had come to share in her big day, a moment Emily would cherish forever. Leona was at his side, wearing a navy wool suit with a fake black fur collar and too much rouge that made the rest of her face appear even more sallow.

Leona had always been there for Emily and would be until she wheezed her last breath, but this attention from a daddy she barely knew had been gold magnified, a doll's treasured dress to be carefully folded away, meant to last for the ages.

Afterward, Leona alone had met her to take her home, hugging her and telling her how much she and her father had enjoyed the play and how proud they were of her.

"Where's daddy?" Emily had whined.

"Oh, he had some business to take care of. Maybe we'll see him later," Leona replied.

Thanksgiving dawned three days later and Emily still had not seen her father. She and her mother spent the day with her Uncle Seth and Aunt Carolyn and their kids in neighboring Harker County, but her daddy had seemingly vanished from the Earth's face.

Emily remembered crying a lot and the smell of her aunt's onion dressing for years afterward had triggered memories of that day. Other than her mother's boundless love there had been little to be thankful for and even that had not registered in her five-year-old head.

Daddy wasn't there; had never been really, in her young life, but his appearance at her play had given her faint hope that he would suddenly materialize and be a what's-for-supper-at 6-pm. kind of father, like all the wonderful parents she saw on television. Her young mind's images of him were elusive shadows - the scent of Vitalis hair tonic, sweat and cigarettes, strong brown hands and arms holding her close to the ceiling, a glimmer of white teeth and sharp laughter. She vaguely recalled his tractor-trailer being parked in the edge of their yard.

Emily never saw her father again after the Thanksgiving

pageant. For weeks afterward she asked her mother about him, only to meet with harsh, red-faced looks hidden behind wads of Kleenex.

Now, as lascivious Ed Browling innocently tried to make his move on her, Emily snapped.

"You don't talk much, but I sure do like what you're wearing," he said, hoisting her sun dress with his leer. Lost years and timeless feelings of neglect boiled out and over and Emily grabbed someone's mug of beer off the bar.

"You like what I'm wearing?" she screamed. "Well wear this!" Splashing the drink in his face, Emily grabbed her purse and stalked out of the place.

George Wallace was waiting for her. He was looking sharp when the deadbolt's clinking signaled Emily's return home. He enticingly lay on his back so that he would be the first thing she saw when she opened the door.

Emily barreled in, still incensed from her bar blowup, and flung her purse at the couch, the door banging shut behind her. Not wanting to intrude or be hurt, George Wallace dashed to a window ledge where he immediately busied himself licking his privates.

Emily was madder at herself than anything else. Sure Browling was an old pervert, but he hadn't really given her any reason to react the way she did. She kicked her sandals into a corner and, ignoring George Wallace's meow for attention, headed into the tiny kitchen to get a glass of grape Kool-Aid - she always kept a pitcher of it mixed and cooling in the refrigerator.

She felt George Wallace brushing around her ankles and reached down to stroke his back. They had been together for about two months, ever since the morning she had first seen the black and white cat sniffing around her garbage can on the lane behind her apartment. She ignored him at first, hoping he would go away, but he was there the next day, peering up at her with knowing golden eyes and purring as if they had been companions for years.

When he did not appear in the lane on the third day when she went out, she reasoned that he had gone home, but then became worried that he might have gotten killed or hurt. Besides, what kind of owner - if the cat wasn't a stray - would let their animal roam free in downtown Savannah with all the traffic.

Emily had had an ornery tabby cat named Rufus that someone had given the family when she was about eight. But all he seemed to want to do was spray or claw the living room furniture and Leona had finally given him away to the Sobiski family, whom Leona despised anyway. "I hope your bladder is nice and full and that you go all over Libby Sobiski's new shag carpet," Emily remembered her mother whispering to Rufus moments before they arrived at the Sobiskis.

This alley cat didn't seem to act at all like old Rufus and if he did show again, Emily had decided to grab him for her own. To her excitement, the cat darted up that night when she arrived home from work. He offered no resistance when she scooped him up and carried him inside, smelling everything with minute care, almost instantly comfortable as king of his new three-room universe.

Fluffy, Boots, Mr. Kitty or Princess. Emily mulled over several names, but wanted something unique. She settled on George Wallace after the controversial Alabama governor and presidential candidate. Leona had admired Wallace because he had been a firebrand segregationist who, after being shot and partially paralyzed, claimed to change his ways and worked for harmonious relations between blacks and whites.

Her cat's fur colors allowed Emily to honor her mother, the late governor and good will among races while giving her a name to scream when the feline tried to squat in her potted tomato plant.

Yet even George Wallace the lap cat could not soothe Emily's frustration this night. She was a single woman in Savannah with no worldly knowledge about dating, or playing hard to get, or bar flirting or men in general for that matter. Minus Lyle, she was a virgin at age 24, innocent of life for the most part, other than the dark side he had bestowed upon her and she, terribly and finally, on him.

She tried to convince herself that she wanted to be swallowed by Savannah's decadence, where gay men kissed and caressed in the squares and streetwalkers lured seamen from Denmark to Hong Kong for $20 orgasms in the shadows.

Deep down, Emily abhorred the seamy side, but the many bars on River Street, overlooking the Savannah River, were always alive with music and dancing and folks from all over creation and a drinks-with-little-umbrellas vivaciousness that she had never before experienced. Including Savannahians, she had met people from almost every state and two dozen countries - tourists, servicemen stationed nearby or sailors whose ships were coming in or leaving the port with cargoes of every description.

She had danced with Marines, Rangers and Seals, most of them really young and really muscular and really naïve, but on leave and hell-bent on a high-beer-casualty count and maybe getting laid. She had been felt up, kissed and propositioned and had yet to spread her legs for anyone.

"You heard about seek and destroy missions?" a fine-looking soldier from Olathe, Kansas, had told her. "My mission is to seek and screw." A Finnish first mate had wanted to suck her toes and a city alderman blitzed on Fuzzy Navels had solemnly pleaded for her to spank him with his Oriental fan collection.

Emily was never fazed. Lyle had kept her in a mind-scarring cocoon of abusive violence from which she had emerged - with Old Lucy's help - but would likely not heal.

Five days a week - Tuesday through Saturday - she worked at the deli from 10 a.m. to 7 p.m. Mastapoulos was the cook while Emily waitressed and worked the cash register. The place was closed on Sundays and Nick used an assortment of temporary waitresses on Mondays. He went through a succession of busboys, none of whom lasted very long. Emily would have gladly worked on Mondays too, but Nick said that some of the other girls needed the extra money.

Nick was good-natured, always with a smile, and best of all, did not ask her many questions about her background. It wasn't that he wasn't interest; he always seemed absorbed by whatever she shared with him, but she sensed that he did not want to pry and risk making her uneasy. Some nights after closing they would sit out at one of the sidewalk tables, talking and watching the passing people and traffic on Broughton Street.

Nick soon became like an older brother to her although they did not socialize away from work. His parents had come to the States just after World War II and settled in Brooklyn where he was born. While in the Army he had been stationed at Fort Stewart near Hinesville, about fifty miles south of Savannah. He had fallen for a local girl, gotten married and stayed down South after his discharge. The marriage had lasted only three years, doomed by their lack of money and Nick's lack of acceptance by his wife's parents. When she walked out on him, there had been much more relief than sadness, the fact that they had been childless even more of a blessing.

Nick had worked in several Savannah restaurants and when his father died four years earlier he had used some of his modest inheritance to open his own eatery. The Zakias would never make him rich, but his sumptuous gyros had earned him a solid base of loyal customers, most of whom jammed the place at lunchtime.

A waitress, at least as Emily saw it, had to be equal parts flirt, diplomat and marathon runner. A well-placed wink here and there could be rewarded with a more generous tip, as could a killer smile or compliment about a banker's colorful necktie, a woman's new purse or jewelry or a regular's change of hairstyle. Many of their diners knew Emily by name and vice versa, but she was careful not to get to know anyone too well. Nick would not have had a problem if she dated a customer, but this was her own unwritten rule, a measure to help her keep her distance from any and everyone.

In good weather, she walked to and from work, a distance of about ten blocks, even though Nick always offered her a ride home. Her car seemed to be on life support, belching clouds of purple smoke and rattling like ball bearings thrown into a washing machine but it was still moving. Not wanting to press her luck, Emily drove it sparingly.

Sometimes after work or on Sunday afternoons she would stop in at the Cotton Boll. She was friendly with a couple of the waitresses there and they would slip her a free drink every now and then. It was here that she met the Ed Browlings of the world, their brains usually in their pants and looking to get lucky with any half-decent-looking female who would give them the time of day. If she went out on Saturday nights, her payday, it was usually down to River Street where the bars were hopping.

So it was that Emily immersed herself in her new life, as if baptized in Lyle's blood and emerging tainted but reborn. The busy, small-town tongues of Pierpont might as well be wagging in Outer Mongolia for all she cared or worried about.

Once in a blue moon her mind crossed to the Gillons and the pain and hurt and fear and anger that twisted their everyday lives as routinely as Tuesday night pot roast graced their dinner table. There was no doubt in her mind that Treat Gillon was a wife beater and that Lyle's evil had been absorbed from his dad. It wasn't some father-son ritual, like backyard baseball or building a model airplane together. Yet Lyle had been mentally maimed and no one had been spared the tragedy.

If Emily thought about anyone the most it was Sarah Gillon - how she had suffered probably years of abuse from Treat and then denied to herself and anyone else that anything was wrong or that her son was cut from the same rotten cloth. Emily had gone through a time where she blamed herself for the violence; she obviously was doing something terribly wrong in their marriage to elicit such awful fury from Lyle.

Whenever she could get an Atlanta or Chattanooga newspaper she read the advice column "Ask Aunt Agnes," and over the course of a year or so had seen other women in similar situations be advised to get counseling, call the police or get out. Emily knew that the last two recommendations would be death sentences for her. The law wouldn't hold him, and to leave Lyle would mean to become his prey, another animal to be hunted, likely to take a bullet in the parking lot of a grocery store or movie theater or even sitting at a red light.

"Why don't we find a marriage counselor," she had asked him one night, bringing out one of Agnes's columns she had cut out of the paper. 'Desperate in Des Moines' sounds a lot like us." She had kept the article neatly folded in the bottom of her jewelry box for three weeks, finally building the nerve to show it to him. Lyle had been sprawled on the couch watching TV, or at least appearing to, since his eyes were half closed in a self-induced Jim Beam coma. The front of his T-shirt was stained and smelly from where he had vomited on himself after leaving a bar earlier. He hadn't told her this, but he had done it so often before that Emily knew what had happened. Harrv the bartender had put out pretzels again, she judged from the brown, shuddering in the thought.

Lyle's eyes had fluttered open as she stood over him.

"Honey, please read this for me."

Lyle had staggered to his feet and snatched the clipping from her, tearing it in his carelessness, and glared at Agnes' stamp-sized photo at the top of the column.

"Well this bitch has got some big hair, but I'd still ream her," he slurred, swaying. "Since she ain't here, I guess it's your turn."

He had raped her with a mop handle that night as she screamed into a pillow and prayed to any god listening for his death.

Thoughts of that night and infinite others just as bad were buried deep in her head, like an ugly dress hanging in the back of the closet. She was bitter that the Gillons had protected their son as they did and sometimes found herself wondering if she would have done the same if Brandon had lived and matured into his own version of Lyle.

Sometimes, lying alone in her bedroom's blackness, amid the delirium of near sleep, she envisioned sitting across the dinner table from a grown-up Brandon and his wife. It would be a fancy affair at the Gillons although her semi-dream never included Lyle.

With his chocolate eyes, just like his daddy's, Brandon

gazed at her over the twinkling crystal and her motherhood would, for a moment, be a heaven of harps and singing angels.

Then she looked at Brandon's wife. Nameless and faceless, the girl stared back at her from behind oversized sunglasses, as if she were another Sarah Gillon, cooking a fine dinner and entertaining perfectly only to submit to a caveman's brutality when the guests had left and there was no one to hear her begging and tortured whimpers echoing through the big house. All this due to the binding, trapping ring on her finger, an awesome rock that Treat had slipped on her hand as if sliding a glittering rope around her pretty neck.

Thoughts of devotion, faith and fidelity swirled in a haze of shocked pain, blood and swelling and Emily always awoke terrified in the moment, gasping for air and shielding her face with her arms against an attack in her mind.

Whenever this vision came, she always wanted Brandon to grow up strong, but compassionate and warm, as if trying to change the end of a bad movie. It had been a loss only a mother could suffer when he died, but as she finally drifted asleep on these nights, she soothed herself with the thought that it was best that her son had gone to the grave so early, rather than perpetuate the violence.

Chapter 3

"**S**o this is George Wallace," the young black aide said, petting the cat's head. "How'd he get here from Alabama? Ride the bus with Rosa Parks?" Emily and Tiffany Bryant laughed together as they both held the feline crouching on the stainless steel tabletop.

"I think the Klan dropped George off at my house to get even with me because Dave Justice was my favorite Atlanta Brave," Emily said. "It was cheaper and easier than burning a cross."

Tif had wandered in for lunch one day and had clicked instantly with Emily. Now she was a deli regular, Emily always piling extra dill pickle slices on her plate. Tif was a veterinary assistant at the Yamacraw Animal Clinic, so when talk got around to pets, she had been very interested in George Wallace. She convinced Emily to bring him in for a checkup, assuring her that the cost of the exam and his annual shots would be taken care of by her connections with the Humane Society. Emily had reluctantly made the appointment for a January day in 1999, knowing that her sparse checking account couldn't handle such an expense.

It was on a Saturday morning that Emily grabbed George as he lay curled and unsuspecting on the rug where the sun always came in that time of day. Emily had prepared for this big moment the night before, punching dozens of ice pick holes in the top of a Peter Pan peanut butter box she found behind the corner grocery. Before sleepy George could react, he was inside, sniffing smooth and crunchy and listening to Emily rip swatches of duct tape to seal the cardboard flaps.

The vet, Dr. Wellesley Craven, was well past retirement age, Tif joking that God told him not to neuter or spay the animals on Noah's Ark. But fifty-plus years in the business gave him a soothing style and touch with George Wallace that comforted Emily as much as her cat, despite the thermometer protruding from under G.W.'s tail. Craven suggested heart worm medicine and after the exam, Tif gave Emily some free prescription samples at the front desk as G.W. meowed mournfully from his box at her side.

"Come on by the deli, Tuesday, Tif, I'll be there and Nick is trying out a new sandwich," Emily called as she opened the reception area door, checking her wristwatch while balancing the cat box. "I definitely owe you. Call me..."

She collided with someone, momentarily losing her grip, but the someone steadied the box in her hands.

"I'm really sorry, miss, I wasn't looking where I was going."

Emily regained herself, slightly angered, and whipped her head up to see the klutz while G.W. excitedly clawed at his cardboard cell.

The man was good looking, no movie star, but well proportioned and in a red and black flannel shirt. Past that, Emily didn't register. She was in a hurry.

"I hope your kitty's okay."

"I'm sure he is. Thanks."

Emily carried the box out to her car and put G.W. in the backseat, his scratching continuing with more vigor.

"I'll let you out as soon as we get home, baby," she cooed to him. She had to hustle. Nick would be waiting for her, and even though she had told him she had a vet appointment and might be a little late, the Saturday lunch crowd would never wait. As she backed out of the parking lot, she glanced back at the vet's office, but the man had disappeared.

"So tell me about your coleslaw."

Emily was balancing five dirty plates on her arm and trying to take this table's order from memory. She had been in a non-stop, no-break waitressing frenzy since she got to work and now some grease-ball guy with white, hairy legs and sandals wanted to know the history of coleslaw.

"Sir, I can't tell you the exact ingredients, but I'm sure you'll like it."

White Legs was enjoying her predicament as he mulled over the menu.

"I see. So perhaps I should order the potato salad instead?"

"I'll tell you what, sir. I'll give you a minute or two to decide and come back to take your order."

"No, no, that's not necessary. Just give me a second."

"I'll be right back."

Emily bolted for the kitchen before he could reply, bashing through the swinging door where Nick was immersed in his daily lunch turmoil. He was cooking sliced mutton, dicing vegetables and making iced tea simultaneously, rushing about the closet-like kitchen as if possessed by a food demon.

"I've got a cockroach complaint at table three," she said nonchalantly.

"You please give them what they want, then, okay?" Nick answered, not looking up from his cutting board. "Walter is a good friend to have."

Emily hoisted two plates for table six and then reached up on a shelf to snatch something from deep in the corner.

"Walter needs a raise, Nick. At least minimum wage."

"Yes, maybe."

She backed out the door into the dining area, catching a glimpse of White Legs glaring at her. She served the folks at table six, a local couple who had recently moved to Savannah from Maryland, and, offering her best fake smile, she sashayed back to number three. White Legs was watching her all the way, slowly drumming his fingers on the tabletop. He had been so obnoxious earlier that Emily hadn't really noticed a plump woman and a boy she guessed to be about ten sitting across from him.

"Just shuffle on over her anytime you're ready, honey," White Legs said with a sneer. "If we were up in Jersey, I'd light a fire under your butt."

"So would y'all like to order now?"

Emily's smile was mint julep sweet and bogus enough to set off White Legs.

"Listen up, trailer trash, you don't know who you're dealing with. I own..."

"Uhhhhhhh." Emily closed her eyes and rotated her neck. "I knew they'd come back."

The White Legs family was frozen in their chairs, watching her.

"The exterminator said if we can't control the rats, we'll have bugs in everything too."

With Walter in her hand, Emily reached behind her back as if to pull him out of the top of her shirt. "Well there's the little culprit," she said flicking a dark object to the floor.

The White Legs leaned in unison to see the five-inch-long cockroach bounce off the beige linoleum tile.

The woman gasped and gagged into a napkin, while the boy asked Emily for a jar to capture Walter. White Legs, meanwhile, had scrambled to his feet and in seconds had hustled his family out the door as several regulars at nearby tables broke out in laughter. A woman Emily had not seen before, however, was staring at her in horror, as if she was about to spit out her lunch. Emily picked up Walter and casually dropped him in her pocket.

"He's plastic," she told the lady. "He just helps us with pest control."

Emily hit River Street for a few hours after she got off that Saturday night and slept late on Sunday morning, awakening to Savannah's church bells summoning the faithful. It was her weekend now and with no particular plans, she reveled in the luxury of burrowing deeper into her pillow and ignoring the clock on the bedside table. George Wallace was curled at the foot of the bed, sleeping contentedly after rousing her face-to-face about 6 a.m. to fill his food dish.

She had traces of a headache because some guy wouldn't leave her alone until she did two shooters of some aqua concoction that the bartender set aflame. Once in a while, Tif would join her on River Street, but usually she was on her own, and Emily actually preferred it that way.

In her travels and at work she had met several city cops who had warned her about walking or riding alone downtown, although she basically ignored them. Still, she knew Savannah could be a deadly violent place. Despite all its beauty and history, ugliness could surface anytime, anywhere. It was as if the gods demanded the occasional sacrifice of an innocent tourist or downtown dweller in exchange for the city's eternal magic. Occasionally, someone would be murdered in the mossy recesses of the old streets. More frequently, there were armed robberies, purse snatchings and rape, many of the latter incidents never reported to police.

Crime was a leprosy as it was for any other city of any size, but it seemed to be worse here, possibly due to the genteel nature and the atmosphere of genuine Southern hospitality Savannah exuded. Emily had heard the story about a young Broughton Street waitress who had offered a co-worker a ride home. The woman vanished, only to be found a few days later in her car, submerged in a tidal creek. She had been raped and strangled. It was much more common for a crack whore to turn up with her throat gashed from ear to ear or some street corner drug mogul to die writhing in his own blood after a drive-by shooting.

Death was life's carved-in-marble finality, no matter if you were black, white or speckled purple and if Emily was careful in always being aware of her surroundings, she also believed that if it was your time to go there was nothing to do but succumb gracefully. Lyle had callused this on her soul on countless nights when she had believed she was seconds from dying as he slapped her into senselessness. She had balanced on the brink so many times that death held no fear for her, and to ride her bike through a rough neighborhood at any hour couldn't begin to rival what she had endured in her life.

Shuffling about in her bathrobe, Emily made a turkey and cheese sandwich for lunch and, finally getting dressed about 1 p.m., found a rusty gallon of paint that Miss Alma had left her to touch up some of the woodwork. Under George Wallace's watchful eye, she painted some baseboards and window frames.

She had just settled into her chair to relax with an icy glass of Kool-Aid when there was a rap at her front door. Half hoping whoever it was would go away, Emily waited until the third series of knocks before she got up and opened the door. There was no peephole so if a bad guy was standing there, so be it, although the thought was always with her when the door whined open.

On her welcome mat this time was not Jack the Ripper but Howie Kleinsul, a college student who lived just down the hall. Sometime in his future Howie might develop into a decent-looking guy. At nineteen, however, he didn't bother to bathe much and his struggling goatee was nothing more than glorified peach fuzz.

"Uh, hi Emily. Sam and me are gonna head down to the park and throw the Frisbee and check out the action. Wanna come?"

Howie reeked of marijuana, from his dirty flip-flops to his crusty Levis to his "Scorpions World Tour 1988" T-shirt, and Emily stared knowingly into his blood-shot eyes. She had never smoked herself, but living with Lyle had given her the experiences of the most seasoned pothead.

"Howie, which planet are you on today? You look like you have been living in a bong for the past two weeks."

He lowered his face and shuffled his feet, embarrassed. "Damn, Emily, you always catch me. I can't believe I'm that obvious."

"You smell like a lit joint and you've got Dracula eyes like always. Let me brush my hair real quick and I'll be right with you."

They rode their bicycles down Whitaker Street to Forsyth Park, Savannah basking in the laziness of a warm January Sunday afternoon. Sam was Howie's live-in girlfriend, also a student, who was from somewhere in the Midwest - they could have told Emily that Nebraska was on the Mexican border and she wouldn't have known the difference - and always very quiet.

The few times Emily had been around Sam she had tried to make conversation, but her attempted chatter had been met with little more than a smile. Emily didn't know if Sam's brain had been fried by reefer or if she was just naturally shy or if, being in college, she thought she was better than some redneck waitress from out in the boonies. Whatever was behind those pretty azure eyes, Emily had stopped caring, smiling back when she had to, but otherwise not wasting her time. She liked Howie, but never asked him any questions about Sam.

The park was busy with other people also savoring the nice weather. While Howie and Sam wandered a safe distance away from her to toss the Frisbee, Emily spread the old bed sheet she had brought along and lay on the grass mattress, closing her eyes and listening to the melodic hum of activity surrounding her. The sun massaged her and she was just dozing off when a voice interrupted her rest.

"Hi there."

Emily's first reaction was irritation aimed at whoever was disturbing her. She squinted against the sun, expecting to see Howie standing over her. There was someone else instead.

"Hi," she replied, shading her eyes and trying to buy time to recognize the man.

"Don't you remember me?"

Emily sat up on her spread now, looking at him squarely and drawing a total blank. The man looked to be in his late thirties, with black sunglasses.

"You and me struck up a conversation on River Street - was it the Rabbit Hutch Bar? I don't rightly recall."

"Maybe so, I can't say that I remember either."

Emily was trying to be pleasant as he squatted beside her. He hadn't invaded the turf of her bed sheet yet, but he was just off the edge of it.

"Your name will come to me in a minute, I just know it will." He looked skyward, slowly tapping his chin with a finger as if in deep thought.

"Annie? No, that's not it. That was my ex-wife's sister." The guy was chuckling to himself now. "Beatrice, Deborah, Pam, Wanda?"

Emily had had enough. This man was no one that she knew or had even bumped in to, like the man at the vet's office.

"Listen, if you're gonna go through the phone book for names, maybe it's not important enough for you to remember, if you get my drift. Enjoy your day." With that she lay back and closed her eyes.

For about thirty seconds there was quiet, other than

the park chatter and noises around her. She began to think that her unwanted companion had left. Where were Howie and Sam anyway? Gradually she relaxed, the sun's embrace returning.

Then the voice close to her ear congealed her blood.

"I guess you forgot about Old Lucy."

A seagull squawking overhead seemed to be the clarion call exposing her awful secret as Emily shot to full, stomach-churning alert. Extreme willpower kept her from bolting upright and, panicking, trying to crush the man's throat in her hands.

He looked at his wristwatch. "Well, I gotta go."

"Listen, I'm sorry. I didn't mean to give you a cold shoulder," Emily said, her words rushing together as if coupled like boxcars. "Do you want to sit down?" She could feel the sweat pouring out of her now clammy palms and felt as if she was trying to breathe in a grocery bag.

The man was standing now, looking down at her with a look that betrayed nothing other than what appeared to be bewilderment although he seemed to be enjoying her fix.

"So did you get your memory back?"

Emily brushed the hair from her face and tried to calm herself.

"Maybe. Why are you rushing off?"

"I just saw you and walked over to say howdy, that's all." He seemed indifferent and impatient now. "Sorry I can't stick around, but I've gotta be somewhere else in about half an hour."

"What was your name again?"

"Dewey."

She tried to look unaffected, turning to watch a rugby scrum of thirty-somethings across the park's green expanse. It was futile. This dude had her tighter than any headlock Lyle had ever tortured her with and she was frantic.

"See you later."

"So what are you doing tomorrow? You want to meet back at the Rabbit Hutch? I'll let you buy me a beer." She winced mentally at the desperation she heard in her words, even as her legs stood her up.

Dewey studied her features and looked at his watch again.

"Tomorrow's Monday, uh, sure, I can be there. About 5:30 okay?"

"See you then. The name's Emily, by the way."

"That's right. It's Emily. I'll see you tomorrow."

She watched the gangly oaks swallow him in the distance, but her eyes seemed glazed over, her mind cartwheeling in emotions and thought. For a moment she contemplated stalking Dewey, if that was his real name, and finding an isolated spot to kill him.

He knew about Old Lucy and everything else and her new life was over. Lyle had somehow reached out of the grave to despoil her one last time with this awful missionary and if she was to survive at all, the blood soiling her hands had to be refreshed by another.

"Hey Em!"

Howie and Sam appeared from nowhere, both sweaty and gasping for air. They plopped onto the grass beside her.

"We're gonna meet some buddies for beer and pizza in about an hour. Wanna come?"

Emily tried to smile, but she could tell from the expressions on their faces that they knew something was wrong.

"Thanks anyway, but I think I'll just head home and take it easy tonight."

"Em, you okay? You look kinda ill." Howie's concern was genuine even if he was an immature pothead.

"Yeah, no problems. I'll see y'all later."

"We'll be at Maxcy's on Congress Street if you want to join us later."

"Sounds good to me. I'll catch up to you. Bye."

They left her alone and she lay on her sheet for a few minutes before gathering her things and finding her bicycle, unlocking the little padlock holding it to the stand.

The sky was a deepening purple and squadrons of chimney sweeps wheeled and chattered among the trees and buildings as if they had suddenly become aerial monarchs of creation. Pedaling along the sidewalk, Emily didn't notice them or a covey of West Virginia tourists she barreled through.

Old Lucy was back to haunt her.

Like most of the bars and restaurants on River Street, the Rabbit Hutch was located in an old brick cotton warehouse. It was always dark and reeked of eye-watering bathroom disinfectant, draft beer and urine from decades of weekend benders and St. Patrick's Days.

Unseen speakers crackled with endless Led Zeppelin, Bob Seger and the like, while the clientele hunkered over their drinks at the bar, most of them pale and at least slightly seedy and looking as if they had burrowed into the Rabbit Hutch to eat their last meal from a happy hour snack bowl. When the front door whined open to emit some blinding daylight, the regulars looked up long enough to squint through a nicotine cloud at whoever was coming or going. Unknowing tourists sometimes peeked in but rarely ventured inside.

Emily had been to the Rabbit Hutch many times, and it had become one of her favorite hangouts on River Street. The dimness offered intimacy and on weekends they had live music, usually just an acoustic guitarist or two on a tiny stage in a small side room.

When Emily walked into the place that late Monday afternoon, she inhaled the second-hand smoke as if it was a purifying elixir. As always she ignored the inquiring stares of the regulars - she called them the "Crusties" - and found a rickety barstool away from everyone else so that Dewey would be able to see her when he came in.

The night before had been nothing but nervous thrashing - which had driven George Wallace out of the bed - and left her to finally awaken exhausted. Any attempt at sleep climaxed with the worried extremes of what she might face and left her mind tingling while she sucked for breath in quick gulps. There was little rest and she rose early from her sweat-soaked mattress, half praying and half wishing that her memory, her conscience and her imagination all would abandon her.

This was certainly no date and she had dressed to unimpress. Makeup would have been a waste of time and effort and her baggy jeans, paint-splotched T-shirt and unwashed hair completed the package of a woman who had nothing much else to lose or gain. Without asking, Timmy the bartender stood an icy mug of beer on a coaster in front of her, read her face and with a brief smile wordlessly retreated to the Crusties, who were embroiled in refighting Vietnam.

"If LBJ had any spine we'd a bombed Hanoi and anyplace else we damned well pleased and won the war," a guy Emily had heard called Toby was saying. "The VC were tough, but we shoulda kicked their yellow asses all the way up the Ho Chi Minh Trail to China."

About this time, Dewey walked in. It took a few seconds for his eyes to adjust from the daylight to the Hutch, but he quickly spotted Emily and, with a wave toward the Crusties, settled onto a stool beside her.

"So how we doin?" he said. "Sure glad you could make it." Dewey seemed to be in a great mood, a hangman who savored his work.

Emily weakly tried to smile at him and string some words together, but Timmy interrupted.

"Well there's my two tequila shooter twins," he said cheerily. "Back together for a reunion?"

"If we're not, it ain't my fault," Dewey said, gazing at her. "This little angel gets whatever she wants."

Emily drained her beer and motioned for another while Dewey ordered a vodka tonic.

He sighed heavily, lit a cigarette and exhaled hard.

"Man, what a day. Always glad to get a Monday behind me, but this one was particularly tough." He took a big gulp from his drink. "So how about you? How was your day? You work?"

Emily stared down at the bar, not ready to look him in the eye.

"No I had the day off. I just kind of hung out."

"You got a little sun out there in the park yesterday."

"Yeah, I guess so."

"So you wanna have a couple of cocktails here and then grab some supper? Bernardo's up on Montgomery Street has got great linguini. Ever been there?"

Why was he torturing her with this small talk? Suddenly she had had enough.

"What do you want from me?" Her words were almost a growl through gritted teeth. "Why are you doing this?"

Dewey's genial expression was suddenly transformed into a look of disbelief and hurt. Across the bar the Crusties were oblivious, immersed in their Vietnam diatribes, and had drawn Timmy into the debate.

"Can't they all just leave me alone?" She could feel her face reddening and the tears beginning to flood her eyes, but submission was not in her nature, not even when backed into a hopeless corner such as this. Balling her fists, she summoned her strength to knock this bastard into next week. After he got off the floor he could arrest her for Lyle's murder, but at least she would have the satisfaction of cold-cocking him in the face.

"What are you talking about?" Dewey's perplexed act was very good. "I just thought we could have a good time together." He ground his cigarette hard into an ashtray and threw his hands in the air. "Why do I always end up with hell's belle?"

Something about his body language and demeanor made her relax slightly even though she was still in attack mode. No one would ever treat her like Lyle had again, she had vowed, and this clown was not going to toy with her at all. Still she hesitated, glaring at him with thinly veiled hatred for all that he represented and all that he conjured from her past.

"Just level with me and get it over with," she blurted. "You know about Old Lucy, so you know everything and that's the end of it, right?"

The Crusties had ended Vietnam now and were a rapt audience for the obviously feuding couple. Timmy was propped against the cash register and at a respectful distance, but was ready to step in if things got out of hand. Dewey rested his chin on his arms folded on the bar and stared into space.

"Listen honey, I'm sorry this didn't work out. We met here a couple of weeks ago, I liked you and when I ran into you yesterday I figured we could get to know each other a little bit more. That's all. Be seeing you." Without looking at her, he rose from his barstool, taking a $20 bill from his wallet and flicking it on the bar. "Take it easy, Tim."

With a wave to the bartender, Dewey was quickly out the door and a stunned Emily followed him into the fading daylight a minute later. Her flipflops clattered on the cement as she ran after him down the sidewalk. Catching up to him about a block away, she grabbed him by the arm and tried to turn him toward her. He stopped and she could tell he was in no mood to see her face again.

"I just need to know one thing."

He was impassive.

"How do you know me?"

Dewey rolled his eyes and stepped away from her.

"You're just a drunk slut, aren't you? We had a few tequila shooters together and I didn't figure you'd remember me because you were so out of it. I wouldn't screw you with my best friend's tool."

By now all of Emily's inhibitions were gone.

"What about Old Lucy?"

"Hey, that was all you wanted to talk about; don't ask me."

"What did I tell you?" If this guy was a cop he had to be among the dumbest ever, she reasoned. Dewey started to walk away but turned back to her, his face crimson.

"Old Lucy?"

"Yeah."

"You just kept talking about her and I figured she was your mother or a sister or somebody like that. Now I'll tell you what. Get out of my life."

Emily stood and watched Dewey trudge up the cobble-stoned street while her mind absorbed and processed his words. She was relieved and thankful that he apparently was some harmless joe whom fate had thrown in her path one drunken night at the Rabbit Hutch. On the down side, she was horrified that she hadn't remembered him at all after a tequila orgy in which her loose tongue had babbled about Old Lucy.

Drained and confused, she headed home. Tuesday was a workday.

"Honey, you sure did make a big impression." Emily was cleaning one of the outside tables and had her back turned, but recognized Tiff Bryant's voice. After her confrontation with Dewey, she had gone back to her apartment and fallen into bed, George Wallace comforting her with rubs, licks and purrs. About twelve hours of sack time had refreshed her and allowed her for the most part to forget about Dewey. She had ridden her bike to work, arriving ten minutes early and now looked up to see her friend coming down the sidewalk.

"Hi, Tif. Nick said you came by yesterday looking for me."

"I did, I did, I just plumb forgot you're off Sunday and Monday. And let me tell you, that girl that fills in for you on Mondays is a real witch. I think I could kick some politeness into her though."

"Yeah, that's Gloria, I don't know too much about her. She's a college kid. Don't worry, she won't last long. What'd you say about a big impression?"

"Yes ma'am, you've got a fan club. That guy that bumped in to you when you were leaving my office the other day, well, he came in and was checking you out through the window and then asked me about you."

Emily had not given the man a second thought after their encounter, but now she remembered him, not wanting to appear too eager for details from Tiffany.

"Oh really?" she said spritzing a chair with cleaner and wiping the seat cushion. "What could he possibly want to know about me?"

"Well he just said that he thought you were really cute and asked me your name. I told him that I couldn't give out that information, but when I stepped away from the desk a minute I saw him looking at the patient sign-in sheet for that morning. You came in so early that the only other person on the sheet was old Mrs. Mulherrin who'd brought her toucan in for a laxative."

"What did you just say?" Emily was squinting at her in disbelief.

"About what? Your guy, Mrs. Mulherrin or the toucan?"

"We'll get to the guy in a second. Your vet gives laxatives to birds?"

"Em, this is Mrs. Mulherrin, who's got to be two centuries old and that toucan of hers ain't much younger. He was a gift from her late husband - I've heard that story a million times - and she wants that bird to live forever. She comes in every now and then and says that Marty - that's his name - is all bound up inside and needs some relief. Doc Craven feeds him some doggie treat or something, tells her it should do the trick and she and that bird go home happy. Now do you want to know about your admirer or not?"

"I don't remember that he had a dog, cat, toucan or anything else with him when I saw him," Emily said. At this, Tiffany gently clasped her arm.

"Em, you have just about succeeded in getting me totally off my train of thought. Will you let me finish my story?"

"Sure, Tif, sure."

"So anyway, I catch this dude looking at the sign-up sheet, even though he's reading it upside down, but I didn't say anything to him. I knew what he was doing and he didn't look like any kind of serial killer. In fact, I thought he was pretty good looking. Otherwise, I'd a told him you were a pregnant crack whore trying to escape from your pimp."

Tif had the ability to make her laugh, one of the reasons their friendship had gotten steadily stronger.

"So you didn't tell him anything about me, what kind of friend are you?" Emily joked. "You probably want him all to yourself."

"No ma'am, not this sister. My daddy would kill me if I brought a white boy home. He was raised in another time."

"So how does a guy go to a vet's office without any animal?"

"Now see, you didn't let me finish about that part. He came in to make an appointment for his dog, an Irish setter so I remember. Said he'd just moved from Waycross back to his daddy's farm out near the Ogeechee River and needed to find a new vet. Somebody recommended Doc Craven."

"So you're going to be seeing him again and get more scoop, is that it?"

"You got it, missy."

Tif had a quick, early lunch and was headed back to her office before Emily even realized she had not asked her the man's name. It didn't matter to her anyway, especially since the Dewey incident. So some stranger thought she was decent looking or cute or pretty or whatever, she'd grown up a lot since moving to Savannah and heard a ton of come-ons, the guy always aiming to get in her panties, at least to her thinking. Sure, some of them might have been sincere efforts just to spur a conversation, but Emily always lumped them together, a tribe of Lyles, each one waiting to screw her and then whale her with fists as he came.

Her emotional wounds would bleed endless rivers years after the welts, bruises and stitches had healed. Man was evil and any son of a bitch would have one hellatious time convincing her otherwise. Of course, she was forced to temper this attitude with the priceless afternoons she had spent shooting and drinking Dr. Peppers with her Uncle Seth as well as the stability she had derived from Nick's gentle demeanor and stalwartness.

Try as she might, deep down she couldn't completely convince herself to castrate the whole male half of the human race.

Chapter 4

As if driven by the Grim Reaper himself, the tan Lincoln Continental always glided into the cemetery about 3 p.m. every Wednesday afternoon. The caretaker and gravediggers for Pierpont's two white funeral homes had become accustomed to seeing the fine car and the pretty lady who returned their waves when she stopped and got out to visit a loved one or friend in Section G-10.

No matter the weather, Sarah Meade Gillon always made the trip out to see her son and grandson. They were buried side by side and she would pull a folding lawn chair from the trunk, along with an umbrella if needed, and set up her vigil. Every other week she stopped at Spain's Florist to pick up small arrangements for each grave.

It was a ritual she had begun the week after Brandon's death at five months and eight days and had assumed even more meaning for her when Lyle joined the baby there. In silence she sat staring at their headstones as if on the front row of a church. Sometimes she brought along a photo album of Lyle's childhood and the precious few pictures she had of Brandon. Occasionally she would bring a small stuffed toy bear for the baby. It always disappeared before her next visit, but Sarah didn't care, hoping that whoever took it gave it to a child.

She was always neatly dressed and wearing dark sunglasses and one day a couple of the $5 an hour laborers caught leaning on their shovels and whistling at her shapeliness as she knelt in prayer at the grave sites had been fired.

Sarah Gillon was a woman of routines. She had a standing appointment to have her hair and nails done at Raylene's Stylon every Wednesday at 4, allowing herself ample time at the cemetery.

Every day of the week the alarm clock on her nightstand always jangled at 6 a.m. and she was out of the shower and into the kitchen in her bathrobe within half an hour to cook breakfast. Treat liked his breakfast at straight up 7 a.m., no matter if it was Judgment Day and Sarah complied as any good wife would. Three link sausages almost seared, a stack of wheat pancakes, a six-ounce glass of orange juice and a pot of magma-hot black coffee were ready with military precision by the time she heard his footsteps on the stairs.

Beside his plate and silverware the early edition of the *Atlanta Constitution* was laid open and folded neatly to display page one of the sports section. Some mornings she stood in the driveway in the dark, tapping her foot nervously and waiting for that no-account paper boy. Treat could be one incensed devil if he didn't have his paper first thing in the morning and she had often paid the price when it was late or wasn't delivered for whatever reason. For that matter, Treat could go off if he didn't like her lipstick color or if the coffee burned his tongue.

Ernest Lyle "Treat" Gillon did not tolerate any way but his narrow-minded way and any variation was a sure backhand to the face or worse. His family had been among the biggest landholders in Bratton County and had owned more slaves than anyone when the Civil War came. Everything changed when Union cavalry raiders burned the Gillon plantation, the now-freed slaves gathering their few belongings and gleefully following in the wake of the conquering Yankees.

Reconstruction did not spare the Gillons any more than it did hundreds of thousands of other white Southerners, but Treat's great-great grandfather and his family had gradually gotten back on their feet through a recipe of hard work, guile and shrewdness. There was no way to recoup their prewar wealth and prestige, yet as the century neared its end, Treat's grandfather Henry had ridden the Gillons' resurgence to a two-term seat in the Georgia House of Representatives. Henry had used his political contacts to wrangle a government contract to manufacture cartridge belts for the army as the Spanish-American War loomed.

By the early 1900s, the Gillon clan operated the

county's largest cotton gin and Treat's daddy, Jefferson Davis "J.D." Gillon, had stepped into his father's shoes as one of the region's prominent civic and business leaders. J.D. was also proud of his activities with the Ku Klux Klan, joining in at least two lynchings and a dozen cross-burnings.

The family endured the Great Depression and World War II, before 65-year-old J.D. and his third wife, a 30-year-old brunette named Henrietta, announced the birth of baby Ernest on a wind-raked January day in 1950. Not wanting to die without a son, J.D. had plucked Henrietta from a low-rent cocktail lounge in downtown Atlanta, where she worked as a coat check girl, and brought her home to Pierpont to give him an heir.

Rarely was she seen in public, not even at the supermarket or church, J.D. telling everyone who asked that she was a sickly girl. Henrietta vanished from Pierpont before young Treat had any recollection of her and J.D. refused to speak of her.

The Gillon men had developed reputations based on their toughness in business as well as in personal matters - a fist fight in a back alley or an underhanded deal both instruments for gain of some kind. J.D. Gillon would raise his son no differently, even if he was a lone parent.

It was in his formative years that Treat had earned his nickname. He had hated the name Ernest since adoring and long-dead great-aunts had fawned over him in his earliest Christmas memories. Little Ernest was a known school yard bully by the time Halloween 1956 rolled around. J.D. had taken him in to Pierpont to trick-or-treat with others in his first-grade class. Dressed as Davy Crockett, he and the others had piled into the back of J.D.'s pickup truck and were driven house to house.

Among his classmates was Sollie Rosenfeld, a matzo-thin Jewish kid whose folks ran a men's clothing store on Main Street. On this night he was dressed as Howdy Doody. As they were leaving one house, Ernest tripped him on the sidewalk, sending Sollie sprawling and goodies from his bag flying in all directions.

"More treats for me! More treats for me!" Ernest sang as

he scrambled to grab up the scattered candy. A nickname was born.

A decade dissolved into 1968 and Vietnam was raging when Sarah first met Treat. She had grown up in Snowville, a one-stoplight farming community about twenty miles east of Pierpont. Since Snowville did not have a movie theater, Sarah and two girlfriends had driven to Pierpont one Friday night to see an Elvis Presley picture. She always forgot which one because she never saw it.

As she and her friends approached the ticket booth, they saw several guys wearing Pierpont High varsity jackets hanging out near the theater entrance. Sarah was especially taken by the boy with stark brown eyes who coolly flicked his cigarette to the curb as if he had just stepped out of a James Dean movie.

Treat at the time had received his draft notice and had to report to the army in three weeks, fully expecting to be shipped to Vietnam. J.D., wheelchair-bound by now if he was able to get out of bed, had told his son that he would use his political pull to keep him out of uniform, but Treat had wanted to serve, believing any alternative would make him less than a man. True Southerners never shrank from a fight when their country called - be it the Confederacy or the United States - and he was honor-bound to go.

Treat had explained all this to Sarah as they sat in his red Ford Mustang convertible parked just down the block from the theater. Unlike the long-haired, dope-smoking peaceniks she saw demonstrating on the TV news, Treat seemed reverent about his convictions, speaking in quiet tones as they waited for her friends to come out of the movie. She was also impressed by his dreamy car.

They went on three dates before he was inducted and boarded a bus for basic training at Fort Jackson, South Carolina, Sarah vowing to wait for him to return.

Treat indeed was sent to Vietnam for a year's tour, assigned to an infantry company that was in considerable combat. Sarah wrote him every other day and in the beginning his letters to her were regular and upbeat. A month after he arrived "in-country," however, his words became increasingly infrequent and despondent, and she sensed a change in him, even though she knew him hardly at all.

Treat proved to be a good soldier who survived to come home with the starburst scar of a Viet Cong's AK-47 round through the fleshy part of his left calf. Sarah had been faithful as promised and was ecstatic to have him back safely. She slept with him for the first time on the night he arrived back in Pierpont, and within days they started making wedding plans.

Reflecting on her life with Treat long afterwards, Sarah realized that Vietnam had not changed him. If anything it had merely stirred the cauldron of a soul in which Jefferson Davis Gillon and Henry Gillon and probably a host of other long-dead sires of the family had poured violent ingredients.

Sarah herself came from good stock, both of her parents small-town people who were devout Southern Methodists, at least on Sunday, and led simple lives centered on little Snowville, where they had lived forever and raised their three children. Sarah's dad ran a small grocery store just out of town, which his father had established when Warren Harding was president. Snowville had gotten an A&P in the early Sixties, but Curtis Meade couldn't compete with any supermarket chain and never made the effort. His place was a gathering spot for locals who congregated around a pot-bellied stove in the back room, laughing and swapping wisecracks and tall tales while swigging long-neck beers. It was a redneck utopia.

Truckers traveling U.S. 81 braked for sandwiches, Vienna sausages and cold drinks while the regulars came for the comradery, and it all amounted to a comfortable living for the Meades.

Sarah remembered her mother, Samantha, taking her to the store when she was very young and how she had hidden her face in the folds of her mama's skirt upon seeing the group of men lounging on creaking wooden chairs in the back of the store. The smell of burning pine logs, cigarettes, male sweat and beer breaths never left her. Samantha was a housewife and Sarah's memories of her were much more pleasant and close to her than anything she recalled about her dad.

Sarah was the oldest child of the Meade's three, born in 1952 when the only doctor in Snowville made house calls because there was no hospital and a black midwife named Chloe had helped bring her into the world. Sarah was followed by her brother Isaac in late 1953 and sister Gail fourteen months later, the boys at the store joking that if there was a Cold War going on, Curtis and Samantha would melt it with all their baby making.

Sarah had planned on going to college and possibly becoming a secretary for some big business in an Atlanta high-rise, but all of that changed after she met Treat. A junior in high school at the time, she was suddenly devoted to a soldier fighting a world away while she tried to conquer biology, algebra and civics. When she graduated Snowville High in 1969, she had already decided to forego college and go to work to build a marriage nest egg for Treat's return. She landed a job as a cashier at the Pierpont National Bank, still living with her parents to save money.

Treat came home from Vietnam to a loving girlfriend and a father who might not live out the hour. Every organ in J.D.'s body was shutting down as if God was using a checklist and flicking off the switches. The old man did not recognize his son, wearing pressed khakis and a rainbow of service ribbons, when Treat walked into his bedroom, kneeling to weep by what would be J.D.'s deathbed within the week.

No depth of war immersion could steel a son for the loss of a beloved father, and J.D.'s last breath eight days after Treat's return devastated him. Sarah tried everything to comfort him, but his grief appeared to be so deep that he seemed almost oblivious to her presence. She, however, attributed his stolid attitude to the double shock of the war and J.D.'s death and decided to patiently wait for him to surface from his gloom.

Two weeks after the funeral, Treat dove into running the gin, doing everything from driving a forklift to the book work to measuring the size of boll weevils trapped in the wagons of freshly picked cotton that tractors hauled in from the fields. While his days were beyond exhaustive during that fall harvest season in 1970, Treat's grief slowly dissolved and he returned to somewhat of his old self.

Treat never out and out proposed, but it seemed as if everyone, including Sarah, had willed their marriage, her love and devotion for the returning warrior being rewarded with a ring.

Like many combat veterans the war had wounded his mind as well as his flesh, but the violence within him had been seething long before he saw men blown apart in the Asian jungles.

Sarah experienced it on more than one occasion in the months before their June 1971 wedding, the first time he hit her an event as memorable as any of the twenty-seven wedding anniversaries that would pass. On a Friday night in mid March they had grabbed a couple of milk shakes and a bag full of hamburgers before Treat drove them to a lovers' lane near Abbott's Mill. It was a mild evening and Treat had lowered the convertible's top before they had climbed into the backseat to make out.

Amid their passion, he had hit his funny bone on the door lock and swore loudly. Sarah had laughed, which was the wrong thing to do. Hovering over her in the dark, his body pinning her to the vinyl seat and ten thousand stars as witnesses, he slapped her face, blood from her lip warming her mouth. There had been no apology from him when he drove her home that night, and lying in her bed later she tearily blamed herself for what had happened. It would become a common pattern for the run of their marriage.

Over the coming weeks, Treat abused her several more times and Sarah began her everlasting ritual of caking on makeup and wearing sunglasses to hide her welts and bruises. She plunged ahead with the wedding plans, tipping along a mental tightrope of not daring to involve Treat and risking his ire by not involving him enough. She told her parents nothing, knowing that Curtis Meade was a man who would not for a second tolerate anyone hitting his daughter. Curtis respected Treat for his war record, but if the truth came out, the hot blood of both men would collide in a terrible froth and one or the other would likely not survive.

Sarah didn't want to take the awful chance that her dad would be killed in an angry confrontation with Treat. She also didn't want to lose her future husband, a man to whom so many years of her young life had been devoted and whom she still believed wanted only the best for both of them, if only she could stop making mistakes that ignited his wrath.

The wedding had been a small, informal ceremony at Gideon Methodist Church where the Meades were members. Sarah always remembered how handsome Treat had looked in his dark suit, standing so erect as if at attention before the altar. She knew he would not have wanted a big event and, despite her own feelings and the protests of her parents, had limited those attending to the immediate family. Treat had only a couple of high school buddies there for him.

They made a two-night honeymoon jaunt to Atlanta, staying at the General Johnston Hotel on Peachtree Street. She would have liked a longer trip and one possibly to a more exotic locale, but Treat insisted that he had to get back to the gin. He moved her into his house, an elegant Victorian lady that had basically been the only woman in the lives of old J.D. and Treat between Henrietta's departure and Sarah's arrival.

The mansion on LaCourt Street, one of Pierpont's stateliest avenues, had been in the Gillon family since Prohibition, tall windows opening onto a large front porch and a wide staircase curving to the second floor. Still, it had a decidedly masculine touch, dominated by dark mahogany paneling and furniture, an occasional stuffed animal head on the walls or oil paintings of stern soldiers or politicians and grim, grandiose battle scenes. A front room had been converted into a den with a stereo, big color TV, bar and zebra-striped, overstuffed pillows, flung about on the orange shag carpet, about as trendy as Treat would allow himself.

For several weeks after they were married, Treat seemed fine, which to Sarah meant that while he was not overly affectionate or talkative, at least he wasn't slapping her. She figured that she must be doing something right as she adjusted to married life and her new home. As the summer baked into late July, he was regularly working long hours at the gin and she was busy at the bank, hurrying home each night to make supper and keep it warm until he arrived.

Their palace of cards was not long in tumbling, however, and it was celery that nearly got her killed. It had been an especially humid night about the first of August and Sarah was waiting for Treat to come home, sitting on an ottoman near the air conditioner in the den. The evening being so oppressive, she had prepared a cold plate for him, with a big scoop of tuna salad, two plump dill pickles and potato chips.

Treat finally trudged in about 8:30 p.m., grimy, sweaty, and with his clothes covered in lint and bits of cotton hulls. He plopped down at the kitchen table and Sarah placed the plate in front of him trying to appear like she was not feeding an angry wolverine. She knew he was tired and didn't bother him with much conversation.

He shoved a hefty forkful of tuna salad into his mouth and began chewing as she sat across the table from him. When Sarah was a little girl, her mother had shown her how to make tuna salad, boiling and peeling an egg, finely dicing a stalk of celery, adding a dollop of mayonnaise and combining it all, sometimes with a spoonful of pickle relish, in a bowl. Mix it all well and chill it in the refrigerator for a few hours and it was a refreshing dish on a hot Georgia day, just like the Kiwanis Auxiliary cookbook said.

Treat wasn't refreshed, his eyebrows arching as he slowly crunched.

"Did you put celery in this tuna fish?" he asked without looking up from the table.

"Well, yeah, Treat, if you don't like it, I can leave it out the next time I fix it."

He was on her with what seemed to be lynx quickness, sending her flying out of her chair and sideways onto the cheery yellow and white linoleum she had mopped an hour earlier.

"Now why would you put celery in my tuna? You know

I can't stand it, Sarah."

Straddling her on the floor he punctuated his words with a punch that likely would have driven her nose into her brain if she hadn't turned at the last second, the blow glancing off her left ear.

"I didn't know, Treat. I didn't know. I never made it for you before!"

The back of his hand came low and hard, his high school ring ripping across her cheek and she screamed and spit blood and a piece of a tooth.

For an hour he had tortured her, alternately slapping or punching her or pressing the muzzle of a pistol against her forehead, threatening to pull the trigger. When he finally went up to bed, she had spent the rest of the night curled on a mat in the downstairs bathroom. Before daylight the next morning, she was up and prepared his breakfast, Treat acting as if nothing had happened and Sarah too fearful to mention it. After he left for work, she called in sick, spending much of the day with an ice pack to relieve the swelling.

Celery would never again be on her grocery list, but a routine that would afflict her for the rest of her married life had been established. Certainly the abuse was rarely as severe as that night, but she never knew when to expect a stone-hard fist or food from his plate hurled at her. Treat was a hard drinker like J.D. and his grandfather and like their future son who would soon be kicking in her belly, but Sarah had taken a vow for better or for worse.

The girls at the bank sensed something was wrong and tried to get her to open up, but she wouldn't tell them anything. She believed in the sanctity of her marriage and wouldn't betray any secrets about their private lives. Besides, if she was the perfect wife, none of this would be happening to her, she reasoned, all the more cause for her to work harder to make Treat happy.

She learned that certain music set him off. There was no method to it, just a painful trial and error that meant that as certainly as the sunrise, she could expect to be beaten if they listened to specific artists. Anything by the Beach Boys, Perry Como, Grateful Dead or Peter, Paul and

Mary almost always ended in an evening of violence. Treat had several hundred records - he refused to buy compact discs for whatever twisted reason - and she contemplated breaking them or throwing them out. She always decided against it, the consequences possibly being even worse than the music.

When Sarah became pregnant just before Christmas in 1971, Treat had made her quit her job so that she could stay home and raise their child. He also was tired of those busybodies at the bank giving him the cold shoulder and hard stares when he went there to make a deposit.

For a time, Sarah leaned on her sister Gail for support, even though she never told her about the troubles she was enduring. By now, however, Gail was out of high school and was in the first months of her freshman year in college. They still talked long distance on the phone but it wasn't the same. Sarah's brother Isaac also was no longer around, having joined the Air Force after graduation and was now serving at a base in Germany.

Sarah birthed their son fittingly on Labor Day 1972 at Bratton County Hospital and Treat had been there through the ordeal, holding her hand. Even as the baby's emergence seemed to be ripping her in half, her hopes were that this creation of theirs would finally bring them together. They had named the boy Lyle - Treat's middle name - and at 20 years old Sarah was a new mother.

Her parents naturally were ecstatic, even though they congratulated Treat with all the sincere affection of rival ambassadors at a nuclear arms summit. Even more so than the bank employees, they knew there was a wormy core to this marriage that even the glorious birth of a beautiful, healthy grandson could not overshadow.

Time and time again Samantha had sat down with Sarah over iced tea and her favorite lemon cookies and tried to penetrate the sunglasses and the eyes of her daughter's soul. Yet even as she enlarged with Lyle, Sarah had resisted her mother's every onslaught, often yielding tears but no confessions. The Meades felt they knew what was going on in the big house on LaCourt Street, but without Sarah's confirmation they were helpless. If his health had not nose-dived, leaving him attached to an oxygen tank on wheels and with tubes in his nose, Curtis likely would have killed Treat or at the very least taken a swing at him.

Still, all of this bile did dry to some degree amid the baby gifts of blue knit caps, blankets, cards of congratulations, rattles and mobiles that signaled infant Lyle's world debut. Even as she stood over his open grave more than two decades later, Sarah always remembered his flawless features as nurses swabbed the blood and other afterbirth from him, and the first time she peered into his pink face.

Heaven was hers.

And so for the next seventeen-plus years she had done her best to raise her son; brown diapers to kindergarten valentines to Little League to the junior-senior prom all interspersed by Treat's horrendous flare-ups. Lyle had always been a good, quiet, kid, but Sarah wondered about his emotional state.

Treat never hit her in front of him when he was a toddler, but some nights she had run to his crib, wiping the blood from her face after her screams of pain had brought him to pitiful wails. Lyle grew into adolescence with none of them speaking of what went on under their roof and at times Sarah felt as if she was raising a stranger. Her love for Lyle was unconditional, but what she couldn't know was that he was becoming a chip off the old block. It would be an unseen and gradual transition, born of endless nights hearing his mother's sobs and the whack of his daddy's hands hitting her and the angry rising of voices behind closed doors that never withheld the sordid secrets behind them.

If Lyle was to follow his father's path to violence, he would not tread after Treat in another way that Treat valued most. Treat would have loved to have groomed Lyle to someday take his place at the cotton gin, but Lyle had absolutely no interest in pursuing this career. He had been fascinated by cars and what made them work since he was old enough to draw and color them with his crayons. Later he would help some of the older boys tinker with their jalopies, earning his mother's scoldings when he came home splotched in crankcase oil or reeking of transmission fluid.

He went out for the football team his junior year at Pierpont High, but it seemed his heart was in some grease monkey's garage rather than on the field and he only played in a few games when the outcome had already been settled.

By now Lyle was dating a pretty tenth grader named Emily Tillman, but he was about to take a major step backward in his life. He had been working a few hours a day at Pete Stuart's dealership, washing cars, sweeping up and filling in when Stuart's regular mechanic called in with all-too-frequent hangovers. When the mechanic finally quit, Lyle asked for the job, both he and Stuart realizing that Lyle had just turned eighteen and started his senior year in school.

Lyle's grades were average at best and he told Stuart that he would get his parents' permission, which he never intended to do. Stuart went along with the charade, after all the kid had assured him he was asking his folks about the move, and Lyle was developing into a first-rate mechanic. More to the point in Lyle's mind, he was an adult now and plenty of kids his age had come home in boxes from Vietnam and he could do what he wanted.

Lyle had already accepted the job and left school when he dropped the bombshell on Treat and Sarah at suppertime on a late September evening in 1989. The boy had quietly told them of his plans while staring at his plate, and Sarah could see Treat's blood pressure rising at every syllable. Her own disappointment, like her being, was subservient to him, even when it came to their only child making what could be the biggest mistake of his newborn adulthood.

There was weighty silence at the table after Lyle had his say, as if all three of them were waiting for an explosion of emotions. Treat's face was cooked-bacon red and his eyes appeared ready to burst from his skull cartoon style, but he said nothing. Dropping his fork noisily on his plate, he rose slowly from his chair, glaring at Lyle as he did so, and left the dining room. Before Sarah could muster her thoughts, Lyle was gone too, out the back door without meeting her eye, the mutter of his car's motor soon lost in the deepening dusk.

Lyle had not talked to Emily before making his decision. Why should he? She was just a stupid tenth grader who worked part time at the Portly Pig Diner, necked with him on weekends and didn't know a four-barrel carb from a hole in the ground, much less anything else about life. His parents were another matter and with Stuart's consent, he had slept in a tiny supply room of the garage for three nights before approaching them again.

Unknown to Emily or anyone else, Stuart's secretary, Eileen Stegman, had kept him company for a couple of hours on the second night. Eileen was old enough to be Lyle's mother, in fact she was three years older than Sarah. But she was separated and needed loving and Pete Stuart was too old, stringy and slimy, despite his endless come-ons.

Lonely and bored, she had gotten off work that day and had a few drinks with a girlfriend before driving back to "Honest Pete's" to seduce Lyle with her body and a six pack.

Before the night was over, she had enticed him into whipping her with a fan belt, getting more than she bargained for in the process. Eileen spent a week recuperating at home, telling Stuart that she was having "female problems." Too embarrassed to report the assault to the police, she quit her job without ever going back to the car lot. Weeks later she left Pierpont forever.

Sarah well remembered the night Lyle brought Emily home for the first time. After the initial shock over his school decision, father and son had seemed to make an unspoken, uneasy peace and Lyle had moved back into the house, much to her relief. If the truce between them was one of silence, the tension separating Treat and Lyle was a vast canyon, emotions heightening on both sides. Even though he slept in his old room, Lyle was barely in their lives now, coming in at all hours of the morning, even when he had work the next day.

The night they met Emily, Sarah and Treat had been sitting in the den when Treat had put a Perry Como record on the stereo and refilled his ninth stiff bourbon of the evening. Sure enough, not ten minutes later, he slapped her for no apparent reason, moments before Lyle and his date unexpectedly walked in. What Sarah did not remember very clearly was anything about Emily, as she tried to shake the cobwebs Treat had knocked into her head, and to stop her tears.

Regaining her composure was impossible, but, mercifully, Lyle and the girl had popped in only briefly before heading upstairs to listen to music. Treat had barely acknowledged them, returning to his bottle of Rebel Yell.

Emily graduated high school in spring 1992, but it was not a time for celebration. Leona Tillman was dying and, having been sent home from the hospital to spend her last days, was not even able to see her daughter receive her diploma. The cancer had eaten up her insides and there was nothing any mortal could do about it except offer up a prayer or a cheery word at her bedside and make sure they had something to wear to the funeral.

When Leona passed on during the first week of June, Emily had never felt so alone in the world, and she clung even tighter to Lyle. She gave him the little bit of money she had saved from her job to help make a down payment on a mobile home for them.

Treat Gillon had money to burn, but if his son didn't want to be in the gin business than he could make his own fortune; Lyle wouldn't have it any other way. Bullheadedness, as well as beating up on their women, were traits that ran deep in the men of the family.

The rift between Treat and Lyle had worsened so much by late summer that Lyle decided there would be no church wedding or even a small ceremony for relatives and close friends. Emily had wanted a big wedding, but she had learned there was no sense arguing with Lyle when his mind was made up.

After their brief honeymoon, they had stopped by his

parents' house and Lyle had made her wait in the car while he went in and told them of their marriage. She was in no shape to see the Gillons anyway, having been raped only hours earlier, the $50 ring on her finger burning as if it was a circle of fire.

So Sarah had a new daughter-in-law, who seemed nice enough, but the feud between father and son sullied their relationship as well. While Emily desperately needed someone to try to fill at least a portion of her mother's void, Sarah was hell-bent not to be anyone's mentor or savior. She had been standoffish from the beginning when Emily became more and more of a presence in Lyle's life. Even after the wedding she wouldn't allow herself to get close with Emily, who was starting out in life to endure from her husband what Sarah had suffered for years. There was not going to be a pity party between them if Sarah had her way.

Baby Brandon Lyle Gillon had been born on an eggs-fried-on-the-sidewalk day in late July 1993, the humidity making everything in motion appear to be in the process of melting. The Gillons were there to be with Lyle for the hours of waiting and finally the three were allowed in to see Emily and the new arrival. It had been a time of indescribable joy for all of them, even Treat and Lyle breaking from their usual stone faces to offer congratulations and give stilted back pats to each other. Sarah's indifference toward Emily dissolved, at least temporarily, as she cuddled her six-pound-eight-ounce grandson for the first time.

In her relief and exhaustion, Emily was blissful too, but her mood was tempered by the expression on the doctor's face minutes after Brandon's cries first greeted the world.

Emily had chosen the name Brandon from a soap opera character and Lyle had not objected. As the first and only grandchild the Gillons would have, he was lavished with attention and gifts, his nursery soon brimming with stuffed animals, stacks of bibs and baby albums. Brandon had Lyle's brown eyes, a flair of light hair and dimples that must have trickled down from some long-forgotten ancestor on one of the family trees. He was a handsome baby, and even though his doctors ordered him to remain in the hospital for observation and tests for almost two weeks after his birth, the Gillons remained upbeat and excited. Yet even after they were allowed to bring the baby home, Brandon was back and forth to the hospital over the next four months.

Brandon's primary physician, a young Pakistani named Yusef Kharfni, seemed hesitant to tell Emily much about the baby's health, other than that there had been "complications." She guessed that he really did not know what the problem was. Already frustrated, Lyle had erupted during one of the few office visits in which he accompanied Emily, and she had been forced to step between him and the doctor, Lyle threatening to hit him. Emily had hustled him out the door, through a crowded waiting room, her face hot with embarrassment.

By this time, Emily had gotten the heart-ripping news from Dr. Kharfni. Brandon's kidneys were weak, functioning at less than thirty percent efficiency due to a rare blood disease, and there was little that could be done for him. Based on Kharfni's instructions, they had taken Brandon to see a kidney specialist, in Columbus, but the diagnosis had been the same. Another nephrologist offered the same sad story.

Emily and Lyle had celebrated Christmas in a room at the Tomahawk Motel in Atlanta where they had brought Brandon for yet another doctor's opinion. It was to be Brandon's only Christmas and Emily decorated with silver tinsel and cheap ornaments she picked up at a K-Mart down the street. They hung a stocking for Brandon on the window latch beside his crib and filled it with candy canes that he would never enjoy.

Brandon died on a chilly morning the following February. At the time, the family was back home in Pierpont and he simply stopped breathing in his crib. When Emily found him, his face was blue and she bundled him in her arms and stumbled to the phone, blurting her crisis to a 911 operator. Emily had ridden to the hospital in the ambulance and Lyle had met her there, coming straight from work and still clad in his soiled coveralls. There was nothing anyone could do for the baby.

The wailing whistle at Gillon's Cotton Gin announced high noon and many of the people of Pierpont took their lunch break on its signal, including Treat, who unwrapped a ham sandwich at his desk. Emily and Lyle had not had time to call him as they rushed to the hospital. The whistle always sounded for ten seconds every workday, and was as much of a town tradition as the August Peanut Festival. On this day, its mournful echoes also heralded the death of Brandon Lyle Gillon.

For the next three and a half years, Emily endured Lyle's tirades and beatings. Treat and Sarah treated them like they had leprosy and vice versa, the men on both sides dictating the barely concealed hostilities, neither confiding in their spouses or showing any signs of wanting an end to the problem. Lyle was submersed in his own world now, either at work or in the woods or drinking and whoring, but managing to fit in an Emily beating every now and then.

Emily worked six days a week at the Portly Pig, starting at 5 a.m. with the breakfast shift and working through the lunch rush. The Calvert family had owned the old diner for three generations and "Old Billy," their grizzled patriarch always sat on a thickly cushioned stool by the cash register where he could gab and swap wisecracks with the regulars. Despite his rheumatism, arthritis and eighty-plus years, he always found cat speed to swat Emily on the butt if she got too close to him, a lesson she had learned since she started working there in her high school days. Any waitress was fair game if she wandered into Old Billy's range.

Emily had always enjoyed working there, but her paychecks were skimpy despite her tips and at no time was this more evident than in the weeks and months after Brandon left them. The baby's medical bills had been immense and she paid what they could, but it was like chipping at a glacier with a teaspoon. In a corner of the spare room that had been Brandon's nursery, Emily soon began piling the unopened envelopes of statements from the hospitals and doctors, building miniature high-rises of form letters demanding money they didn't have.

Certainly there was nothing to spend on decorating the trailer and about the only thing on the dark, wood-grain walls, other than dried spaghetti Lyle had flung there were a few cheap prints of fruit bowls or pastoral scenes that had come with the home. With little else to do in her spare time and her Saturdays off, Emily tried to spruce up the nursery where Brandon's crib still stood. From seed and flower catalogs and old magazines she clipped photos of roses, her favorite flower, and taped or glued them to the wall over the crib, starting at the ceiling and working down.

Emily had always loved roses. In all of the crackling old black and white movies, the glamorous, gold-sequined starlets always received stunning bouquets and she fantasized that one day she would have some of her own, even if she had to buy them herself. Her wall montage had them in all sizes, shapes and patterns, alone and in bunches. It became her hobby to try to find additions for the collection and add them to her "rose nursery" as she called it. Soon her wall blossomed with Gallicas, Damasks, Noisettes and Teas. There was no need to believe that Lyle would ever spring for the real thing, even if he had the money, which he didn't, so this was likely the closest she would get to the grandest material gift she ever wanted.

Occasionally she dreamed of roses, slowly breathing their succulence as if savoring the aromatics of a pedigreed wine she would never sip. From her thin pillow her mind danced with Albas, Chinas, Bourbons and Portlands, their keen brilliance transforming her slumber into a delightful garden. Awakening from one of these flights was a harsh free fall to her brutal existence with Lyle before she ended it with a flick of a trigger finger.

Brandon's loss had twisted a dagger in Sarah Gillon's soul and she knew that Treat was tormented as well although he was too manly vain to admit it. The baby's passing, however, had served as a revelation of sorts for Sarah. She slowly began to acknowledge how much she hated Treat as well as herself for the waste of more than twenty-two years of her life, a tally that mounted each day.

Yet at this stage even if Emily had picked up the phone and begged to talk to her about her problems with Lyle, Sarah would not have listened. Her denial, as well as her scars, were deeply ingrained and it was as if she had performed her duty in a private war, a bloodied but unyielding survivor. Emily had to do the same.

Of course Sarah had no way of knowing what went on between Emily and Lyle; they were rarely together, but Pierpont was not big enough to prevent them from running in to each other downtown or seeing each other driving on the street. And as much as Sarah told herself Lyle was not like his father, she could see that she and Emily were members of a sunglasses sorority of two.

Chapter 5

The roses were the size of a sultan's baubles, richly red, moist and kissed with the exquisite aroma like no other flower. Emily buried her face in them, a thorn nicking her cheek in her oblivion, a few drops of blood a small admission to her personal Eden.

She had arrived at work to see the bouquet, wrapped in clear plastic, lying as if on display on a table in the middle of the restaurant. At first she believed they were for a customer, but then she saw Nick beaming at her from the kitchen.

"Open them, fairy princess, they are yours," he called over the clatter of the dishwasher.

For a few moments the awesomeness of the gift outweighed the need to know the name of the giver. Eventually - about thirty seconds - Emily looked for a card, but there was none. She thought about who liked her enough to give her such a magnificent arrangement; no one came to mind. Was Dewey playing games and trying to return to her good graces? She didn't think so, but who else could it be?

Nick could see that she had no clue and neither did he.

"The delivery guy said he didn't know who sent them. He just had instructions to bring them to you. Somebody must like you very much, Em. You cheating on your Nick?"

She laughed, even as her mind tried to identify the sender.

"No, no, Nick. You're the only man in my life. Unless somebody better comes along."

"I pray you find one of us."

All through her shift that day, Emily couldn't take her eyes off the roses, presiding over the deli like a visiting empress from a shelf behind the cash register, Nick having found a glass vase for them somewhere in the bowels of the storeroom.

The deli was swamped at lunch and several regulars had noticed the bouquet and made comments to Emily, who had beamed and squirmed and said nothing before hustling away with their dirty plates.

What could she say? She had no idea who sent them and the distraction had caused her to botch two orders. Nick had not said a word. Emily was a great employee who rarely made mistakes and, even as they worked through the midday jam, he knew the mystery roses had jumbled her head.

Emily had ridden her bike to work that morning and Nick gave her a ride home, the roses radiating from her lap as if she had suddenly become some fertility goddess. She carried the flowers up the ten steps from the sidewalk, grasping the vase with both hands. It was an ascendancy to the stars and Emily felt that she was glowing like a giant firefly, her euphoria flooding over her.

Next to the day Brandon was born, this was the happiest time of her life, she decided, entering her apartment and carefully placing her treasure on a yard-sale cherry wood table near the painted-over cupids. George Wallace greeted her at the door, his pink nose quickly sensing the regal fragrance that was suddenly sweetening their little home.

Emily kicked off her shoes and settled into her favorite chair to gaze at the roses. In the deepening shadows she gingerly pulled one of them from the vase and sat back down, her fingers running over the delicate satin petals and gently pressing the thorny stem. The cat sprang to the chair arm to be petted and relish the flowery perfume as well. Her ringing phone snapped the spell and Tif Bryant's voice came through the line.

"So, how was work today?"

"Uh, it was good, actually great, Tif, but since when have you ever called to ask me about my day?"

"You said great, right?"

"Yeah, it was great! Somebody sent me roses!"

Amid her excitement, Emily suddenly realized that Tif knew something.

"Roses, huh." Tif's tone was nonchalant. "Wish somebody thought enough about me to spend that kind of cash."

Emily was playing along and listening now, waiting for Tif to spill the beans.

"Yep, sure wish I had a secret admirer who would all but bribe a friend to find out more about a baby doll he's interested in. Guess the next thing you'll be getting is a Rolex watch or some fancy diamond ring."

"Give me some details, Tif."

"So are they pretty? I woulda come downtown for lunch, but we got real busy and I couldn't get away."

"Yeah, they're just gorgeous. Now will you tell me what's happening?"

"Can't leave you hanging out to dry no more, I guess."

"Thank you."

"You remember the guy who came into the office and was asking about you, right?"

"Sure Tif. Is that who sent the roses? What's his name?"

"Don't jump the gun, missy, but yes it is - unless you got a real ultra-secret, secret admirer out there that I don't know nothin' about. You think that's it?"

"Tif, how about if Mrs. Mulherrin or whatever her name is just happens to find out that your vet is giving her toucan doggie treats instead of bird Ex-Lax. You want to deal with that?"

"Lord, Em, you are fighting dirty now. Here's all I know. This fella's name is Travis Hawthorne. He asked about you the day y'all ran into each other at the office, remember I told you?"

Emily was becoming impatient.

"Will you get to the point or let me get back to my roses and my cat. Nick thinks you got a crush on him by the way."

Tif ignored her.

"Anyway, he brought in his dog yesterday, this pretty Irish setter, and Doc Craven checked her out, but in the meantime, this dude was trying to check you out through me."

"Go on."

"So him and the dog are in the waiting room and he

walks up to the desk and starts chatting me up like he did the first time he came in. Very friendly and easy going and he says something like, 'Well, have you decided to tell me about your friend?' and I pretend that I don't know who he's talking about at first."

"Uh huh."

"I guess he sees that I'm a little suspicious or hesitant or whatever and he says that he only wants to send you some flowers to introduce himself and says there's no harm in that, right? I agree with him and since we got all his personal info in our records, I tell him your name is Emily - I didn't tell him your last name - and that you work at the deli. After he's finished with the doc, he comes out and pays and asks me what kind of flowers he should send and then asks if you might like roses. I tell him what girl wouldn't."

"But there wasn't a card with them. Did he tell you he was going to have them delivered today?"

"No, but he seemed mighty intent and serious about it and I just figured you might get a surprise. I betcha he just shows up out of the blue, Em. Like I told you before, I thought he was good looking. No Mel Gibson or Denzel Washington, but not bad for Savannah."

"We'll see what happens, Tif. I'll keep you posted. Come by the deli or let's get a drink one day this week."

"Okay, Em, just one other thing. You decide to throw this one back in the pond, tell him to come see me. It's been a long time - like never - since a man sent me a bunch of roses. I ain't too proud to take leftovers."

For the next two days Emily floated among the deli tables waiting for Prince Charming to come in and order a gyro wrap, pickles and coleslaw. She considered herself tough and indeed she was, but unexpected roses from a mysterious, handsome stranger were something straight out of a sappy romance novel. It was a charming intrigue like she had not experienced since her junior high and high school days of puppy love daydreams, a return to an innocence long since ground into the dirt that had been her marriage.

She cared for her roses with the diligence of a new

mother, checking the water level, giving them plant food and moving them to spots in the apartment where they would have sunlight, always warning George Wallace to stay away from them. Her workdays were very busy, but there was no word from or appearance by the person she most wanted to see. Nick kept an eye on her when he could, not wanting to pry, but wondering like her about who had sent the bouquet.

By day three - a Thursday - the roses were beginning to show their cut age and Emily knew that no amount of tender care would prevent the inevitable. Her roses mirrored life, time eroding youth and physical beauty of all things mortal and to try to quell the measured flow of the hourglass was timelessly futile.

The first petal had fallen from a bloom that morning before she went to work and she had cupped it like a baby robin tumbled from its nest. Not wanting to be late, she tucked it into an envelope so that she could later paste it into a memory book she kept. The book had been a wedding gift from the Calvert family at the Portly Pig and it was nicely embroidered with gold and lace trim and a fine red ribbon to wrap around it. The only problem was that Emily's good memories were sparse and to this point there was nothing in the book other than a few, mostly blurred Instamatic shots of Brandon. Death had taken her boy before any cutesy studio photos could be arranged.

No matter if she ever saw who sent them, the roses were the second-best thing to happen in her life, her tough side told her, but her heart wanted resolution to the matter of why she had earned them. With no one coming forward to kneel and propose, Emily began to wonder if one of Nick's regulars was playing a trick on her or had a secret crush on her.

She had several suspects and shuddered to think it was any of them. There was Terrence Cockburn III, a local lawyer with a bad toupee who always dressed in seersucker suits and gave her the eye, but he was "an old white fossil," as Tif called him. Vincent Romano was a salesman at one of the men's stores on Broughton Street and God's gift to women, at least in his own mind. To Emily, he was barely a step up the evolutionary ladder from Lyle and still couldn't walk upright. A younger man she knew only as Jimmy delivered prescription orders from Mecklin's Pharmacy on his bicycle and stopped in for lunch at least once a week. He "wasn't quite right," as her mother used to say, and Emily had felt sorry for him before the cops had arrested him for exposing himself to a little girl in Forsyth Park. Certainly there were other customers, but they were too married or too old or too gay or just plain not interested, she knew.

The Thursday lunch crowd flooded in starting about 11:45 a.m., as it always did, and things were hectic but not out of control. If it was a routine day, it would be very busy until about 1:30 p.m. Emily scurried about, taking orders, bringing plates of food from the kitchen, refilling glasses of iced tea or cups of coffee and getting lost in her work as she always did. She was irritated and getting hotter because the new busboy, a college kid named Ernie, didn't clear the tables very quickly and she vowed to talk to Nick about it.

She was sweating and fuming and watching Ernie out of the corner of her eye when she rushed up to one of the sidewalk tables where a man had sat down and was reading a newspaper. She probably would not have given Ernie so much attention if she also hadn't been hacked off with two guys who had stiffed her for a tip after making her recite the beverage selections about four times.

"Hi, can I bring you something to drink?" she asked the new customer, barely glancing at him while watching Ernie closely examine a ketchup-stained fork as if it was the key to his future.

"Yeah, I'll have unsweetened tea, thank you."

"I'll get that and bring you a menu in just a sec."

"Great. Uh, by the way, how did you like the roses?"

Emily had wheeled to dash for the kitchen, the words freezing her in her Reeboks. She turned to look at her admirer, who was calmly grinning up at her.

He appeared to be about her age or slightly older with a nice face accented by straight brownish-blonde hair that crept over his ear tops and a walrus moustache of the same color. A white Izod golf shirt enhanced a medium tan and a nice build, his jeans and black tennis shoes rounding out the first lasting picture Emily had of Travis Hawthorne.

"Wow," was all Emily could manage, staring at him, a reaction to the moment more than to his question. For all of a three-second eternity she couldn't move as he gazed steadily at her.

"So I'll have unsweet tea and a menu," he said finally, clearing his throat and trying to prompt her to action. "I hear y'all have great food here."

"The roses were perfect," Emily blurted. "Just so beautiful and I thank you so much."

"Glad you liked them. My name's Travis Hawthorne by the way."

She fumbled with her order pad and pen before shoving a hand forward to shake his.

"I'm Emily."

"I know. Your friend Tiffany helped me out in trying to find you."

Lunch was winding down, but there were still customers inside and Emily had to attend to them, Hawthorne sensing her rush.

"Tell you what, I know you're busy so do what you gotta do and I can see you after you get off, if you don't have any other plans. What do you think?"

Emily's defenses suddenly bristled and her Cinderella demeanor disappeared in a poof of reality. If her hell with Lyle had taught her nothing else, her mistrust of all men reigned, and this smooth talker was no different, roses or not.

"How do I put this politely," she said, staring at the floor.

"I'm moving a little too fast, is that it?"

"That could be it. Listen, I'll bring your tea and a menu. Just give me a minute to think, okay?"

"Not a problem. I can come back tomorrow if you want."

"No, you stay right where you are."

Her mind was in overdrive as she hustled to the kitchen,

poured a glass of iced tea from a big plastic pitcher and grabbed a menu. Nick watched her wordlessly and she was so absorbed in her thoughts that she was oblivious to him. By the time she raced back to Hawthorne's table, however, she had a plan of action.

"What do you think of this idea," she said to him, placing the tea and menu in front of him. "The Cotton Boll Lounge is about three blocks from here on Broughton. It's nothin' fancy, but I go there a good bit and we can sit and talk. I get off at seven and could meet you there."

He laughed. "I see, I've got that ax murderer glint in my eye. Chop you into pieces and throw you in the river. No, seriously, that's fine with me."

"Okay."

"I gotta tell you one thing right now, though."

"What's that?"

He was staring at her now.

"You're just as pretty as you were when I saw you the first time."

"Well it's only been about two weeks," she answered, not comfortable with compliments. "I hope I haven't aged too much since then."

"Not at all. I'm glad you liked the roses."

Unlike lunch, Nick rarely made money at the supper hour. Downtown Savannah emptied out starting around 5 p.m., the office workers heading home to the suburbs and most of the Broughton Street stores closing. Nick considered closing the deli in the afternoon or shifting to offer breakfast, but until he did so, he had to be satisfied with the few patrons who wandered in for a gyro, salad or sandwich for their dinner.

Hawthorne had ordered a grilled cheese and french fries and seemed to enjoy them. His small talk with Emily had continued through his lunch as she was back and forth among the other customers. He had left her with a "See you later," a big smile and a $5 tip under his tea glass.

Emily spent the rest of her workday with the myriad chores of a restaurant with a small staff, including cutting up vegetables and helping Nick restock the coolers with packages of sliced lamb, ham, turkey and hard salami. He had seen her talking with the stranger and had held his tongue through the afternoon, but finally could not contain his curiosity any longer.

"So was that your gentleman friend who sent the nice and pretty roses?" he asked Emily as they refilled napkin dispensers. "You don't have to tell me unless you want."

Emily had been in la la land all afternoon, so distracted that she had almost started to wash the front window with mustard rather than cleaner.

"That was the guy, Nick. What did you think? Did you get a good look at him?"

"I did not, Em. From the distance of the kitchen he seemed okay. The better question is what did you think of him?"

"I thought he was good looking," she answered, reflecting as she spoke. "He had nice eyes and looked at me when he talked, that's important. He liked his grilled cheese, by the way."

"Another sacrificed customer - I mean satisfied."

"Yes he was, Nick. Even you can't screw up a grilled cheese," she joked.

Unlike the River Street bars, the Cotton Boll was a cut above in class, with a massive mahogany bar brooding over an interior in which floor-length windows presided over views of the passing people and traffic on Broughton Street. It was a gathering place for many professional people who worked downtown and stopped in for a drink or two or eight before heading home.

Nick let Emily off a few minutes early and she primped in the deli women's room before walking down to the Cotton Boll. She was nervous and excited, but also cautious about this encounter, wanting to make a good impression and see where fate led them. After all, this guy had fulfilled one of her life dreams, modest as it was, in sending her roses, and had gone to some length to find her, mainly through Tif, so she figured she at least owed him a chance. Also, she thought he was kind of cute.

Emily had on a blue jean miniskirt and a pale pink blouse one of the "uniforms" she always wore to work. She had her hair pulled back in a ponytail and had refreshed her makeup, but after a day at the deli she certainly knew she wasn't the freshest American Beauty in the garden. She figured that if Mr. Travis Hawthorne liked her anyway, it would be the first brick in a foundation for them. She also calculated the bricks would have to number in the thousands.

Most of the first wave of the happy hour crowd had moved on by the time Emily walked into the bar just before 7:30 p.m. and spotted her would-be beau sitting alone at a table. His face brightened when he saw her and he waved and stood up to greet her. She threw him a smile and glanced about the lounge, thankfully not seeing Ed Browling among the twenty or so patrons. A confrontation with a spurned suitor who remembered the sting of a thrown beer in his eyes was the last thing she needed right now.

"I'm glad you came," Travis said, giving her a quick hug, which even in its briefness made Emily stiffen like petrified wood. "I figured you might back out, but I hoped you wouldn't."

"Why would I not at least come out and have a drink with a man who sent me roses?" Emily said, thinking that she sounded like some nameless bimbo actress in an old spy movie.

Travis had a beer in front of him and a waitress quickly appeared to take her drink order. Emily usually would have asked for a beer but, wanting to impress Travis, or at least not wanting him to think she was lowbrow, ordered a gin and tonic instead.

"Did you have a busy rest of the day?" he asked cheerily as they both settled onto their chairs. With so many other people around, Emily's nerves calmed somewhat as well.

"No, it wasn't so bad. Nick and me have got a pretty good system going so the work flows along. He's a great boss." The waitress brought her drink and she stirred it a few times before taking a big swallow, its strength making her eyes water.

"Whoa there party girl," he said laughing. "I can see I might not be able to keep up with you."

"So you just moved back here from Bainbridge?"

"No, Waycross. I worked for a small newspaper down there, but decided to come back up here and keep up my family's farm. It's just a small spread between here and Statesboro."

"Yeah, Tif said it was along the Ogeechee River, I think. Is that right?"

"You do have a good memory."

Emily gulped another mouthful, swallowed hard and looked at him squarely.

"So why did you send me the roses, Travis Hawthorne?"

He leaned back in his chair and surveyed the room as if everyone was listening for his answer, Emily not taking her eyes off him.

"The day that I ran in to you at the vet's office, I thought you were a fine-looking lady and I wanted to get to know you. I didn't mean to offend or scare you. Your friend Tif helped me out a little and that's how I found out where you worked. I sent the bouquet and intentionally asked that they not include a card with them so that I could handle the introduction myself; so then I dropped by the restaurant."

He had wrapped everything up with a simplicity that appealed to Emily, but she wasn't ready to let him off the hook yet as she ordered another drink.

"So do you still think I'm a fine-looking lady? Even after I've been on the go and in and out of a hot kitchen all day?"

Travis looked at her steadily and seriously.

"Emily, I've never been one for fancy women. I don't like the opera or ballet or a lot of fancy jewelry or makeup and I don't see any of that in you. I think you are naturally pretty and nothing that Max Factor or Revlon or any of those other frilly companies ever made would do anything for you. You don't need them."

Emily could feel herself starting to melt like butter over hot popcorn but she maintained her defenses.

"That's awfully nice of you to say. I mean, I'm a waitress

who drives a beat-up Escort when it's able to move and I don't have a lot of money - hell, I really don't have any money - so I can't imagine what else would attract you to me." Her unexpected frankness embarrassed her and she swigged her second drink and busied herself poking at the ice cubes with the little straw. "I'm sorry. I'm not used to getting a lot of compliments."

"There's nothing to worry about," he said as softly as he could in the talky bar. "If we hate each other after tonight then all you've lost are a couple of hours and me, I sprung for a dozen roses, which ain't going to break me. But I also took a chance and got to meet a girl who I was attracted to and I'll never regret doing that."

They talked and drank until a few minutes before midnight and Travis drove her home, kissing her on the forehead as she climbed out of his pickup truck. The roses had made Emily soar and her emotions were in the same realm as she entered her apartment, George Wallace meowing a loud welcome and alarm over an empty food dish.

No man had ever treated her with the respect and kindness that Travis had shown in one evening. Could it all have been an alluring ploy to attract her? Absolutely, and she was wary of that. Still, he had said and done all the right things and was kind and gentle in a manly, mildly awkward way and had not made any effort to take advantage of her. They had left matters that he would call her in the next day or so and the lack of pressure from him was a comfort to her.

Woozy from six drinks, Emily slumped into her chair and tried to focus on her roses, her eyes telling her they had grown from twelve to twenty-four to thirty-six as she blinked and squinted at them. From the kitchen she heard the cracking sounds of George Wallace enjoying his dry Friskies before he bounded onto the back of her chair like a furry and purring acrobat.

In the distant blackness a church bell chimed one o'clock and a freight train rustled over the rails somewhere along Savannah's west side, but Emily did not hear them.

The gin, her hard work and the anxieties of the day had carried her into sleep's embrace, wondering, in her last conscious thoughts, whether she had been dreaming while awake.

A silvery drizzle cloaked the city in mist near daybreak Friday as Emily stirred from her chair, the cat nose to nose with her. She mentally scolded herself for falling asleep before making it to her bed and stumbled to the shower while trying to shake a minor headache out of her skull. The hot water, a couple of aspirin and two heavily peppered scrambled eggs mixed with bits of sharp cheddar made her feel better and she flicked on the radio while getting dressed for work.

There would be no sun for the roses today, their deepening burgundy mute evidence of their decline, and she cleared the fallen petals off the table, placing them in the envelope with the others.

She replayed the evening in her mind, trying to recount every word of the conversation and the implications of Travis' body language and tones of voice. Had their first meeting gone as perfectly as she imagined or was she so starved for something good to finally happen to her that she was overreacting?

At the moment it didn't matter; she had savored a taste of happiness and she wanted more. Before heading out the door, she looked at the calendar and noted the date: January 27, 1999. Maybe one day the anniversary of their meeting would be an occasion to celebrate.

The morning's dreariness and cold did not faze Emily as she drove to work, the thermometer having plunged some twenty degrees since the day before. Reaching in her coat pocket as she navigated through traffic, she felt the cocktail napkin on which Travis had written his phone number. At a stoplight she pulled it out and studied the loops and curves of his penmanship as if Elvis himself had given her an autograph.

She pictured Travis' face and what he wore and recounted what he had told her about himself. He was seventeen months older than her, and had grown up on his family's farm. Even as a youngster he had wanted to be a writer and he had gotten a job covering high school football for the Statesboro Clarion newspaper, even though he was only in the tenth grade. After high school he had gone to Georgia Southern for two years, but his grades had been dismal and he had dropped out to take a job with a daily newspaper in Waycross. He had worked there through years that brought his mother's death and the deterioration of his father's health. Dealing with three siblings who seemed to be too far away and too unconcerned about their daddy, he had told his editor that he had to go home to care for his father. Travis had left Waycross the previous June and returned to the farm. When his father died about three months later, Travis learned that the old man had amended his will to give him the home place.

Travis had been staying out there ever since, fishing in the Ogeechee, batting around ideas for a novel and generally trying to get his head together amid the awful reality that his parents were gone and that he was on his own.

By the way he talked and the nice truck that he drove, Emily sensed that Travis wasn't hurting for cash, not that it mattered to her. A woman who married or screwed for money was a two-bit whore, plain and simple, Leona Tillman had taught her daughter, and Emily had never forgotten the lesson. Better to be poor with dignity than to sell your body and soul for mortal riches, she preached.

Emily vowed to herself that she would not call Travis. He would have to make the next move, even though he had already walked the narrow limb in sending the roses and then popping in to see her at Nick's.

Travis' place was about a forty-minute drive from downtown Savannah and Emily did not really expect him to show up at the deli on such a bad-weather day. Nevertheless, as the clock ticked toward noon, she became more and more excited, hoping that he might continue his string of surprises.

The drizzle turned into a cold, heavy rain by late morning and cars and city buses swished along Broughton

Street with their headlights reflecting off store windows amid the gloom.

"The business will be no good," Nick said despondently, staring out the front door at the water splashing off his canopy and onto the sidewalk. "We not make money today, Em." About two minutes later he held the door open for a lady who was shielding herself with a gray trench coat - Tif Bryant.

"Thank you, Nick. Lord, I just about washed away trying to get here; I hope you appreciate that," she said, hanging her coat on one of the hooks near the cash register and finger-combing her hair.

"I greatly do, Miss Tiffany. I make you a special sandwich today. As you like it."

Nick hurried to the kitchen.

"And besides," Tiff continued, eyeing Emily, who was putting salt and pepper shakers on the tables, "I got to find out what's been happening with Snow White here. Apparently somebody's suddenly got a love life."

"Tif, I'm sorry. I was gonna call you last night, but I got, uh, occupied."

Tif snorted in laughter and sat down at a table up front.

"Oh, I figured as much, Em. A man don't send roses and then don't show up to strut and crow and take credit for it. It's not natural. I tried to call you at home this morning but I didn't get an answer and I was about to bust to find out so I came down."

"He came in yesterday, Tif," Emily said in a low voice, sliding into a chair across the table from her. "Shocked the hell out of me, to be honest, just popping up out of the blue like that." She paused for dramatic effect. "But it sure turned out to be worth it."

Tif's eyes widened and her mouth fell open.

"You didn't take this boy to bed yet, did you, crazy girl?"

"I don't know, Tif," Emily said in singsong, toying with her friend. "He was mighty nice and after all, he did send me a big bunch of roses."

Tif quickly saw through her.

"Don't feed me that junk food. I know you like a book, Em."

"He came in near the end of the lunch rush and I didn't even notice him at first," Emily said, turning serious. "Asked me how I liked the roses and Nick just about had to peel me off the floor I was so surprised."

"So what'd you think of him?"

Emily reached across the table to touch her friend's wet forearm.

"Tif, I don't think it could have gone any better if some guy from olden times who wrote fairy tales had sat down and made it all up."

As cats and dogs drenched Savannah, Emily unwrapped her eventful evening for Tif, and they mulled over what would or should happen next, like two generals plotting the course of a campaign to take and hold Travis Hawthorne. Tif agreed that she should wait for him to call her, but her lunch hour was too little time to fully discuss such a weighty matter. After she ate her triple-decker BLT, she had run out into the flood to get back to Doc Craven's, Emily watching her dodge puddles until she reached her car.

Stay cool and be patient, had been the strategy they decided on. If Travis seemed too good to be true, then maybe he was, Tif had stressed. Time and experience would give her the answer.

The day dragged with the rain continuing to come down in waves, effectively drowning out most of Nick's business. The two of them sat up front, all the water making it almost seem as if they were watching a street scene in Atlantis.

The clock was straight-up 3 p.m. when the phone rang and Ernie the busboy, who had been supposed to be tidying up the storeroom answered it.

"Hey Em, it's for you," he called to her sleepily. She trotted to the phone and took the receiver from him, hoping that Travis' voice would greet her. It did.

"I didn't want to call you earlier because I know how hectic lunch can be," he said.

"Oh, that's okay. It's raining like crazy here so we

haven't had too many customers."

"Emily, I just wanted to call and tell you that I had a great time last night and I hope you did too."

"It was a lot of fun. You're easy to be with." Emily wanted to say more but words forsook her.

"I'm glad you had a good time. Listen, I'm kind of tied up for the rest of the day, but I was wondering if you would want to get together tomorrow. I know you work on Saturday, but we could have dinner or drinks or something."

Emily hesitated to say yes only in trying to string her thoughts together, but Travis pounced on her pause.

"Unless you think it's too soon. I don't want to pressure you at all."

She finally found her voice.

"I don't feel any pressure from you Travis. We can go out for dinner if you give me time to get home and grab a shower."

"Awesome. I'll pick you up at your place at 8:30 or should I make it 9?" he said, Emily sensing his excitement.

"Make it 8:30. I'll be ready."

Emily would have preferred one of those post-first-date calls where she lay on her bed, coiling and uncoiling the phone cord around her index finger while she and Travis cooed at each other like tenth-graders who had explored each other's tongues in a makeout spot the night before. Instead it had been straightforward with no gushing and no commitment, other than to a second meeting, and the more she thought about it, the more she realized this approach from both of them was for the best.

Emily figured she had to be patient and that if Travis was the right one after she had wasted so much of her life with the wrong one then she was due for a reward - a lasting, loving relationship. If he wasn't, then she would cast him back into the dark waters where Tif could fish for him if she wanted and Emily herself would bait a hook and try again, something she had never done.

If Travis shattered her pieced-back-together heart and Emily let him go, Tif or any other woman wouldn't have a problem finding him in the vast dating pool where most men were bottom feeders anyway. They would only have to look for the tear-darkened rose petals floating on the surface.

Chapter 6

With the weather continuing its nastiness into Friday night, Emily went home after work and curled up to work on her memory book. Under George Wallace's careful supervision from his perch on a windowsill, she meticulously glued the rose petals onto three pages following Brandon's photos and wrote above them in pen: "Roses from Travis Hawthorne - January 25, 1999."

To let the glue dry, she lay the open book on the table beside the vase, the roses now withering and drooping in their last glamorous act. The droning rain pattered on the roof, a lullaby from nature that Emily had enjoyed since she was old enough to remember. Even though it was only about 10 p.m. - early by her standards, particularly on a Friday night - she decided to crawl into bed, watch some TV and let the rain serenade her into a cozy sleep. The cat quickly joined her, padding out a nest near her feet and unhurriedly blocking her view of the little 13-inch television set on her chest of drawers.

In her widowhood, Emily had started sleeping in the nude - something Lyle would never have allowed - and she loved it, another freedom that she relished. On messy winter nights like this it was all the more wonderful, burrowing under the sheets and blankets and curling like a fetus until she warmed up.

The only thing missing was a lover that she had never had. Even on the most brutally cold nights she had never been able to seek Lyle's body heat. To the contrary, any contact with him, in bed or otherwise, made her shudder.

Travis would be so different, she thought to herself, closing her eyes and listening to the rain. His gentleness, at least what she perceived of it after one date, would endear her to him sexually, a far contrast from the only man she had ever been with. Travis also had hands that smothered hers and she always remembered what the other waitresses at the Portly Pig said about men with big hands.

She thought about what it would be like to make love with him, or any man really, who wouldn't snarl threats and insults in her ear as he thrust and then slap her after the brief act. Even if the violence had vanished, Emily would have preferred putting away groceries after a supermarket trip to having sex with Lyle.

On coffee break when the other girls at the Portly Pig had sat down for a smoke and had talked about their men, she had hung back at first. Gradually she had shared stories about Lyle's "little midget buddy," much to their yelps and giggles. She suspected that waitress Nell Windom had experienced the midget first hand and she only hoped Nell - two-timing whore that she was - had laughed in his face.

Emily guessed that Travis would be another man altogether, and in the dim room illuminated by the television images painting the walls, she touched herself and thought of him.

Emily slipped into sleep disappointed that Travis had not called her in the evening, but as she arrived at the deli Saturday morning the sun was torching away the clouds and there were peeks of blue sky off to the west. It was hard to be down when the weather was clearing and a Saturday night date with a seemingly nice, handsome guy was only hours away.

Business was better than Friday, but Saturdays were never much of a moneymaker for Nick either since he depended so heavily on the 9-to-5ers during the week. Saturday usually attracted a few locals and occasional tourists, and there would be more of both with spring approaching.

As if on schedule, Travis called at 3 p.m. to make sure that Emily still wanted to go out.

"Are we going someplace fancy or just out for a beer and maybe chicken wings?" she asked. "I need to know how to dress."

"If you have a preference, tell me, Emily," he replied. "I'm about as easy as an old shoe."

Emily was beginning to believe that he was just that, a complete shock to her system from her late, hated husband. They decided to go to an Italian eatery on Victory Drive that both had heard was very good.

The hours crawled by, but finally Emily was off and she raced home to get ready, Nick wishing her luck with her date as she began her weekend.

Travis was prompt, which she liked, and she invited him in to see her apartment. He was wearing jeans and a heavy green flannel shirt and gave her a hug when she answered the door.

"You look really pretty," he said, eyeing her from head to feet. She had pulled on jeans herself, the tightest she could find in her closet, and had on her favorite blouse, a lavender number the Gillons had given her for her first birthday with Lyle. It had been big on her then, but she had grown into it, only wearing it on what she considered special occasions.

"So you've lived here since you moved to Savannah?" he asked, surveying the living room.

"Yep, other than the cat, who's hiding from you, you're the first man to ever see my palace." she said, feeling slightly embarrassed about the poorness of her home. On their first night out, Travis had not asked her a lot about herself, which Emily had appreciated. She knew a lot of girls would have taken it differently, thinking a guy wasn't really interested if he didn't want to know more about them. In her case, however, a lot of questions would have understandably made her uneasy and uncomfortable. He had seemed content to tell her whatever she asked about him and to make small talk. This had put her at ease and attracted her to him even more.

"The roses you gave me are fading away, but I'm still enjoying them."

"Looks like they're about past their prime, that's for sure. Some folks have probably said the same thing about me."

"I'd say they're crazy."

"Well that's nice to hear from somebody whose opinion I respect." Travis sat down at her table, but didn't seem to notice her memory book, which she had closed after seeing that the glued rose petals had dried. "Your cat doesn't like visitors?"

"He's just real particular about who he associates with, and he's never seen you before."

"Sure he has," Travis laughed. "I'm the guy that crunched into him when y'all were leaving the vet's office. That's why he's under the bed or wherever he is."

"George is a real tiger. You sit there long enough and he'll rip off your head - only if I tell him to, of course."

Marconila's Restaurant was jammed and they had to wait about twenty minutes before being seated at a tiny, candle-lit table in a back alcove. Despite the noise of a hundred conversations, the air was basted with the smell of burnt olive oil, steaming rigatoni, and baking pizza which, with the candle burning through some of the dimness, made the setting as romantic as Emily had experienced in her life.

Travis chose a bottle of Chianti from the wine list and they ordered their dinner, the cacophony making it difficult to carry on a conversation while they waited for the food to arrive. The waitress brought heaping plates of Chicken Cacciatore and fettuccine Alfredo and they feasted, feeding each other forkfuls across the table. They agreed that they loved the restaurant and that the entrees were superb, but it had been too loud and crowded for them to talk much.

"I don't think I can breathe," Emily gasped as they walked across the parking lot to his truck. "Do I have oregano oozing out of my ears?"

"Let me check," Travis said, brushing her hair away from her neck and drawing close to her. "No, just a little Parmesan, that's all." He gave her a quick, gentle kiss on her earlobe, Emily responding with a shy smile. As always, he opened the truck door for her, and as always, she marveled at what a gentleman he was.

"Can I interest you in a nightcap before I have to make my long drive home?"

"Sure. I'm game for anything."

At her suggestion, they ended up back at the Cotton

Boll, Emily not wanting to chance running into one of her unsavory acquaintances down on River Street. Unlike Marconila's, the lounge was much quieter, a pianist Emily knew only as "Classy Tommy" greeting them with a wave as they entered. Tommy was in on weekend nights, playing standards by Ray Charles, Count Basie and other favorites from the big bands.

They sipped their Budweisers and watched a well-dressed older couple celebrating their fiftieth wedding anniversary slow dance as Tommy played a Cole Porter tune at their request. Then Travis asked the question she had anticipated with loathing.

"So why don't you tell me a little bit about Emily? We haven't really talked too much about you."

"What would you like to know?" she replied, trying to appear receptive and conceal the sudden nervousness that zigzagged through her.

"You make the call," he said nonchalantly. "What would you like for me to know about you?"

"Okay, let me see." She was choosing her words carefully. "I'm a waitress at a Greek deli. I've got a cat named George Wallace."

"No, no, no," he interrupted, laughing, "don't hand me all that. Tell me about you - where you're from originally, your family, stuff like that."

"Well, I grew up in Bratton County, which is a few hours west of here. My small town where I lived was called Pierpont. Ever heard of it?"

"Sure, I know where Pierpont is. I bet I've been through there at one time or another. They had a tire factory there that went belly up a few years back, is that right? I had a friend whose daddy got laid off there and they ended up in Statesboro."

"Yeah, when the Hercules plant closed, a lot of folks lost their jobs. My dad was one of them," she lied.

"Man, I'm sorry to hear that. What did he do after that?"

The question caught her off guard and she took a drink, her mind grasping for a believable answer.

"He worked odd jobs for a few years. Carpentry,

electrician, things like that. We got by."

"Wow, that must have been tough on your family."

"It was a rough time. Anyway, that's where I grew up."

"So you ever been married or been serious about a guy? Other than me, right?"

"Travis, a man who sends me roses and is sweet like you are deserves my attention." Emily paused for a moment to signal the waitress to bring another round of beer and give her time to think about how much to reveal about herself.

"I, I was married for a little over five years." She watched for any change of expression on his face, but there was none.

"What happened?"

Again, Emily gulped her beer before answering. The anniversary couple had finished their special dance with Classy Tommy adding a flourish at the end of the song as they kissed to applause.

"He committed suicide."

Travis winced as if her words had slapped his jaw.

"Aw, Emily, I'm sorry. I didn't mean to dredge up something like that. Man, that's terrible. Did y'all have kids?"

"I had a son, but he had a lot of health problems." Emily could feel her lips trembling. "His name was Brandon and he was just a beautiful child."

Seeing her reaction, Travis looked horrified and unsure of whether to ask any more about Brandon, but Emily was not done. She dried her eyes with a cocktail napkin.

"He died before he was a year old. He was the only child."

Travis appeared to be almost teary himself while taking her hands in his. "You've had a tough row to hoe, Emily. I wish there was something I could do for you."

"You're doing it, Travis. Maybe it's best that you take me home."

January frosted into February, but Emily's relationship with Travis didn't cool despite her revelations. Travis did not ask any more questions about her background, but

Emily told him that she herself was an only child and that her parents were no longer living. She had no idea if her daddy was alive and had gotten past the point of caring.

During her work week, Travis called her every night to talk over the day's events and they saw each other every weekend. He was working on his first book and keeping up the farm, but occasionally found time to drive in and have lunch at the deli.

They kissed for the first time on their third date, as he was saying good night at her front door, but Emily felt it was too early for her to go any further than that and he had made the drive home without protest. "I'll never put any pressure on you, Em," he had told her.

On their third weekend together she asked him if he wanted to spend the night with her. It had been an anxious decision for her, since her sexual resume began and ended with Lyle and she was very much afraid that she would disappoint Travis in bed. Their first kiss had been wonderful and she yearned for physical intimacy with him, but the thought that she might not perform well and could lose him because of it was a tremendous worry to her. On this particular night, she asked him after they had been out for dinner and a few drinks and had come back to her apartment.

"Emily, you don't have to do anything you don't want to," he replied. "I hope you realize that by now." They were sitting on her ratty sofa and he had his arm around her.

"You've always shown me respect, Travis and that's a big reason why I care for you so much."

"Do you really want me to stay here tonight? I would love to, but I need to know that's what you want too."

Emily rubbed her face with her hands as if the decision had drained her mentally.

"This is all new to me, Travis. I've only been with one other man and to tell you the truth, I'm scared." Tears washed her eyes.

"You're not afraid of me, are you?"

"No, not at all. It's just, well, it's just that I'm afraid that I'll disappoint you because I don't have much experience."

"Are you sure that's all there is, Em?" he said, slowly

running his fingers through her hair. "I get the feeling there's something more to all this."

Emily balled herself on the sofa beside him and wiped her eyes with her hand. "There is more than you'll ever know."

For a few seconds they sat in silence, the wind groaning through the trees outside as if winter's banshees were gasping their last before spring.

"Do you want to tell me about it?" Travis said finally. Emily sensed that if she didn't level with him now, things might never again reach this point between them. With all else she had suffered, the thought of life without Travis was suddenly devastating to her.

"It was my husband," she sniffled.

"Tell me, Em."

She buried her face in his side, raising her head only enough so that he would be able to hear her.

"He beat me, Travis. He beat me long and hard the whole time we were married. For no reason at all that piece of trash tortured me for years and for that I hope he is rotting in hell." She was sobbing uncontrollably now.

"Any man who would hit a woman for no reason is a piece of trash," Travis said, gently rocking her. "I'm sorry I wasn't around to protect you, Em."

"You would have, I know."

"Was he a big drinker?"

"If he was awake, most likely he was drunk."

"Did he just hit you when he was drinking?"

"No, it didn't matter what he was doing or anything. He abused me for years and he had no right or reason to do that. He stole my life from me."

Travis kissed her on the top of her head. "I tell you what, we'll talk more about this later, but I gotta ask you one other question."

"I'm listening. Go ahead."

"You're not afraid that I'm going to beat you, are you Em? I mean, that's not the reason why you're a little uncomfortable with me staying over tonight."

"That's not it at all. Travis, you are the first person I've ever told this, but Lyle, my husband, he, he..."

"Let it out, Em."

"He raped me." Her tears were flowing as rapidly as her words while Travis held her and listened. "He raped me on our honeymoon and other times. A husband's got every right to expect loving from his wife, but nobody should be forced to do it or be raped with mop handles and things. I hate him for what he did to me!"

Travis tried to soothe her, embracing her tightly as her sobs heightened. There was no need for more words just now, a strong hug from a caring companion the best remedy Emily had never had before. For about five minutes they sat entwined on the sofa and she gradually regained her composure.

"I'll say this about the whole thing, Em," he said softly and deliberately. "Your husband committed suicide and I think that's about the best thing that could have happened to you and your marriage."

Emily sat up to look at him.

"Like you said Travis, it was for the best and it really doesn't matter if he pulled the trigger or not. He's out of my life forever."

There would be no wild sex with a new lover this night for Emily. Exhausted from baring much of her soul to Travis, she went to bed, expecting him to join her, but too mentally tired to really care. He had almost carried her into the bedroom, helping her out of her clothes down to her underwear and tucking her in. He kissed her and switched off her bedside lamp before he quietly left the room.

Her next awareness was of the sun streaking through her window blinds in early morning. She was alone in bed and, wondering what had happened to Travis, staggered to her feet, donned her bathrobe and went out into the living room. Travis was asleep on the sofa, an afghan covering him and George Wallace crouching like a guardian angel with a twitching tail on the floor next to his boots.

Talking to Travis about the black side of her life had been like opening an emotional dam for her, the stagnation of her being pulsing out in words and tears. He had steered her on to the long road to recovering from all the evils of her past, and as she stood over him she decided to reward him for everything from the roses to this moment.

Wordlessly, she tapped Travis on the shoulder, rousing him, and placed her finger to her mouth to tell him not to speak. The cat wove through her bare legs in greeting and a request for food, but he would have to wait. Emily grasped Travis' hand and, pulling him to his feet, led him to her bathroom. He had slept in a T-shirt and his briefs, his other clothes piled on a chair.

She turned on the shower and opened her robe to him as the first wisps of steam clouded the air. He came to her and the hands that had consoled her hours earlier now kneaded and stroked her flesh. Together they climbed into the shower, the hot water sliding over their bodies, and soon the sounds of their lovemaking sent the spooked cat scurrying for cover under the bed.

"Now that's what I call the way to start a Sunday morning," Travis said, toweling off. "You okay in there, Em?"

Emily was still in the tub, hiding behind the shower curtain until he left the bathroom. She had never known physical pleasure like she had just experienced with him, but she was shy about her body.

"I'm fine, Travis, more than fine. You made me feel wonderful."

"I can sure say the same about you, sweetie."

Even though it had seemed to be the most natural thing in the world, Emily had been somewhat rigid when they first got into the shower. On top of everything else, Travis was only the second man she had ever seen naked. It was as if she was a virgin whose innocence had never been lost in the nightmare with Lyle.

Travis, however, had not rushed things, caressing her with gentle words and kisses and slowly soaping her body, using his own to spread the lather. Gradually she relaxed, the tension quickly replaced by a tingling of lust that torched through her amid a frenzy of slippery hardness and softness, circling tongues, and yelps and grunts of primal pleasure.

"Hey Em. I gonna go get some orange juice or whatever I can find to drink in the fridge. Can I get you anything?"

"No thanks, Travis. I'll be out in a minute."

By the time she dried herself, put on her bathrobe and padded to the kitchen, Travis was sitting at the table with a glass of milk, some of which he had poured into a saucer for George Wallace.

"I had to make friends with him somehow," he said, the cat purring and lapping up his treat.

"You had me purring too, buster," Emily said. "Tell you what. I'll fix you some breakfast if you want, but then I've got a request."

"I'm all ears."

"Can we do it again?"

By the fifth anniversary of Brandon's death nine days later, Emily was more serious than ever about Travis and each day seemed to deepen her feelings for him. The calendar, however, always was a bleak reminder of the baby she had buried and no amount of good times, sex and security from any man living could make up for a mother's loss such as this.

Travis spent that particular night holding and petting her, but her lost son haunted her mind. Brandon always did, really, but the anniversary was always much harder to deal with, regardless of the passing years.

She figured that she was probably the only person who still cared about Brandon, remembering Sarah Gillon's weekly trips to the cemetery, but wondering if Sarah was still alive to make the visits. Treat had likely killed her by now and for the lack of help or advice Sarah had given her, Emily felt no sorrow about what might have befallen her ex-mother-in-law.

Emily harbored no guilt about Brandon's tragedy. God had willed him to live five months and a few days and there was nothing she nor the finest doctor on the planet could have done to save him. She believed that, even telling herself that God had taken Brandon from her because of Lyle's wickedness. What Emily regretted immensely was that in leaving Pierpont, she could not at least visit his grave, as Sarah did.

Looking at his photos in her memory book, she vowed to return to Bratton County and the resting place of her infant son.

Chapter 7

The Georgia countryside was abloom in early spring, the smell of the awakening earth perfumed by dogwood, honeysuckle and wild azaleas as Emily and Travis headed west on Interstate 16. Emily's yearning to be with her baby had prompted her to ask Travis to drive her to Pierpont. It was the first weekend in March and they decided to make it an overnight getaway, leaving early on Sunday morning.

She was completely at ease with Travis by now as if he had pulled her out of a life-draining cocoon that had been spun around her. He was easy going and charming and always seemed to know when she needed her space or quiet time.

They had spent Saturday night on his farm, located on sixty acres backed up to the Ogeechee River. This had been Emily's first visit to Travis' home, since he usually drove into Savannah and, as their intimacy had evolved, had stayed with her. The Hawthorne place wasn't anything fancy. The two-story, white clapboard house had been built about 1920 and had been in Travis' family since just after World War II. His daddy had raised corn and soybean and a few acres of cotton, along with keeping some hogs, cows and a scattering of chickens. There were no crops now and had not been since his father had been able to run the place, cocklebur, dandelion and other weeds choking the abandoned fields. The livestock was gone as well and a dirt-coated John Deere tractor, with jagged patches of rust beginning to eat at its green, was parked in the old barn, its work days long over. Travis used a smaller tractor to keep the grass cut around the house.

He had converted the den into his office where he had begun work on his first novel. Emily wanted to see what he had written so far, but he wanted to get further along with the project before letting her see it.

The night had been especially warm for that time of year and they had wandered down a path through tall grass and pines to the banks of the Ogeechee, the river's brown water like tarnished copper in the half-moon's glow. The river at this point was about fifty yards wide, the opposite bank ominously dark among trees tangled with stoles of Spanish moss. They had sat by the silently moving water and talked and laughed, having no concept of time as they were cradled by the night, Emily basking in the serenity of it all. Later they had spread a blanket in the back yard and made love, afterwards lying on their backs and gazing into a black sky sequined with countless tiny diamonds.

With a bag of jelly doughnuts on the seat between them, they were on the road by about 8 a.m. Sunday, the pickup's heater quickly chasing off the bite of a morning chill.

Almost ten months had passed since Emily left Pierpont, and she wondered if the town had changed. Yet overriding this mild curiosity and her desired closeness with Brandon were feelings of fear and foreboding about what might loom for her - this was where she had spilled blood and snuffed out a life, worthless though it was. On TV detective shows and a mystery novel she read in eighth grade, a killer always returned to the scene of the crime. Emily was doing just that as Travis exited the interstate onto U.S. Highway 63, which led through Pierpont some thirty miles away. It was early afternoon now and they stopped at a Hardee's near the exit to stretch their legs and grab a quick burger. Twenty minutes later they were back on the road, Emily becoming increasingly nervous as the miles clicked off, bringing them closer to Pierpont.

"Are you okay, sweetie? You're mighty quiet," Travis asked finally. "Anything bothering you?"

"No, no, Travis, not really. It's just that I'm going back to where my one and only son died and it's just hard on me."

"I understand. And then old Lyle did himself in, but that wasn't no great loss to anybody." Travis paused as he passed a faded blue church bus filled with smiling, waving black children. Emily waved back to them.

"Can I ask you a question about that, Em? I mean, if

it doesn't upset you. I'm just the curious sort."

"Ask me whatever you want, Travis."

"How did he do it? I'm talking about the suicide. Was it with a gun or drug overdose or closing the car in the garage or what? Again, I'm not trying to dredge up bad memories, I just figured it might do you good to talk about it, plus I'd like to know. We've never discussed it before."

Emily stared down U.S. 63, the white center line zipping under the speeding truck like someone had strung aspirin on the two-lane asphalt. She could make out the smoky purple eminence of Tatum's Mountain in the distance.

"A shotgun," she replied as if in a trance. "He used his favorite shotgun."

They were about eleven miles from Pierpont now and the locals called this stretch of the highway Gum Creek Road because of a minnow-slim branch that fed into the Hookachee River. Emily knew it well since it had been part of the route she had taken to kill Lyle.

"Wow, did you have any idea he was in that frame of mind?" Travis asked, not taking his eyes away from the windshield. "I guess he left a note, right?"

"No, he didn't write a note. He didn't leave me anything but a chance to climb out of hell." Emily's tone was almost hypnotic, the passing landscape and the mountain blocking out more and more of the sky while refreshing a portion of her memory she had worked so hard to cleanse.

"How did you stay in your home after he did something like that there?"

Roadside signs now boasted the pitifully few attractions for any traveler to have ever slowed down in going through Pierpont. Flaked-paint billboards advertised the Hercules House, an inn whose heyday had been when the tire factory was in robust full production in the early 1950s. Others tried to lure motorists to the Georgian Motor Lodge and Restaurant which, Emily knew, had burned to the ground when she was ten, and Big Mattie's Truck Stop, which had long been boarded up.

The sign for the Harbor Sunset Motel drew Emily's eye and mind, the horrors of her honeymoon mingling with recollections of the pleasant Pakistani family who operated it and who sometimes ordered take-out dinners from the Portly Pig. They had never had any idea of what Lyle had done to her in Room 21 and the father was always friendly and gave a good tip when he came to pick up their order.

The truck was less than two miles from Jenson Lane, which was no more than a little-used farm road cutting through the fenced pastures and woods where Lyle hunted and had built The Hootch.

"He didn't do it in the house. He went hunting. It was up in his deer stand. It wasn't really that far from right here where we are now."

"So who found him?"

"I'm not sure, Travis." Emily was becoming irritated. "Why should it matter who found him and why do you care? Isn't it enough that he's gone?"

The pickup passed the Jenson Lane turnoff.

"I figured I might be pushing my luck too much. I'm sorry, Emily." Travis reached over and softly patted her on the knee. "Sometimes I ask too many questions, I guess."

"You didn't mean any harm, Travis."

Minutes later, the pickup rumbled over double railroad tracks and Travis drove slowly through Pierpont's business district, such as it was. On a Sunday afternoon, there was no deader place on Earth than a small Southern downtown and in this regard Pierpont was no different than ten thousand other dots on the map. On the seventh day of Creation, God rested and the churches filled for worship and there was a tranquility and strength about it all that had endured for centuries.

Certainly other little towns across America, from Hawaii to Maine, closed down on Sundays, but the South did it best, relaxing amid lace finery, and smite-the-devil sermons. There was fried chicken or baked ham for dinner around 1:30 p.m. and sweet tea, fat yams, good manners and shady hammocks to make the seventh day a luxurious drawling laziness from the rest of the week - mixed with a heaping dose of religion, of course.

Emily was silent as they passed the storefronts, all of which held memories for her from her childhood to her flight from Pierpont. She remembered that her mother while shopping had pushed her down these same cracked sidewalks in a stroller. All the old familiar sites rolled by her open window and soon they were driving through Pierpont's westside where LaCourt Street held the monarchy of Treat Gillon. Just seeing the street sign made Emily shudder.

The Olivet Hill Cemetery held the dust of more than a century's worth of Pierpont's Methodists. It was located just off Highway 63 about two miles on the other side of town and had been a burying ground long before Pierpont was established. Countless unmarked and long-forgotten graves were in the woods outside the low chain-length fence of the modern cemetery's boundaries. Emily remembered Lyle telling her about deer hunters plodding among these trees and occasionally kicking up old skulls and pieces of bones.

"So you're gonna be all right handling this?" Travis said as he turned into the cemetery. "With your baby and, uh, him, buried right next to each other, this would be tough on anybody."

"I'm dealing with it." Her tone was unintentionally terse. "We need to go to Section G-10."

Emily was trying to appear as strong as possible, even if her emotions were gushing out of control internally. She didn't recall telling Travis that Brandon and Lyle were buried side by side, but fate had blurred a lot of things in all that life had piled on her. Travis drove slowly, scanning the rows of granite and marble on both sides of the narrow paved lane before stopping.

"That's them, isn't it, Em?"

Emily knew that it was without even reading the markers. Wordlessly she swiveled out of the truck and stood before all that was left of her treasured son and loathed husband.

There was nothing fancy about either headstone, both slim and about waist high. Treat could have certainly afforded much more elaborate tributes to his only son and grandson. This area of the cemetery was treeless, but both graves were well-tended, a small brown teddy bear, that looked to have been recently placed, propped against Brandon's marker.

Clutching a plastic shopping bag, Emily slowly approached her son's resting place and knelt on the grass beside it, gently touching the letters and numbers carved into the granite. Travis had gotten out of the pickup by now, standing at a respectful distance from her as she looked to be praying. Emily had her back to Lyle's grave, not even wanting it in her peripheral vision. In no way had she come here for him and if she had been alone here at night, she probably would have pissed on him again like she had after his funeral. It had felt so good.

Her full attention now, however, was on Brandon and her brief memories of him flickered through her head like a movie fast forwarded. From the bag she pulled a stuffed toy butterfly she had bought to bring to him, remembering the way his face had brightened in fascination and delight when she had put a butterfly mobile on his crib. She gently laid the butterfly beside the teddy bear as tears filled her eyes.

Suddenly she realized there was no sense staying here any longer. There was no comfort for her in staring at a chunk of stone with her little boy's name cut into it or the brownish-green grass beneath which his tiny form had been placed in a miniature casket and buried. Brandon was no more here than he was cradled in her lap; he lived in her heart and mind and this place now meant nothing to her.

Sarah Gillon must obviously still be alive, since no one else Emily could think of would have put the teddy bear there. If Sarah found solace in visiting the graves then so be it, but Emily would never return to Olivet Hill Cemetery.

The budding trees dressing the slopes of Tatum's Mountain basked in the dropping sun's orange brilliance as Travis drove back into Pierpont.

"Thanks for doing this for me," Emily said. "I'm glad I finally got it out of my system."

"I'll bring you back here any time you want, Em, you

know that."

"You're a good man to keep around Travis, that's what I really know more than anything. I don't think I'll ever want to come back. Maybe someday we can find enough time to go visit my mama."

Leona Tillman rested in a country church cemetery outside Chattanooga where some of Emily's other relatives on her mother's side also were buried. The Tillman family was rooted deep between the rocks of that mountainous, wild land and Leona never strayed from her desire to return there once death kissed her. Emily had not seen her mother's grave since the modest funeral, Lyle refusing to take her or to allow her to go back on her own. Travis would go with her, she knew, but they would have to decide when to make the trip.

This Sunday, however, there was to be one final stop in what Emily believed would be her last journey to Pierpont.

"Travis, I figure we can stay at a motel out near the interstate if that's all right with you, but I've just got one more request."

"Whatever you want, Em."

"I want to see The Hootch."

Pierpont's city limits sign was shrinking behind them as Travis' truck sped toward I-16.

"The Hootch?"

"That's where Lyle did himself in. Do you mind?"

"No, not at all. Just give me directions."

Travis did not seem affected by her wanting to go there, nor did he ask her any more questions.

"The next paved road to the right is Jenson Lane. We'll turn there and then it'll be a few miles." They rode in silence for the next few minutes, as the day rapidly began to slip toward twilight. Jenson Lane was named for a local farmer whose fields of corn, cotton and soybean bordered it near the main highway. The most traffic it ever saw was at the various harvest times when tractors and combines were common and during hunting seasons when camouflaged pickups rattled toward the killing zones.

It was a long, straight, roughly paved road that seemed to go nowhere, eventually looping around by

Lazarus AME Church and back into U.S. 63 on the far side of the interstate. There was nothing much to distinguish Jenson Lane other than the ever-changing farm fields and swatches of pine and oak woods which it divided and the fact that Lyle Gillon had blown his head off while hunting nearby; that was how the locals would have described it anyway.

Why she wanted to retrace her lonely route to murder Lyle, Emily had no idea; it had been basically an impulse to ask Travis to make this detour into her darkness. Perhaps deep down she wanted to share the madness of her marriage with a man who had been her savior and who might somehow understand the desperation of her bloodletting. Well over a year had vanished since that November morning, yet this area of Bratton County had changed very little. A few houses were scattered about, but this land was for crops and game, the deer, wild turkey, dove, mallard, quail and other fowl coveted by the legions of hunters.

"We're coming up on the turn, it's a dirt road," Emily said after they had gone about fifteen miles. By now the shadows were surrendering to gloom and Tatum's Mountain was dark against the faintly rouged sky. At Emily's word, Travis steered onto a dusty dirt trace. On each side of the road were cornfields, which had not yet been cut after the last harvest, the shriveled stalks standing in rows like a dead army guarding Lyle's last stronghold.

Pete Stuart the car dealer owned some of this land, even though Emily's cat probably knew as much about farming as he did. Stuart had bought about a hundred acres some years back, planning to build a country home for himself, but selling used Pacers and other junk on four wheels hadn't exactly been a mother lode for him. "Pete's Place Ranch" had had to wait, but Stuart always let some of his buddies, including Lyle, do their hunting out here. Emily always wondered if Pete knew that Lyle was using The Hootch for hunting and screwing, but it mattered little now.

Travis had been quiet, following her directions, and she was glad of it, not in any mood for conversation. Her heart was thumping against her shirt as he stopped the truck in a weedy area between an open field and a cluster of mixed pine, elm and blackjacks.

"Now we've just got to walk a little bit," she said, climbing out without looking at Travis. This was the place she had parked that morning and she could still envision Lyle's pickup there, a couple of old, crumpled beer cans in the grass probably among the last he drained in this life.

The narrow path leading to the deer stand looked to have been little used and there were more briars than she recalled. In a nearby thicket, a murder of crows was settling into the evening roost, some of them fussing unseen among the new spring leaves. Dark was coming quick and hard now as Emily pushed down the trail with Travis a few yards behind her.

Suddenly she emerged into the clearing and saw the unmistakable outline of the regal oak that held The Hootch - the only thing missing was the stand itself. Emily was confused momentarily, thinking that she had come to the wrong place, but this tree was old, with uniquely twisted branches and she quickly realized The Hootch was gone.

"What's wrong, Em?" Travis moved close against her, softly clasping her arms. "Is this the spot?"

Emily did not answer immediately, taking almost a full minute to scan the blackening forest. "I'm pretty sure this is it," she said finally, wading through some tall grass to reach the oak's base.

This was it. On the tree trunk were the wooden slats Lyle had nailed there to be able to climb up, only now the ascent would have merely been into the boughs of the oak itself. Looking up, Emily saw that the only other remnant of The Hootch was two small pieces of old plywood dangling from limbs. Someone had gone to the trouble to ensure that The Hootch was destroyed.

"It was right there, about twenty feet up," Emily said, pointing into the branches. "That's where Lyle died."

"Not much to see now, is there," Travis said, standing beside her and peering upward.

"Not much to see even then," she replied. "It was just like a big tree house that kids would've built. "All he did up there was shoot at deer, drink and whore around on me, best I can tell."

Night was on them and a thousand insects intensified their screeching operettas as Emily walked around to the other side of the oak, stumbling over something half buried in leaves and pine straw.

"What did you trip on?" Travis said, pulling a penlight from his shirt pocket.

"I don't know, probably a piece of log or something."

The pencil-thin beam of light played over the ground and came to rest on the object.

"There it is," Travis said. "Looks like part of an old plastic milk crate. We ready to get out of here, Em?"

Emily was frozen, staring through the light at the faded blue fragment of the crate. It had to be part of the same one Lyle had fallen over as he attacked her that morning and it lay unburied like the guilt that had suddenly flooded over her again. Travis clicked off the penlight and they stood a few feet apart in the darkness cloaking them.

"I killed him, Travis." Emily's voice was calm but shaky.

"What?"

"I killed him. I shot Lyle."

"It was suicide, Em. You said the cops ruled it a self-inflicted gunshot, death by his own hand, right?"

"That's what they said, Travis, but I know different. I, I did it."

"Em, I think you're mixed up right now. Let's go and find us a nice motel room and get in some serious snuggling tonight."

Emily barely heard him. The Hootch was no more but Lyle's blood was cascading down the oak's trunk, gurgling over its massive roots and crashing through the undergrowth to wash around her legs in an unseen rising red mass.

"I murdered him, Travis!" she blurted, in tears now. "Take me away from here! I staged his suicide and he deserved what he got."

"Emily, I..."

"Old Lucy was his favorite shotgun. I used it on him."

She was shivering and crying as Travis hugged her close and guided her back down the path toward his truck.

Little more than an hour later they checked in at the Empress Motel on the interstate at the U.S. 63 exit where they had stopped to eat what seemed an eternity ago. Emily had cried a lot and said nothing more as Travis left the killing field, returning to Jenson Lane and back to the main road.

Appearing exhausting, she had not wanted anything for supper and he had put her to bed, leaving the television on as he stepped outside the room.

It was almost midnight but I-16 still roared with the occasional semi, barreling into the night, leaving or heading toward metro Atlanta.

Travis stood on the little porch in the darkness and pulled his windbreaker tighter against the night chill. He fished a long cigar and a box of wooden matches out of one of his pockets and fired it up, the smoke curling blue in the darkness.

"Finally got her," he murmured to himself before going back into the room.

Chapter 8

Treat Gillon was smoking himself to death and Sarah made sure that he always had enough cancer sticks in the house to keep him in business. In addition to his drinking, Treat had been almost a non-stop smoker since well before she had met him. Both vices conspired against him to the point that his wheezing cough was becoming more constant as his blood pressure continued its steep ascent. He was almost forty-nine, but the years had not been gracious and he had the weathering of a man two decades older.

Sarah had two reasons for keeping at least two cartons of Salem filters in the kitchen cupboard at all times. First, if Treat was in need of a smoke and opened the cabinet to find none, his wrath could be terrible to endure. Second, even though they were approaching their twenty-eighth wedding anniversary, if Treat wanted to kill himself, she could hasten the process and be rid of him with a clear conscience. She watched him puff away and swig at whatever alcohol was within arm's reach of his trembling hands and tried to imagine that every poisonous breath and swallow pushed him closer to hell's portal.

The beatings were less frequent now, Treat getting older and slower. But what they lacked in regularity, they made up for in fierceness, as if he had saved his strength to whale on her and would do so until the phlegm overflowed his lungs and unknown tumors conquered his wracked body.

What was becoming more common were the times Sarah found him bent over the toilet, heaving up nothing but with a force that should have torn loose some vital organ and sent it plopping into the water. Experience had taught her not to try to help him during these spells or to even suggest that he see a doctor; a Perry Como song wouldn't have sent him into a comparable rage.

To his credit and despite his abuses, Treat always was up early and in his office Monday through Friday and most Saturday mornings. Sarah had learned long ago that the cotton gin was his real bride; she was merely a trophy mistress that his golf buddies at Brattonwood County Club slobbered over in their locker room banter and Treat himself used for a punching bag. At forty-seven she could look in the mirror after a shower and see why those needle-dicked hackers lusted after her; she was religious about her aerobics class and never left the house without looking like she had just stepped out of a Phi Mu reunion photo.

If Sarah longed for him to roast for eternity, Treat was burning internally for an answer that he intended to have before he set foot in any netherworld. He was convinced that his son had not committed suicide. No Gillon had ever done away with himself and Lyle wouldn't, no, couldn't, be the first.

Treat was convinced that Emily had killed him and every time he stared up at Old Lucy, on its mahogany mounts over his den hearth, he seethed for payback, usually exacting a measure of revenge on Sarah.

It was this searing torch within that had driven Treat to contact Travis Hawthorne, a private investigator based in the Statesboro area. He had gotten Hawthorne's card from a cotton broker who had used Travis' services. The broker had suspected his wife of being unfaithful and Hawthorne had supplied a trove of evidence, including nude photos of her with her lover, copies of cancelled checks and credit card transactions from motels where they had been together.

Thus it was within two weeks after Emily disappeared from Pierpont that Treat was on the phone with Travis. Days later they met and Treat laid out his story in detail, also giving Travis several photos of Emily. His job would be not only to find her, but to gather enough evidence for the district attorney to charge her with capital murder and send her to death row.

It had not been any great feat for Travis to trail Emily

to Savannah; she had not covered her tracks very well. In searching the abandoned trailer, he had found notes she scribbled about job possibilities and places to live there. One expense she had to maintain was her car insurance, and she had sent her change of address to her agent in Pierpont, one of Treat's country club cronies.

So then it had just been a matter of staking out her apartment for a few days, watching her comings and goings, her work routine at the deli and her forays to River Street or the Cotton Boll.

Never a man of patience, Treat became Job now. He was euphoric when Travis called with the news that he had located Emily, but the mission was only half complete. He wanted to nail her to a cross and Travis would be the man to give him the hammer.

Treat did not mention any of this to Sarah. For all she knew, he was going about his usual business of cotton, booze and nicotine, all in bale-size amounts, in between taking swings at her. To Sarah, Emily was gone and all that was left of that journey in their lives was to make sure the weeds were plucked from the graves of Lyle and Brandon.

Travis, meanwhile, waited for the prime moment to spring upon his prey, finding it on the January morning when he followed Emily to the veterinarian's office. He had waited for her to come out, intentionally bumping into her and then asking Tiffany Bryant about her. The dog he later brought for Doc Craven to examine belonged to a colleague.

The roses had been easy. Any woman who pasted cutouts of them on the walls of her rundown trailer was desperate for a bouquet and Travis had sent her one, adding it to Treat's ever-lengthening bill.

The farm on the Ogeechee did indeed belong to the Hawthorne family, and on the Monday night after he and Emily returned from Pierpont, Travis sat typing his notes into his computer and reflecting on all that he had told her about himself. Most of it had been true, but there had been significant alterations, bald-faced lies, some would call them.

It was true that he was more than a year older than Emily and that he had wanted to be a writer when he was a teenager. He had worked for the Statesboro paper as a sports stringer and enrolled at Georgia Southern where his book smarts failed him.

Here, fact and truth separated. Travis had never taken a reporting job in Waycross, instead finding his niche with Pinnacle Investigations, a private detective agency in Atlanta, run by an old friend of his father. The hours were long and the pay wasn't great, but it had been a natural fit for him and he quickly became very good at what he did. After about a year, he was assigned to work Pinnacle's Savannah region, since he was familiar with the area.

Travis had not particularly liked Treat when they met, even though his new client was trying to bring his son's killer to justice. Travis knew that the Bratton County authorities had ruled Lyle's death a suicide, but the circumstances were certainly suspicious and just maybe he could find out what really happened. Still, in Treat Gillon Travis saw a man not so much grieving over his loss as being gnawed by an all encompassing hate shrouding everyone, including himself.

Now, on this March night Travis mulled Emily's confession of murder, adding it all, in his own words, to the case file he had compiled against her over the few weeks he had known her. He had worked with the Bratton County district attorney, Elton Livingston, on two other cases and felt that he was well respected by the prosecutor. He knew that once he handed over his files to Livingston, the D.A. likely would charge Emily with murder. At minimum, the county sheriff would have to reopen the investigation.

If and when the case went to trial, it would be Travis' word against Emily's and there would be no guarantee of a conviction, the evidence being primarily hearsay. But he had done his job, getting Emily to admit her guilt, even if his methods would be ethically questioned.

She trusted him with all her heart, giving him her soul and body and as a lazy breeze nudged the trees along the Ogeechee, Travis thought of the thirty pieces of silver he would receive from Treat Gillon. It was a momentary lapse;

he was a first-rate professional who was being paid for his great work and he had achieved what he set out to obtain. What he could not shake, however, no matter how hard he tried this evening as he pieced together his crime puzzle, was his growing affection for Emily.

A predawn thunderstorm watered Savannah on Tuesday and puddles along the streets were ringed yellow with pollen as Emily rode her bicycle to work. Her weekend had been emotionally exhausting and she would have liked to have taken the day off, but she needed the money.

As always, Nick sensed her sourness and did not intrude while they prepared for the lunch rush hour. For her part, Emily merely went through the motions, dicing vegetables, making sure the coolers were stocked and the tables were clean. She had mentally bared herself to Travis, but there was no inkling that she had placed herself in any danger. Her myriad thoughts were more centered on his reaction to her revelations and the dreaded notion that he might leave her because of what she had done.

Can't you understand that I had to do it? There was no other way.

It had been awful enough to visit Brandon's grave and see again where Lyle lay and she wondered why she had put herself through the ordeal in the first place. Now she faced the prospect of maybe losing her possible soul mate because she had shared the plague of her being, the girl he had known a killer instead of a lover of cats and roses.

Even as Emily waited tables that day, Travis was punching in Treat's number to tell him of her confession. As always, he called Treat at the gin and had winced and held his cell phone away from his ear as Treat gave a triumphant, shrill whoop upon hearing the news.

"Mister private detective, you have made me a real happy man today, I grant you that," Treat said. "Now we can go about the business of putting little missy where she belongs. I want her to fry long and hard until she's extra crispy."

Travis had not shared his glee but made arrangements

to drive to Pierpont the next day, meet with Treat and pick up the check. He was walking in to Treat's office about the time that Sarah Gillon stopped in Section G-10 and noticed with much curiosity that someone had placed a toy butterfly next to the teddy bear she had left the week before. No one other than her had ever left anything for Brandon before and it was almost as if a tiny cry seeped out of the packed earth, telling her that Emily had returned to Bratton County.

She also knew in the instant that she knelt in prayer on the crewcut grass that Treat would surely kill Emily himself if she had come back to stay.

In the days leading up to Savannah's massive St. Patrick's Day bacchanalia, Emily saw very little of Travis, even though they talked on the phone at least once daily. He had told her he was busy with work around the home place and had reached a critical stage in the writing of his novel. For her part, Emily did not mind; she had needed some space from him after their trip to Pierpont and guessed that he did as well because of what she had revealed. But she thirsted for Travis' support and in her breakdown at The Hootch had sprung open the Pandora's box of her life, praying that he would comfort her with strong arms and gentle words and not slink away in horrified revulsion.

She did not want his pity for what she had endured and how she had ended it, but she craved his understanding of it. If there was ever to be anything lasting between them, he had to realize that she had been a cornered animal who attacked Lyle with lethal effect when she felt she had no other choice.

They had not mentioned her cleansing since returning from that weekend, even though Travis had spent several nights with her and they had made love as if nothing had rippled their lives as a couple. They made plans to be together for St. Patrick's Day, watching the parade and likely plunging into the party mayhem of River Street that afternoon. The holiday fell on a Wednesday this year, and Emily had gotten the day off, Nick telling her that the college girl who took her shift on Mondays needed the extra hours. Emily certainly could have used the work too, but she also needed some time with Travis to see where they stood.

Alone on his farm, the private investigator had a very different take on the world he had sculpted with Emily. There was no novel and never had been, his work instead being the careful compilation of his notes in the case. It would be a book unto itself really, documenting with precise times his contacts with Emily, the evidence she had revealed on each occasion and his conclusions, all to be handed over to the district attorney in a tidy package, wrapped in a serpent's embrace for Emily from Treat Gillon.

About all that was missing from his file were the frequency and length of their lovemaking and the depth of Travis' feelings for Emily. He knew that any criminal defense lawyer worth his salt would try to discredit the prosecutor's evidence by uncovering and attempting to exploit his intimacies with "the defendant." This could be a major flaw in the case if it went to a jury trial.

When he sat down with Treat to lay out all he had learned about Emily, Travis had not mentioned how he felt about her and certainly not that he had slept with her. Treat had listened intently, his eyes glistening like a vulture landing on a plump road kill. "Go for the throat, boy," Treat had repeated, pounding an untidy mountain range of papers on his desk with his fist. "Go for the throat."

Travis had walked out of the gin office with a check for $25,000 made out to Pinnacle Investigations. No matter if Emily was found guilty or innocent, he had done his job. But pocketing the check as he stepped into the glaring Georgia sunshine, he felt as if a thousand showers would not cleanse him of the filth he imagined caking him.

The pregnant nuns stumbled on the slick ballast stones and their big Igloo cooler crashed to the pavement, spilling a crushed glacier of ice and spewing beer cans. "Damn it all," one of the "sisters" shouted as Emily and Travis watched them scramble after the rolling cans.

It was St. Patrick's Day - a Savannah tradition since

the early 1800s - and the fragrance of reborn azaleas mingled with the stench of urine from portable toilets and five hundred thousand beer breaths. To many of the city's blooded families March 17 meant a religious observance with a courtly and solemn mass to honor the patron saint of Ireland. To hordes of others it was a chance to enlist in an army of booze swilling leprechauns that invaded Savannah, making its headquarters in the River Street bars.

Fountains in the squares gushed emerald and green grits and whiskey flowed from about 6 a.m. until pass-out-time, whenever that was, clocks and the calendar seeming to stand still amid a fog of yipping rednecks, shrilling Celtic fiddles and bare breasts. St. Patrick's was always a dice roll weather-wise; March in Savannah could bring snow flurries, a summer's wilting heat or a windy monsoon depending on the year and nature's fickleness.

Irish eyes were smiling this day, however, as Emily and Travis found a spot to watch the parade at the corner of East Broad and Bay streets. Spring had indeed sprung and an early morning nip had turned into a sun-washed, humid afternoon by the time they joined the revelry on the packed waterfront.

Emily and Travis held hands to keep from losing each other in the masses of green-clad partiers, Emily being groped and pinched by unseen hands. People were jammed so tightly on the street that it was almost impossible to move, much less talk in less than a shout to the ear. The Rabbit Hutch was beyond reach and they decided to get out of the beer-sloshing mob, picking their way up one of the ballast-stoned ramps back to Bay Street which was not as crowded.

"I gotta say that was my first and last time on River Street on St. Pat's Day," Emily said, brushing the hair away from her face. "Let the amateur drunks have it."

Travis gulped the last of a $6 beer and watched a pair of Savannah police officers lead away a handcuffed, staggering man who had been involved in a fight.

"So you're saying you're a pro?"

"You know what I mean."

Both of them had had several drinks by this point in the afternoon and the real world might as well have been Mars with a flotilla of spaceships belching green imps into the red dust. Travis was caring less about legalese and more about libations and getting laid. Emily had come out of her self-imposed coffin, the alcohol simultaneously stimulating her and mellowing her about all that had been said and done.

"Yeah, I've been coming down here, not every year mind you, since I was about fourteen," Travis said. "It's always something to see, that's for sure."

"I liked the parade and you know I like to party, but not with a bunch of yokels. Am I wrong?" Emily's tongue was loose, as was her attitude.

"Not at all, Em. A lot of these folks come in looking for trouble, trash the place and wake up with one mother of a hangover or in jail like that guy. Or they puke all over themselves and brag about how blitzed they got. You know, buy a t-shirt, head back to New Jersey and tell your buddies all about it."

Emily laughed.

"You're right. Add in how you drilled Scarlett O'Hara under a magnolia tree and they'll buy you a round or two of whatever they drink up there."

"You ready to get outta here?"

"Sure. I'd love to go back to your apartment, but I'm sure George Wallace has got the place packed with a lot of partying pussies. I know I would if I was him."

"Well you're just a bad boy today, aren't you Mr. Travis. Big George I can put off my couch. Besides, he's neutered. You, I'm not so sure of."

"What, the part about the couch or the neutering?"

"Come with me; I'll tell you later."

Savannah blushed and reveled in the height of her jade glory as they reached Emily's apartment. It was hot inside and they were moist with sweat from their walk, their flesh sticking together as they undressed, groped and fondled, George Wallace watching impassively from the couch.

They kissed and caressed in the familiarity of lovers who knew every mole, smell and curve of the other's body, both devoted to satisfying urges and needs, intent on pleasuring and being pleasured. The Golden Rule certainly applied to lovemaking as much as anything else, and Travis and Emily were holy rollers in the devotedness of their screwing. The whoops of yahoos on the street below flooded through Emily's open bedroom window, her yelps lost in theirs.

Yet even as Travis exploded inside her, his conscience could not rest.

Treat Gillon had suddenly become the hot topic of conversation in the men's locker room at Brattonwood Country Club. The last week of March was the shank of the spring golf season, and while there was the usual talk about handicaps, irons, long putts and bunkers, Treat's good mood also was breaking news.

"Old Treat must be finally gettin' some lovin' at home," chuckled Jimmy "Puggy" Lawson, who was in Treat's regular foursome.

"Something's definitely in the water. He's a changed man, I agree," added Terry Donelson, Pierpont's only dentist. "I can't remember him ever being this chipper since I moved here in `84."

"Maybe Treat's finally found religion; man, won't the devil be sorely disappointed," Randall Herman said, shaking his head while pulling off his shoes. "Whatever's happened, it ain't improved his short game or his looks."

In the manly confines of the club's mahogany inner chamber, the three talked openly about Treat, who had shot his usual, respectable but forgettable eighty-eight or so, showered and left before they had reached the nineteenth hole at the club bar. None of them had the guts to ask Treat directly why his attitude had suddenly unclouded, no more than any had had the balls to ask him to leave their foursome.

In reality, to them at least, Treat wasn't a bad sort if he kept his temper, but he had a short fuse on the course. All of them had war stories of having to duck to avoid his flying clubs and the time he intentionally drove a cart into a water trap after missing a putt in the 1991 men's invitational was a Brattonwood legend.

Sure, they had all heard the rumors about Treat and Sarah, but what a husband and wife did under their own roof was no business of theirs. Besides, it was much easier to ignore such ugliness, even if it was true, and rattle on endlessly about that dogleg on Number 16 or which wedge to use in the rough or the high school girls in their short shorts who drove the beverage carts.

It also was much easier just to go along with Treat when they met for their game at high noon every Saturday, rain or shine, and pray he had a good golf day. But for the past two weeks, Treat had been bearable rather than a bear and while it was a major distraction to his buddies, none dared question him about it.

Why, Treat, the ever-present Tampa Nugget he always clenched in his teeth on the course, had even congratulated Herman for making an eagle on Number 8, one of the club's toughest holes. They all had figured on a lightning strike out of the blue that day.

If the "Three Stooges," as Treat called them, were cowed by him, they were equally enamored by Sarah. Puggy Lawson in particular had the hots for her and when Treat wasn't around they spoke in reverentially low tones about her hourglass body and the little dresses she wore on the Brattonwood tennis courts. Puggy always brought up how the sweat must trickle between her breasts when she was running down a wide forehand.

It was as if they reverted to fifth graders ogling a crumpled centerfold one of them had smuggled out of the house and brought to school.

If none of the Stooges could confront Treat about golf, certainly none would ever do more than fantasize about Sarah. Herman already had the adulterer's mark on his life - he'd had a brief fling with one of the Brattonwood bartenders - but trying to seduce Treat's wife would have been tantamount to sticking your member in a high-speed blender.

So if Treat was a new man of sorts, whatever invisibility

brought him to this point was welcomed by the Stooges, whose bravado vanished when they stepped outside the locker room door.

This spring of 1999 would be different, at least for Puggy Lawson. His fantasies about bedding Sarah were about to consume him.

The fat earthworm was too tantalizing to resist. In the Ogeechee's brackish undercurrents, the bass chomped, the barbed hook and bits of the worm tearing through its mouth.

Eight feet above the struggling fish, Travis stood up in his boat and worked his rod and reel to haul in his catch. The remains of a giant tree trunk had rested half in the water and half on the bank for a number of years, forming one of Travis' favorite fishing spots. He wet his line here often, not so much to fill his fry pan as to enjoy the river's solitude and forget the rest of his world's troubles.

In the time since Emily's confession to him, he had been spending more and more time floating and casting and thinking. It was as if he hoped that an answer to his dilemma would snatch his hook in the cocoa water and could be pulled into his boat to save him from a terrible choice.

His Ogeechee trolling had netted him a few good-sized bream, bass and crappie, which he had scaled, gutted, breaded and cooked, but it had not brought him any peace of mind on what to do about Emily. Now more than a week after St. Patrick's Day, his fishing also had taken him away from his case report, which he had yet to finish. Travis had promised Treat that he would have his files ready to hand over to the district attorney by April 1, but that seemed unlikely with so many filets still waiting to be caught; at least that was his excuse to himself.

While he had mailed Treat's check to his agency, he had not sent any copies of his files in the Emily T. Gillon murder probe to his boss, telling him on the phone that he still had loose ends to wrap up. This was true, but he had put the bare bones of his investigation on paper and computer diskette, and what he had would likely have sent D.A. Livingston and the county sheriff scrambling for an arrest warrant and paperwork for a murder indictment.

He had seen Emily once since St. Patrick's, spending a night with her in Savannah. To his knowledge she had no sense of the danger looming for her from him. She seemed comfortable with the way their relationship had grown and did not appear eager to press for anything more serious. She had yet to speak of what happened in the haunted woods where she had unraveled the darkest ribbon of her life to him, and he began to wonder if she remembered the event at all, possibly blocking it from her mind.

That night Travis sat in his wooden rocking chair on the back screen porch, listening to the orchestras of the swamp and unable to see his hand before his face. He had no need for light and the odors of his cigars and fried bream owned the air. Life altering decisions had to be made, but his head was swimming like an Ogeechee catfish. The gin and tonics were going down too easily these days and he realized it, but few men ever had to decide a lover's fate or had the power to do so like he did.

Travis' choices were complexly simple: finish the job for which his firm already had been paid, and let Bratton County justice take it from there, or forget it all for Emily and what they had together.

Big raindrops from a passing thundercloud spattered sparsely but noisily on the porch's tin roof, as if God had rolled down a few gumdrops to jar him out of his mental malaise, but Travis was still confounded. The night crawled past midnight and he rocked and drank.

While he was unsure if he actually loved Emily, he had deep feelings for her and sympathized with her for all her suffering. But whether Lyle's killing was justified - some defense attorney would likely craft it as self defense by Emily - was a matter for judge and jury, Travis refusing to offer his heart an answer.

Even when he was making love to his wife, Puggy Lawson closed his eyes and imagined that she was Sarah Gillon. He had lived in his daydreaming romper room for about three years, each passionate squeak of his bed meant only for Treat's wife.

Other than the gutter talk among the Stooges, he had not mentioned his infatuation to anyone - although he was planning to do so to the only person that mattered - Sarah. It had taken him many months to build his nerve to this point and he knew that he would have only one shot at getting it right - like holding a six-shot revolver loaded with five bullets to his head and snapping the trigger.

He and Marie had been married for thirteen years and had created two beautiful kids - eleven-year-old Connie in the fifth grade and James Jr., who was about to finish kindergarten. Both had their mama's gorgeous gray eyes. Family was all that Puggy knew, but he was about to embark on a course that could ruin it all, simply because his desire for another woman was catapulting him over the edge of his 1996 Rotarian-of-the-Year reality.

The Lawsons had relocated to Pierpont from Atlanta in 1989, Puggy being transferred there in his capacity as an executive with Peachtree Electric & Power. For the ensuing decade he and his family had become naturally ingrained in the community - Rotary, the Methodist church, Connie's Brownie troop and Girl Scouts and Marie's circle of friends from her round robin tennis group at Brattonwood. It was all-American life in a small town.

Yet Puggy had ideas schemed by devils and Sarah was foremost in his thoughts. She was on a doubles team in the club tennis league and he had first seen her at a Brattonwood party where Marie had introduced him to her. Puggy had been enchanted ever since, not smitten by love, but absorbed in a lust that almost maddened him over time. He would never resort to anything as primitive and repulsive as rape; such an act was beyond his realm of civilized thought, but tying Sarah to a bed and having his way with her was certainly within the bounds of his fantasies.

He knew Treat - black-souled Treat with the weak short game - would likely blow his head off just for ogling his wife; the results of an affair with Sarah would be unthinkable if Treat found them out.

Of course Puggy was well ahead of himself in this

frame of mind; no one had an inkling that he intended to put his locker room dirty mouth into real action, taking the hugest gamble of his life.

Even as March faded, Savannahians were figuring they might be in for a tough summer. Already the barometer was in mid-August mode, registering humidity in the high nineties, the sweat season coming early this year.

Emily went about her business with no particular worries. Tips at the deli had been good lately, although Nick couldn't afford to give her a raise. She and Travis were humming along nicely, although she would like to see him more often. Tif Bryant and others had told her about the difficulties of long-distance relationships, even those of forty miles or so, but she was persevering. The telephone was their umbilical cord.

March 27 was the two-month anniversary of their meeting, but she did not mention it to Travis when they spoke that night and the date apparently did not register with him. He promised to see her on the weekend and that was good enough for her. She had no idea of the turmoil churning Travis, his ability to hide it and her naiveness adding up to her lack of awareness.

Emily also had no clue about the hatred mounting daily for her three hundred miles away as Treat Gillon looked to the hour when her executioner pulled the switch. For him, the smell of Emily's seared flesh as she did the voltage dance in the electric chair would be the aroma of angels.

Travis did not meet his April 1 deadline, but his boss granted him an extension of one month to complete his Emily Gillon file for the district attorney. This had not set well at all with Treat, who was becoming increasingly impatient for the county authorities to become involved.

In his contract with Pinnacle, Treat had agreed not to mention anything about the private investigators or the case itself to D.A. Livingston until Travis had finished his work. But his anger and frustration over the delay resulted in him going against his word. It was a muggy Tuesday during the second week of April when he met with Livingston over lunch at Brattonwood and told him how he was preparing to hand him Emily's head like that of a luau pig.

Livingston was expressionless, letting nothing interfere with his fork and knife work on his veal chops and mashed potatoes, but he listened intently as Treat put all his cards on the table.

Elton "Jimbo" Livingston had grown up in Bratton County and was in his fifth year as district attorney. He had graduated law school at the University of Georgia and come home to practice. He was now into his second term as D.A. of the Fortieth Judicial Circuit, which included Bratton, Larson and Paxton counties, all mostly rural. In his mid-forties, he was of average build, his most distinguishing features being a dime-sized purple birthmark on his right cheek and the bright red bow ties he always wore during trials.

Livingston certainly knew and respected Travis Hawthorne and his work in previous cases. He also had known Treat for many years although their paths rarely crossed. Like everyone else, he had heard the rumors about Treat and Sarah, but was too busy to worry much about the gossip.

When Lyle Gillon died, Livingston had been involved in a double-murder trial in neighboring Larson County. He had relied on the investigative work of Bratton County Sheriff Gerald Brewer and Coroner Jeffrey Montague who ruled Lyle's death a suicide. Brewer had been sheriff since ancient times and his retirement party on the last day of 1997 had been set long before Lyle's shooting.

For a little while there had been talk, largely fueled by Treat, that Brewer and his chief investigator, Deputy Earl Kronig, who was also near retirement age, were coasting through their last year in office, and that it was easier to rule Lyle a suicide victim rather than find a killer. Montague had held an inquest, but the hearing was little more than a rubber stamp on Brewer's findings, and Emily Gillon had not even been called to testify.

As Treat rambled on, Livingston tried to recall other details about the death. The autopsy had shown nothing more than the obvious: that Lyle's head essentially exploded from a single, 16-gauge blast of shotgun buckshot at point blank range. There were powder burns on the front of his hunting jacket and Lyle had apparently been lying on his back in the deer stand when he fired, Brewer stating that Lyle likely engaged the trigger with his left sock foot. Lyle's boots were found in a corner of the stand and some of his buddies told investigators that it wasn't uncommon for Lyle to remove them to warm his feet near his lantern on cold mornings.

Livingston had talked to Brewer, Kronig and Montague about two weeks after Lyle's body was discovered. He had known Lyle and Emily had waited on him several times at the Portly Pig. Frankly, his caseload at the time was such that if the sheriff ruled it a suicide, he had no reason to believe otherwise or the inclination to try to prove him wrong. Still, if Hawthorne brought him new evidence, including a confession from a trusted private detective, he would have to consider reopening the case, probably meaning that he would have to get a court order to have Lyle's corpse exhumed for a second autopsy.

"You've given me a lot to chew on here, Treat," Livingston said, calmly eyeing Gillon across the table. "So you're saying that Hawthorne is going to be in touch with me? How soon can I expect to hear from him?"

Treat speared at a chunk of rare steak on his plate and fidgeted on his chair. He seemed agitated to Livingston.

"Now that's the tough part about this whole deal, Jimbo," he said through a grimace. "The kid don't have to have it all ready for you until May 1 is what they're telling me. Should have been the first of this month, but he got an extension."

"I see."

"Me, I'm getting damned frustrated with waiting, but that's just my nature as you might have heard." Treat tossed back the last of his third martini, wiping his mouth with his hand. "I'm just a law-abiding fella who is trying to go about things the legal way and get some justice for my poor murdered boy."

Treat motioned to a waiter to bring him another drink as Livingston continued to watch and listen.

"And to be honest, Jimbo, it's costing me a shitload of money for this private eye to do what y'all, I mean old Jerry Brewer, his half-dead deputy and that sack of manure they call a coroner should have done from the get-go; that is, arrest that bitch for killing my son."

Livingston tried to snap the sudden tension with a slight laugh.

"Now Treat, you know old lady justice can move pretty slow sometimes. You have Hawthorne contact me and we'll see what we can do. I promise you that I'll take a good long look at his case and we'll proceed from there."

"Proceed from there?" Treat's anger was rising as was his voice and people at a few of the other tables began to stare. "What kind of crap talk is that? I want little missy - who couldn't give me a healthy grandson and took a shotgun to Lyle - I want her to barbeque in hell for what she done."

"I understand that, Treat."

"Working with the laws, that's the best way to go about things, wouldn't you say, Jimbo? Give the system a chance to work, I believe I heard one of your lawyer friends say somewhere or another."

"That's exactly right, Treat. Justice can be slow, but it's sure."

Treat glared at him, his voice lower now, but his words bristling.

"Well here's something to be sure of too, Mr. D.A. Old Treat might be slow, but nobody screws him over and gets away with it." He stood up. "Jimbo, I didn't like some of your answers today, but you get Hawthorne's report and we'll talk again. That okay with you?"

"We'll leave it at that, Treat," Livingston said, rising to shake hands. "Just know I'll do anything I can for you."

"I hope that'll be enough."

Treat was walking to his truck minutes later when he paused and pulled a slip of paper out of his shirt pocket. He unfolded it to read his sweat-smeared ink writing on it: "1634 East Bryan Lane" - Emily's address, which he had obtained from Travis.

The courts and that smug district attorney could

stomp along like a three-legged mule in a muddy field, but lady justice had other, uglier faces. His daddy had told him about watching the "niggers twitch" from trees and telephone poles while torch-lit lynch mobs screeched in the jubilation of white mastery. He still had one of J.D.'s moth-riddled old Klan robes folded away in an attic trunk.

Treat ached to avenge Lyle, and he had paid a hefty fee to Hawthorne's agency to provide the damning goods on Emily. Travis had done a good job of uncovering the truth, at least in Treat's estimate, but now he wasn't sure that the Bratton County screwups would follow through on their end.

Only one thing was certain to him as he settled into the driver's seat of his pickup and pulled a Smith & Wesson pistol out of the glove compartment, touching the weapon with a loving gentleness Sarah Gillon had never known from him. Sometimes justice came from the hand of the wronged and Treat was more than eager to go to Savannah and snuff out Emily like a lame cockroach battered by a Sunday newspaper.

Then again, Treat thought, why should he stop with Emily? If the ambulance chasers or prosecutors or whatever they called themselves couldn't find it in their seventy-pound law books how to put a murdering whore on death row, he had plenty of bullets for them too.

Livingston, Hawthorne, Brewer, the coroner - they would all pay.

For now, however, he would have to settle for Sarah. The feel of his hand hitting her flesh, her stifled, pained cries and the dominance he enjoyed over her sent him tearing out of the Brattonwood parking lot. If Treat had to wait to see Emily die, either by his hand or the system, Sarah would be his consolation prize - a bloodied kewpie doll who was always there.

Chapter 9

Puggy Lawson stood on the edge of his personal cliff, ready for the dive into unknown waters. He would either crumple on the rocks or plunge into the glorious realization of his sexual fairy tale. It was his lunch hour and he drove out into the country and parked behind an abandoned sharecropper's shanty well off the main road. He had scouted this location a few days before and it was here that he would call Sarah.

The cell phone almost slipped out of his hands, his palms were so sweaty as he ground his teeth and punched in the number for the Gillon residence. He waited, almost imagining that Treat would reach out of the circuitry and grab him by the throat.

Two rings and he was about to hang up, but then...

"Hello."

Puggy swallowed his insides and found his voice.

"Um, Sarah, this is Puggy. Is Treat home?"

"Hi Puggy. No, he's at work. You've got the number there, don't you?"

"Yeah, I have it. I'll call him there. How are you?"

"Doing real well, thanks. Y'all playing golf this weekend?"

"As long as it doesn't rain hard, snow or hail. Standing date, you know."

"Sounds good. Tell Marie I said hi."

Puggy knew he had to recapture his momentum.

"So how's your tennis going? You got a nasty two-handed backhand, I know. I've seen you and your doubles partner, Carla, on the courts. Y'all beat Marie and Kim Walden a few weeks back."

"Yeah, in the Lady Brattonwood Azalea Classic. I remember seeing you there, sitting behind the fence at the base line. I thought how sweet it was for you to give up your golf and come see Marie play."

Puggy closed his eyes as he spoke.

"I didn't come to see Marie play. I came to see you, Sarah."

"What?" Sarah snickered. "You and Treat got some kind of joke going?"

"This is no joke, Sarah, I'm very serious. I'm attracted to you and have been for a long, long time."

"Puggy are you crazy? You got to be kidding, otherwise Treat would kill you. What about Marie?"

"Sarah, she's a wonderful woman and the mother of my two children. We've been married for thirteen great years, but there's got to be more to life than working all day and supper at 6:30 every night and helping the kids with their homework. Everybody needs some spice, am I wrong?"

"You've floored me, Puggy, you really have. I don't know what to say. I guess I should hang up on you for starters."

"Don't do that, Sarah. Don't you realize what I'm risking on this phone call? I could lose everything because of you!"

"You made the call, Puggy. So what do you want? Are we going to run off to Aruba or Acapulco or somewhere in Europe together?"

"I can't say that I've thought it all out that far ahead. What I can say is that when I look at you, I just start to think about things that I shouldn't."

"And what's that, Puggy? You've gone this far, you might as well tell me."

"I just think that you are one of the most sexy women I've ever met, that's all. And I'd like to get to know you better."

"So why am I so sexy?"

Sarah had moved beyond her immediate shock to curiosity, like a kitten pawing a stranded earthworm. Yet every second he had her on the line without her hanging up on him, the more Puggy was emboldened. He closed his eyes again and opened himself to her.

"I want to smell your hair and hold your hand. I want to watch you disrobe in front of me and kiss every inch of your luscious body and hear your moans for me while I lick you and bury my face between your legs and..."

The sound of Treat's pickup coming down the driveway suddenly distracted Sarah.

"Puggy, I have to go. Bye." She hung up, leaving Puggy clutching his phone in one hand and himself with the other.

The Brattonwood bartenders knew to make all of Treat's drinks doubles and with four high-octane martinis in his brain and belly, he was on fire after his meeting with Livingston. For the next hour after he swayed through the back door, Sarah had no chance to think about her wild conversation with Puggy. Instead, Treat put her through a hell aerobics of abuse that left her face down on their bed, wondering how much swelling she would have to hide as Perry Como's romance emanated from the den stereo. She cringed at the sound of another bar glass smashing against the wall and tried to calm her panicked mind to remember what she had to cook for Treat's supper.

Puggy was shaking and short of breath when Sarah hung up, the tightness in his pants subsiding quickly. For five full minutes he sat motionless, thinking about what he had done, not knowing whether to shout to the heavens or be ashamed of his unfaithfulness. He started the truck and turned on the air conditioner full blast.

Marie would likely never forgive him if she found out about this and panic momentarily wracked him at the thought that Sarah had immediately called his wife to tell her about her perverted husband.

Just as bad, Sarah could squeal to Treat, which could lead to any number of scenarios, all of them terrible and probably deadly. He imagined sitting down to supper with his family, Connie describing her school science project and little Jimmy's lips a ravioli orange. There would be a knock at the front door and Puggy would answer. Standing on the welcome mat was Treat, a shotgun leveled at his waist. A titanic roar blasted Puggy backwards, all before the eyes of his horrified loved ones.

The vision made him wince, but, he reasoned, he had realized the stakes going in and had still stepped into this minefield where his marriage could be blown to the winds or his life ended by wickedly jealous Treat.

All of Puggy's energy had been concentrated on summoning the nerve to phone Sarah; there was no step two in his mind, other than his playboy Everest of conquering her. He couldn't fathom what Sarah could be thinking about him. Was she flattered or flabbergasted? Intrigued or angry?

Driving back to town, Puggy decided to lay low for a week or so and see what happened before making another move, not that he had an inkling what it would be. For now, he had to get back to his office and pray that Sarah, Treat, Marie, and his children were not already spreading the news to every household.

For the next two days Sarah nursed herself, not leaving the house. She cancelled her hair appointment and missed her weekly trip to Olivet Hill Cemetery for the first time. She watched Treat eat his breakfast with a dead-fish blankness, ticking off the seconds in her head until he left for work.

Now more than ever she was the slap-around inflatable doll who had suffered his brutality with a silent scream that thundered through Pierpont, rattling pictures on the walls of every marital bedroom and those living together in sin, as the church-goers put it. The face in her mirror stared through the time of a naive schoolgirl smitten with a returning war veteran, through the highest elation and deepest gloom framing the births and deaths of Lyle and Brandon, and the hope for a good end for which she always prayed. The violent miasma of Treat's punishment tinged all.

She didn't know what to make of Puggy. Treat could have put him up to some cruel prank they could all chortle over while scratching themselves in the club locker room, but that was unlikely. Treat rarely laughed, his sense of humor somewhere in the range of pulling the legs off toads for amusement.

It wasn't uncommon for her to receive subtle compliments from men when Treat was out of earshot, everyone at Brattonwood, and in Pierpont for the most part, believing that he was a volcano brimming with rotgut and lava hate and overdue for an eruption.

And so it was amid the ice packs and caked makeup that Sarah puzzled over Puggy's advance and marveled at his profound stupidity or bravery, sometimes a fine line separating each, and wondered what would happen next. She had never been even remotely attracted to Puggy and other than the fact that he was in Treat's foursome, she had a difficult time remembering much about him other than occasionally seeing him at Brattonwood.

At one point, she looked up the Lawsons' number in the club telephone directory, thinking that she would talk to Marie about what had happened. They were acquaintances through their tennis group, but that was as far as it went. Sarah quickly decided not to make the call; if this wasn't a joke, Treat would blame no one but her for flirting and flaunting and cheating and it would be an awful time to be alive, if she indeed survived it.

By Friday she was ready to rejoin the community, as much as she ever did, and sunglasses on and a tennis hat pulled low, went shopping at the Piggly Wiggly. Her life was going on even though she had no idea what prompted Treat's outburst, but that was the nature of this puny-dicked beast; little had changed in more than a quarter-century of their "togetherness."

She stacked eight cartons of Salem 100s amid the groceries in her buggy and on the way home stopped at the red dot store to pick up wrist-straining bottles of Jack Daniels, Jim Beam and Wild Turkey so the liquor cabinet would be fully stocked. If Sarah didn't have the nerve to pump a bullet in his brain or sprinkle rat poison on his beloved rib eyes, she could at least give nature a boot in the ass by keeping Treat immersed in a hazy pond of toxic smoke and hundred proof.

Like Puggy Lawson with his phone call, Travis Hawthorne also had reached a dusty crossroads in his life, the dirt likely to cling to him forever if he took the wrong turn. It was the last weekend in April now and even as

Emily napped in his bedroom, Travis was poking away at his computer keyboard, finishing his investigative report about her. His phones were switched off, for good reason. Treat had become increasingly impatient with him, almost threatening at times, and was calling him daily about the status of his report. He had been calling Travis' office in Atlanta also, but Travis' boss had refused to talk to him, referring him back to Travis, which seemed to fuel Treat's inner flame. With Emily spending the weekend with him, Travis certainly could not chance her hearing an ugly or incriminating answering machine message from her former father-in-law.

Indeed, she already sensed that something was not right with him and had asked him about it that Sunday afternoon while they were taking a boat ride on the Ogeechee. The day had been hot and they had put on their swimsuits to work on their tans, Emily sitting on a cushion in the bow while Travis operated the motor from his stern seat. They had been out for about an hour when he steered into a sycamore-shaded cove, one of his favorite fishing spots. Emily spoke up in the quiet void left by the shut-down motor.

"Travis, I need to ask you a question."

"I'm listening, Em."

"You seem sad or preoccupied or both lately. Is there anything bothering you?"

He pretended to check the gas tank, not meeting her eye. "We got a little air in the gas line. No big deal. Uh, no there's nothing eating me, Em. I'd tell you if there was."

"I'd like to think that you would, Travis, but sometimes I have trouble reading you. I know we haven't been seeing each other as often these days, but you've been busy and I've been busy and it's not like we live right around the corner from each other. I mean, forty miles is forty miles."

"Em, I'm sorry if I haven't paid more attention to you lately, but like you said, both of us have been kind of tied up. My place is a lot of work to keep up as you can see, and I've been writing a lot on the novel."

"So when are you going to let me read some of your masterpiece?" Her seriousness seemed to lighten.

"Not until it's done. You remember our deal about that, right? You wait until I finish it and you'll be the first one to read my book."

"Yeah, yeah, I remember. I was just hoping to catch you in a weak moment."

"I don't have too many of those, Em."

"Tell me about it. But Travis, I just need to know that everything is okay with you and between us. I..." She hesitated, looking into the brown water. "I, I think I love you."

Emily had never uttered those three words to anyone other than her mother and she listened to herself say them, her voice seeming to carry above the trees as if borne on the wings of a fat spring robin.

Hearing her feelings for him immediately bathed Travis in dread and happiness, both battling to conquer him. He slumped against the Evinrude, a sharp metal edge of it spurring into the small of his back, but he didn't notice.

The river passed them in its endless solitude as if the world's millions waited with a collective held breath for his reaction. "Oh, Em," was all he could manage, easing his way toward the bow and embracing her with a long, deep kiss.

They had gone back to his house and made sweaty love on his screened-in porch before she had drifted inside for a cat nap.

Now Travis sat with his thoughts and emotions and the words - his words - on his computer screen ripping him in half with their bluntness.

"Victim died of a close-range shotgun blast to the head... Cause of death was ruled self-inflicted gunshot wound... Mrs. Gillon then admitted to this investigator that she killed her husband..."

His file for D.A. Livingston would be about one hundred pages and include copies of the autopsy report, a transcript of the coroner's inquest and sheriff's department documents. He realized that Livingston already would have seen most of this paperwork, with his confession from Emily obviously being the most new and damning evidence.

The tangerine sun was impaled on the western treetops like a burning beach ball as Travis closed and rubbed his eyes. It would surely come down to his word against hers in court. There was no one else under that big tree or in those deep pine thickets when Emily spilled her guts to him.

Travis opened a desk drawer to look at his ace, holding the little cassette tape between his fingers. Her confession on tape should be enough to convince any jury of her guilt.

For almost two weeks, Puggy Lawson did nothing to follow up on his call to Sarah.

He had been transformed into some farm-field Casanova in blurting out his feelings to her, but his life had not changed when he returned to his office that day and his home that evening. The routines were the same, as if the electrical surge of his spoken lust had done nothing to disrupt the rhythm of his quiet existence in Pierpont. A week of suppertimes came and went, as did a Rotary meeting and a Saturday golf outing where Treat was his usual glowering self - a relief to Puggy.

Time's passage not only eased his tension, but invigorated him. Sarah had not broadcast his advances, which meant one of two things to Puggy: either she was interested in him and waiting to hear from him or she had decided to forget the whole episode. Puggy chose to believe the former, thinking that he had to contact her again as soon as possible to stoke the rising fire of their new relationship.

He and Marie talked briefly about summer vacation, with Connie getting out of school in less than two weeks - maybe Disney World in Orlando or Washington, D.C., or the Pennsylvania Amish country - they would have to decide soon.

One night before bed, Marie had casually mentioned that she had a doubles match at the club that week.

"Who are you playing?" Puggy had been too wired to camouflage the excitement in his quick response and Marie had looked at him in amazement.

"Why Puggy, when have you ever given a tinker's cuss

about my tennis?"

"I've always been interested, what do you mean?" He crawled into bed and flicked the remote at the television. "Don't you remember me coming out to watch that tournament you were in a month or so back? The Lady Brattonwood, wasn't it?"

"Well you are just scoring some major brownie points tonight, Mr. Lawson," Marie laughed softly. "Are you sniffing around Kim? You got the hots for my doubles partner, don't you."

Puggy pulled the sheet up to his throat and, closing his eyes, listened to David Letterman launch into his monologue.

"No way, Marie. She's got piano legs and a butt the size of Texas; I don't care if she does serve like Sampras." Puggy yawned loud and long before turning on his side, away from her.

"You coming?" he said wearily, listening to her pad out of the bathroom and rustle out of her robe.

"Don't you want to know who we're playing? You did ask."

"I did. Who is it?" He was relaxing into sleep.

"Pippie Moyers and, let me think, her regular partner Barbara Rodgers is out of town for her middle daughter's wedding in Nashville so she's got a replacement."

"Great, honey."

"You know Barbara and Tom. Isn't he a golfer?"

"Must be about a forty handicap. Just terrible." Puggy had totally lost interest now, relenting to the pleasure of near slumber. He felt Marie nestle in next to him, the room suddenly illuminated only by the TV as she switched off her night stand lamp.

"That is going to be some fancy wedding. Their daughter, Marian, don't you remember her? Well she's marrying a boy who belongs to one of Nashville's first families, a lot of old, old money, they say. He's not much to look at, I hear, but neither is she, to be honest."

"Nice."

"Anyway, Pippie had to find a new partner or forfeit the match. Now who did she get? Lord, my mind is going."

"Forget it, Marie. I'm gonna turn off the TV unless you wanna watch it. I'm pooped."

"Turn it off, Puggy, but it'll bug me to eternity if I can't remember who's filling in for Barbara." Letterman vanished in a black screen and Marie curved her body around his in the still darkness.

"Now I remember," she said, bunching her pillow. "Sarah Gillon."

Marie fluffed her pillow and, wrapping her arms around him, burrowed as closely as possible into the back of her now-awake husband, kissing him on the neck.

"Good night, Puggy."

And so it was that on Friday, April 30, 1999, fate, the gods, and pure luck - good and bad - entwined energies to change lives hundreds of miles apart but linked by a thin necklace of events.

As Emily pedaled her bicycle to work that morning, she thought of Travis and their relationship.

On his farm, Travis put the finishing touches on his report, proofreading it for errors and making a fresh printout.

In Pierpont, Treat Gillon was up and out early, while Sarah went over her mind's list of the day's errands and prepared for her 1 p.m. doubles match at the club. One of her opponents, Marie Lawson, was busy also, making sure Connie caught her bus, getting James Jr., to kindergarten, and running home to pay a few bills and check her email before heading to Brattonwood.

Puggy had been his usual chipper self before setting out for his office at 7:35 a.m., promising Marie that he would make the almost-unheard-of effort to drop by and watch some of her match if he could squeeze away from work.

All of them savored a sparkling Georgia spring day, the humidity mercifully low as the last blustery remnants of thundershowers crackled and rumbled north over the mountains around Dahlonega and Resaca and Summerville.

Emily had no reason to expect anything but a routine,

if hectic, shift. Friday was payday for many of Nick's customers and the deli was normally very crowded for lunch, with people standing in line for tables or waiting for takeout orders.

What she was very much unsure of was what was happening between Travis and her. Emotionally, there was nothing else she could do, having told him how she felt about him in the most intimate, innocent and pure manner that she could muster. She knew no other way and was surprised how easily it had been for her to voice her feelings. Yet the naturalness of her words had been offset by Travis' lukewarm reaction and Emily had spent hours wondering if she had moved too quickly. Complicating her thoughts was all that she had revealed to him, but she did not in the least suspect that he had been anything but honest with her.

She decided to ease up on the "love stuff" as she called it, not wanting to make Travis think that he was being backed into a matrimonial corner where the only way out was to slide a big ring onto her finger. In her mind, Emily wasn't sure if marriage was what she wanted anyway; it was too early in their relationship to make that decision and she intended to tell Travis just that the next time they were together. It was perfectly all right with her to be friends and lovers and let that suffice for the time being.

For now, however, she had a deli full of hungry customers to deal with and she flitted among the tables, unaware that her boyfriend, a thick file folder tucked under his arm, was at that moment setting out for Pierpont to see Treat Gillon.

Marie arrived at Brattonwood about an hour before her match, quickly downing a light chef's salad and then taking the court to loosen up and practice her volleys against a backboard. She and Kim Walden were ranked near the bottom of their ladies' group, but Marie had only been playing a couple of years and was pleased with the way her game was coming along. Most of the club's female members played golf, but there was a core group of about twenty that played tennis.

Puggy had kissed her and the kids that morning and hustled to work. He had to be on time because a pencil-pusher from Atlanta was in town to give a first-quarter report on company finances. Puggy had to be there bright, smiling and alert to set an example for the rank and file and Marie thought it was sweet that he would try to get by to see her play.

Kim and their opponents, Pippie Moyers and Sarah Gillon, arrived separately but almost simultaneously about fifteen minutes before match time. The girls were all friends - Pierpont did not have many social circles - and the tennis round robin was a chance to catch up on news and hot-tongued gossip.

Certainly Sarah could have dropped an atomic bomb on Brattonwood the likes of which had not been felt since 70-year-old Raylette Hawkins had been caught screwing a teenaged black busboy on the club kitchen floor twenty years earlier. She had not mentioned Puggy's call to anyone, but could not help but think about it when she gave Marie a gentle hug of greeting.

"So how's Treat?" Kim had piped cheerily as the four exchanged small talk and pleasantries.

"Bitch," Sarah thought to herself. She knew they all had heard the rumors and stories about what went on in her house and even if Kim's remark was innocent, it was still cutting to her. She shrugged and looked at her Nikes.

"Treat's Treat. What can I say?"

The other girls laughed nervously.

"Aren't they all," bubbled Pippie.

"As long as we let them have their golf, well, it keeps them out of our hair, right?" Marie added.

"Y'all ready to play?" Sarah said, more than anxious to take off someone's head with her forehand. "I'll spin the racquet to see who serves first."

Puggy looked into his rearview mirror and finger-combed his hair while busily sucking on a breath mint.

"Just stay calm and cool, big boy," he whispered to himself. Across the Brattonwood parking lot he could hear the hollow twack! of struck tennis balls punctuated by the grunts of the women hitting them.

For a few seconds, sitting in his truck, he closed his eyes and listened to their outbursts, imagining them to be Sarah's gasps of pleasure as she bucked atop him. The thought and the mental picture made him shudder before he returned to the reality of the moment. He had taken a late lunch hour and arrived at the club about twenty minutes after the match had begun, not wanting to appear, at least to Marie, too eager to be there.

"Showtime," he said under his breath, as he stepped out of his truck and walked toward the courts.

Pippie and Sarah had won the first set and were up a service break in the second when he settled onto the aluminum bleachers, the lone spectator. The women didn't immediately notice him until he clapped politely when Marie hit a lob that Pippie could not return. All of them gave him a quick wave - except Sarah. At the changeover between games, the foursome met briefly at the sideline bench to towel off and drink some Gatorade or water.

"There's my sugar," Marie called to Puggy. "Sorry I'm not doing better. These girls are just too good."

"You wanna pinch hit for me, Puggy?" Kim said. "My knee is just killing me."

"All of y'all look like you're ready for Wimbledon to me," he answered. "Honey, you just gotta learn how to cheat more, like we do on the golf course."

No sooner had he said it than Puggy was regretting his poor choice of phrases. His words scalded Sarah and she cut her eyes at him, a glance of daggers.

"But I'd say the way y'all hit the ball, you could probably beat any of us guys fair and square," Puggy said, feebly trying to recover.

"What a diplomat you are, Puggy," Pippie laughed. "You gonna run for mayor?"

"My serve," Sarah said briskly. "We're up four-one."

"Well Miss Sarah seems ready to get on with her business," Kim said, picking up her racquet and walking back onto the court.

"No offense, Kim, I'm just not in the mood to dilly-dally today."

Puggy had not been able to take his eyes off Sarah since he sat down. He had always loved the curve of her tanned calves and what seemed to be the extra shortness of her tennis dresses and the way her body rippled and moved when she tried to track down a ball.

Watching her guide in a weak second serve that Marie netted, he thought about what it would be like in the women's locker room. An eight-shot rally ended with Kim stroking a backhand wide and Sarah quickly closed out her serve at love, but Puggy's thoughts were still in the women's locker room, a forbidden land where only his fantasies had been.

He imagined Sarah there after a long, hard match on a steam-bath afternoon and how he would silently approach her in the shower mist, meticulously tonguing the sweat off every inch of her gorgeousness.

A collective groan from the women brought Puggy back to the court where Kim's serve had been broken, Pippie and Sarah winning the match. They all shook hands at the net and, collecting their bags, racquets and other gear, headed toward the gate.

"Good match, girls," Puggy shouted, clapping.

"Whew! That was a workout," Pippie chirped. "Y'all are getting better, Marie. You're a much steadier player this year."

"Thanks," Marie answered, wiping her face and shoulders with a towel. "I might be getting better, but I also might be getting too old for this. Knitting is looking real good about now."

The four of them laughed and Kim draped an arm around her.

"Now Marie," she said, "don't talk like that. Who would be crazy enough to be my doubles partner if I didn't have you?"

"You just tell Mr. Puggy over there that he'll have to find his fun somewhere else the night before your matches," Pippie joked. "He can't be wearing you out, right, Sarah?"

A grim smile crossed Sarah's lips.

"Yeah, he'll surely have to find his fun somewhere else."

"Then we all agree," Kim added, trying to keep the banter upbeat. "Puggy, it looks like you're in for a dry spell, at least till tennis season's over."

"I heard all that," he called back. "Y'all ain't playing very fair, four against one."

The women chatted briefly before splitting up, Kim and Pippie going toward the locker room to get cleaned up and changed while Sarah headed for her car.

"Thanks for coming, honey," Marie said, giving Puggy a sweaty hug. "It means a lot to me even though we lost." Over her shoulder, Puggy snatched glimpses of Sarah walking across the parking lot. "How was your meeting this morning?"

"Huh? Oh, dry as dirt, a lot of numbers before this geek gets to the bottom line, telling us we were slightly in the red for the first quarter, same as this time last year. A couple of people asked about any plans for layoffs. He said Atlanta didn't have anything set in stone, whatever that means."

"As long as you think your job's safe, I won't worry."

"The place would have to close down without me, I'm so important. You know that, Marie."

"You're right, Mr. Lawson, sir. So what would you like to do about supper tonight? Connie's spending the night with her new friend Bonnie Curtis, who I don't think you know, and I checked to see that the babysitter was available if you wanted to go out. If you just want to fire up the grill, that's fine too."

Puggy's mind was not on supper or his daughter's sleepover or getting the babysitter. Being so close to Sarah had rekindled his libido and the mundaneness of his family life paled in contrast.

"Puggy?" Marie was sitting on the bleachers next to him now.

"I'm here. I was just thinking. Whatever you decide is fine with me. We can cook out or get the babysitter for Jimmy and come to the club or go to Alfredo's or just order a pizza and stay in. Makes no difference to me."

"Well haven't you all of a sudden turned into an easy touch. Tell you what, I'll pick up a couple of thick filets for the barbeque, a Happy Meal for Jimmy and you stop and rent a movie. Nothing too bloody. That okay?"

"Sure, sure, Marie. Listen, I got to get back to the office. I'll see you later."

"Thanks again for being here for me, Puggy. I mean it." She kissed him.

"I told you I'd be here, didn't I?"

Puggy left the club, but he did not go back to work. On his cell phone he told his secretary that he had decided to take the rest of the day off. He drove past the fine houses on LaCourt Street, looking to see if Sarah's Lincoln was in the two-car garage, but the door was down. He decided to prowl the town in search of her.

For Travis the road to Pierpont would be a journey of decision. The drive would take more than four hours so he would have a good chunk of time to contemplate his choice. On the truck seat beside him was the completed Emily Gillon case folder, ready for the perusal of Treat Gillon who, as the client, would have the first look at it before Travis called for an appointment with the district attorney. Also on the seat was the mini-cassette tape of Emily's confession which would be the icing on Treat's cake, since he had not previously known it existed. He would probably cavort around the cotton gin office in wild delight when he heard the tape, Travis thought.

Travis felt very fortunate to have obtained the confession with so little work. He had switched on the little recorder and held it in his hand in the clutching darkness of the blue-gray woods that night as Emily stood beneath the giant oak. She had never suspected a thing and still didn't, to his knowledge. Yet in his uncertainty between love and justice, he had not made any copies of the tape; the original was all that he had.

Before he set out this morning, he had phoned Emily at the deli and told her he had to make an unexpected trip to Atlanta and should be back on Saturday. She had seemed to understand and had given him a whispered "I love you," because Nick was dicing broccoli nearby. They made plans to see each other Saturday night or on Sunday, depending on when he returned.

Travis had no doubt that Emily had fallen for him. Her eyes seemed to dance when she looked at him and she touched him with the soft familiarity of soul-bound lovers never to be dulled by the ages.

He had intense feelings for her as well, savoring their physical pleasures and saying to her in return the three words any sane human wants to hear. Yet around his heart there was a wall, mortared with a thick concoction of legal principles, Old Testament virtues about killing and the sterling traditions of duty, honor and loyalty.

What Travis could not reconcile was how easy it was for him to invoke the thirteenth commandment, "Thou shalt not kill" but ignore all of the Bible's declarations against unmarried sex when he and Emily were screwing as if Armageddon would sear the next dawn.

Among her thoughts this Friday, Sarah contemplated her upcoming wedding anniversary. She and Treat would be married twenty-eight years on June 17, and she knew that he would not acknowledge it in any way; twenty-seven previous dates on calendars had taught her that lesson.

After her tennis match, she had left Brattonwood with nothing in particular to do. Beating Marie and Kim had basically been like shooting half-dead fish in a barrel. She and Pippie had never been close friends, but it had been invigorating to run, focus, work up a good sweat and knock the hell out of the ball.

Certainly it was a tad unnerving for her when Puggy made his appearance, but compared to Treat he was a Cub Scout masturbating for the first time. So he had made a stupid mistake by calling her; no harm had been done and she certainly did not feel threatened by him.

The sun cooked through the windshield and the air conditioning soothed her and in the solitude of her car Sarah found the calm she always craved. There was no snarling Treat in her face and none of her own blood to wipe off the upholstery and no pain for doing nothing more than trying to be a good wife.

Having missed her Wednesday visit to see Lyle and

Brandon, she decided to go to the cemetery. Stopping by Spain's Florist, she bought small arrangements of assorted flowers for each grave. By the time she drove out Highway 63 toward Olivet Hill, a hot breeze had wafted in from the west like an invisible outrider heralding Travis Hawthorne's approach from the other side of town.

Sarah pulled over at the usual spot in Section G-10 and dragged her lawn chair out of the trunk, unfolding it and placing it so that she could see the inscriptions on both headstones. So much of the history of her life lay in the ground here.

She placed the flowers on each grave and, opening a big golf umbrella for shade, settled into her chair, self-consciously tugging down her tennis dress. She second-guessed her decision to come here, dressed as she was, and hoped that no one, alive or dead, was offended by her attire, not that there was another living soul to be seen.

A school bus came to a throaty stop on the highway about two hundred yards away and the laughter and shrill voices of children happy for the weekend washed over the monuments. Hearing this and staring at Brandon's marker, Sarah could not help but think that her grandson would be nearing his sixth birthday had he lived.

She would have had a precious few years' worth of photos of him in party hats and smeared with devil's food cake or taking his first steps. She would have had boxes of crayon-scrawled nonsense from a little mind and construction paper-and-glue wise men or broom-riding witches in harvest skies.

She would have had the warmth of a grandson's love, the priceless, timeless embraces, the fascinated, learning eyes, the faces of every young emotion sticky with candy or green peas.

Sarah never questioned why God had taken innocent, beautiful Brandon and left Treat to tread the world as her personal Satan. No man deserved to be eaten alive by charnel worms more than Treat, but her Methodist upbringing did not allow Sarah to ask herself why his reign over her was nearing another anniversary that no card or bouquet or fancy dinner, or Perry Como music could begin to commemorate - or haunt.

In Savannah, Emily sat at a table and counted the last of the bills and coins from the $72.75 crammed into the tip jar. Her feet hurt, but it had been a good, busy day and she thought about what she would do after she got off work. It was about 3:30 p.m., and she wondered where Travis was on the road to Atlanta, hoping that he was safe. He had promised to call her once he arrived and at least leave a message on her answering machine.

Travis was indeed safe, but he was well past Atlanta and just reaching Pierpont, slowing down and waving to a cop clocking him with a radar gun just inside the city limits sign.

Treat was expecting him, Travis having called him en route, but not divulging anything about the report he was delivering.

Wiping away tears, he drove down Main Street toward the cotton gin. The time and miles and thought behind him had brought him to a heart-ripping conclusion: he would testify against Emily. Twice he had been forced to stop on the road shoulder and clear his eyes, using an old shirt he found behind the seat. He had been paid to do a job and it had been his fault that he let down his guard in sympathizing with, and later falling for, the target of his investigation. He was embarrassed by his weakness and his inability to recognize it before matters reached this point.

How could he have let himself become so personally involved? Personally involved, hell, he had been on the verge of falling in love with Emily, if he hadn't already.

Travis had never put himself in such a position before and words like pride and professionalism welled in his brain, trying to overwhelm his feelings for Emily.

He would show his case to Treat and call the district attorney on Monday to get the legal ball rolling.

Puggy had driven everywhere in Pierpont he could think of but could not find Sarah - the Piggly Wiggly, the park, the downtown business district, such as it was -

she was not to be seen. For an hour he searched without success, unknowingly meeting Travis' pickup heading to Treat's gin.

It wasn't easy to miss a tan Lincoln Continental in Pierpont and Puggy's mind sailed on a stream of wild ideas.

Maybe he had done the wrong thing by showing up at the tennis courts; his boldness possibly sending Sarah over the edge. Maybe she was telling Treat the whole story at that very moment, crying in his arms while he plotted ways to kill Puggy.

Maybe she and Marie were sitting together somewhere in a tearful embrace, telling each other what an adulterous monster he was, Marie vowing to take the kids and move in with her parents until the divorce was final.

Maybe the whole suddenly worsening mess had ended in the worst way, with Sarah taking her life, riding the car in a killing plunge into the Hookachee River to drown all her troubles.

The latter scenario had Puggy almost panicky as he drove by Mount Olivet, nearly screeching to a stop on the highway when he noticed Sarah's car in the cemetery. He had heard some of the Brattonwood women mention in casual chatter that she frequented the grave sites of her loved ones, but despite his infatuation with her, it had not occurred to him to look for her there.

He saw the Lincoln and then the figure seated under the umbrella and instantly knew that it was her. Driving around a bend in the highway, he made a U-turn and drove onto the grassy shoulder, stopping so that he could see the cemetery's main road from about a quarter mile away. Puggy considered approaching her immediately; after all, she was alone, but thought twice about disturbing her, especially not knowing how she would react, while she was visiting her dearly departed. He decided to wait for her to leave the cemetery, follow her and see how things panned out from there.

It was just after 4 p.m. when he saw the Continental glide down the hill and turn back toward Pierpont. Wiping his palms on his khakis, Puggy popped his last two breath mints into his mouth and wheeled onto the highway several hundred yards behind her. He closed on her as they neared town, but stayed back a few car lengths so that he was not right on her bumper.

He had never done anything like this in his life, but Puggy was thinking with the little head in his pants now and the silver-plated flask of Wild Turkey he kept in the glove compartment was his rocket fuel.

Chapter 10

"Like they say in that old beer commercial, it don't get no better than this."

Treat Gillon had just listened to his former daughter-in-law's surprisingly clear taped confession to killing his son.

"I want to be on the front row when they fry that bitch and I want my big smile to be the last thing she remembers from Earth when she's tangoing with the devil."

Sitting in a chair in front of Treat's desk, Travis leaned forward to click off the tape recorder. Just as he expected, Treat had reacted with the excitement of a first-time father when he knew for sure that they had the goods on Emily.

"Treat, I've also got my written report that documents the whole case. I think this and the tape should offer the district attorney some pretty strong evidence."

"Now you're talking like some seersucker courthouse lawyer, Hawthorne," Treat said, hustling around the desk to slap him on the back. "Man, you have made my day. How about a drink to celebrate?"

Treat opened a small refrigerator atop a file cabinet and snatched out a beer.

"You want something harder, I got that too."

"No thanks, Treat." Travis was almost sullen.

Treat was staring at him now.

"What's the matter, boy? You look a little puffy around the eyes. You got a cold or something?"

"No, it must just be an allergy, nothing to worry about."

"Allergy, eh. Well I got some prime-time moonshine one of my gin hands gets that will either cure you or kill you. How about it?"

"Maybe some other time."

"Bottoms up, just like I like my women." Treat drained the beer and crushed the can with a fist while still looking at Travis and not batting an eye. "Not much of a drinker, are you, Hawthorne."

Travis didn't answer. All of this was tough enough without Treat's gloating.

"I'll tell you what, then. I'm a straight-up man who calls a spade a spade, if you know what I mean, and I don't mince words about nothing."

"I hear you, Treat," Travis managed.

"Most folks pussyfoot around issues and other things that require a firm hand, but that ain't Treat Gillon. No sir, that ain't old Treat at all." He pulled another beer out of the refrigerator and took a healthy pull from it, wiping his mouth on his shirt shoulder. "And that is why, Mr. Hawthorne, that for the past year and ever-how-many months since my son was murdered, I have bided my time and gone after the trash who killed him. It's been kinda like a droopy old bloodhound trailing a fat possum and finally bringing her to bay in a tree so the hunter can put a bead on her. I am that hunter and I'm ready to pull the trigger. I'll even pull the switch if they'll let me."

"So would you like to go through my file before I hand it over to D.A. Livingston? That's why I'm here. You are the client and the contract says you get to see everything first."

"You're damn right I want to read every word of what you got. It's going to be one of my greatest pleasures in life." Treat patted his empty shirt pocket and scanned the clutter on his desk. "Well I just really don't believe this."

"What's the matter?"

"My reading glasses, they should be right here." He rustled through some papers and then looked on the floor around his swivel chair. "Although I didn't have no call to use them this morning after I read the newspaper at home."

Travis helped him search through the office, but the glasses were not to be found.

"I'll tell you what, sport. This is real important to me to be able to read all the juicy details. I must've walked out the door without my specs this morning, so I'm gonna run home, get them and be right back. You got any problem with that, Mr. Hawthorne?"

Travis shrugged.

"Like I said, Treat, you're the client. How long am I gonna have to wait?"

"Oh, I should be back in about twenty minutes. Pierpont ain't that big."

Treat's empty beer can clanged off the rim of a corner wastebasket and clattered to the floor. "Dang, I usually make that shot." He headed toward the office door. "There's a couple of hunting and fishing magazines over there on that side table that you can read while I'm gone."

He paused at the door.

"And I almost forgot one real important detail in all of this."

Travis looked up at him from his chair.

"Yeah, Treat?"

"Have you told our friend Emily the whore anything at all about this?"

"What do you mean?"

"I mean, does she know you're a private dick and that you got all this evidence on her and plan to use it to put her away?"

Travis frowned at him.

"Of course not, Treat. First off, if she knew, she might try to run and that could be a problem. Second, it's not my place to tell her anything. If the district attorney reviews the case and it eventually goes to court, she'll hear everything that I got when I'm called to testify, providing there's a jury trial."

Treat listened, leaning against the door frame while studying his gnawed fingernails.

"Now that's just real tidy and interesting. Just about as clear cut as anybody could ask, wouldn't you agree?"

"What's on your mind, Treat?"

"I'm gonna throw a little kink into your plans, Mr. Hawthorne, and it's worth an extra $5,000 of my money to do it."

"Let me hear it," Travis said, sensing trouble.

"I want to see the look on little missy's face when you tell her that you have her taped murder confession and that you're giving all this evidence to the authorities."

Travis sprang out of the chair, banging it to the floor

in the process.

"Treat is this some kind of really bad joke or have you totally gone off the deep end?"

"Oh, I don't horse around about stuff like this, Hawthorne. In fact there ain't much that I take much more seriously - graveyard serious."

"There's no way this is going to happen. This girl has been through enough without putting her through some torture just so you can get a few jollies, Treat."

"Is that a fact? You seem to be mighty defensive about her, Hawthorne. Yes sir, mighty sensitive indeed. Tell me, you get in her pants while you were on the case? Is that how you got the goods? Poked her silly a few times until she talked?"

Travis was boiling now and, standing with white-knuckled fists, it was all he could do to keep from attacking Treat, who was enjoying his dilemma.

"Now son, you look like you're about ready to explode or try to kill me. Getting all purple in the face like that is bad for your blood pressure. If you got the confession in the sack, makes no difference to me. More power to you."

"It's not happening, you redneck jerkoff. I've done my job and you got what you paid for and I've got a good mind to see how far I can punch your nose back up in your face."

Treat was unfazed.

"I appreciate your honesty, Hawthorne, I really do. So maybe you will appreciate mine." He scooped up the cassette tape of Emily's confession and dropped it in the shirt pocket where his glasses case should have been.

"You really don't have any more say-so in this. I decided days ago to put a bank hold on that $25,000 check until I totally got what I want. Your boss agreed when we talked on the phone and he was even more agreeable when I mentioned the $5,000 bonus. He didn't tell you because I told him I wanted to break the news to you. That cost me another $500, but what the hell."

"I'm out of here, scumbag," Travis said, grabbing the case file off the desk and roughly brushing against Treat in the doorway.

"Kiss all your work and all that money good-bye, Hawthorne and your job too. And just keep this in mind - that I'm gonna taste the blood of that murdering, lying slut one way or another, be it legally or with my own skinning knife, and right now, I'm leaning toward the knife."

Travis stopped in his tracks, seething and trying to think. Treat came up behind him and put his hand on his shoulder, like a caring father, which he had never been.

"No need to get all bent out of shape about this, Hawthorne. It's just business, right? I never believed I could be this patient about anything. Now why don't you just slide back in there, sit down and have a drink and let me get my glasses to read what you got. Ain't that the most sensible thing to do? Give yourself some time to think."

Without a word, Travis turned and went back into Treat's office.

Puggy followed Sarah's car down LaCourt Street, realizing that she was going home. He imagined that she knew he was behind him and was leading him to a love nest, braking seductively to let him draw tantalizingly close. There was no turning back now.

Sarah turned into her driveway and pressed the garage door opener on the Lincoln's sun visor, watching the door slowly rattle upward for her entry.

She pulled in, parking on the right side, as Treat always demanded, and was about to get out of the car when, in her rearview mirror she saw a pickup truck coming down the driveway. She didn't recognize the driver at first and the slightest apprehension crept through her. It certainly wasn't Treat's truck. Was this a repairman she had forgotten about? The pickup edged closer and she recognized Puggy, her alarm instantly turning to annoyance. She sat in the Lincoln, watching in the car mirrors as he got out and slowly walked down the driveway to the mouth of the garage.

"Now what does he want," she whispered to herself. "Puggy you're beginning to be a real pest." Standing a few feet from the rear end of the car, he obviously was waiting for her to emerge, and she obliged in a flurry of mounting irritation.

"So you just figured you'd stop by, Puggy? To what do I owe this unexpected pleasure?"

Puggy knew this was the most dramatic point of his life and that the point of no return was somewhere well behind him.

"I told you how I feel about you, Sarah." He tried to quell the nervousness saturating every syllable. "When I look at you, I just get all hot and bothered and I can't think of anything else."

Sarah rolled her eyes and folded her arms.

"Didn't your little phone call get all that out of your horny system, Puggy? Don't you know what Treat would do to you if he found out about all this?"

Puggy had walked slowly into the garage as they talked and stopped next to the door leading into the laundry room and the rest of the house. Suddenly, he reached up and pressed the button on the garage door control mounted on the wall. The garage door shuddered down as Sarah looked at him in astonishment.

"What on Earth are you doing?" she yelled.

"I'm going after what I want, Sarah; something I've never had the guts to do before."

Before she could think of resisting, he rushed around the car and was on her, kissing her on the mouth, his hands roaming her body.

"Stop it, Puggy, stop it right now! I mean it."

Off balance, their bodies smacked against the garage wall, knocking a rake to the floor.

"Don't fight me, Sarah," Puggy said, kissing her throat. "I just want to love you."

"No, Puggy! No! No!"

Travis sat stewing in Treat's office. He called his boss who confirmed everything that Treat had told him. Travis considered resigning during their heated conversation, but thought better of it; he needed to get his act together and not do anything rashly.

He thought about trying to talk Treat out of his demand about Emily, but decided it would be a futile effort. His decision to turn in Emily had been one thing, but to heap salt in her already deep wounds was quite another. Yet there were few options and Treat knew it just as well as he did.

Pounding his fist on the desk, Travis realized that he would have to deliver Emily to evil.

Humming along with a Hank Williams, Jr., song on the radio, Treat owned the world this sunny afternoon as he drove through downtown Pierpont. He had given young Hawthorne his comeuppance, and finally had Emily spread-eagled in the bulls-eye. Four beers into the day he was a victorious king wreathed in a mantle of Salem smoke.

Tomorrow was Saturday and it would be good to be on the golf course and drink and swear and punish the little ball, using many of the muscles he had honed over the years in his violent workouts against Sarah.

A frown suddenly cracked Treat's face and he pulled in behind the aqua pickup parked in his driveway. The garage door was down, the house looked to be closed up and no one was to be seen.

A Georgia license plate and a Brattonwood parking decal on the back window - Treat had seen the truck on a hundred Saturdays. Puggy Lawson drove it. The tailgate bore the telltale scrape where Puggy had whacked it with a driver after a particularly poor round last fall. What the hell was Puggy doing here and where was he?

Treat punched his garage door opener and climbed out of his truck as the garage door whined open. Sarah's car was there and movement in the shadows caught his eye.

"Sarah? Is that you?"

He walked cautiously closer, shading his eyes with his hands to better see inside as the door completed its ascent.

"Who's there?"

"Um, it's me, Treat." Sarah emerged into the sunshine. "We've got company." She looked disheveled, like she sometimes did after one of his sessions with her, and her voice wavered.

"Puggy dropped by to see us."

"How ya doing, Treat."

Puggy walked out of the garage, hands in his pockets and red-faced, and Treat immediately saw the traces of lipstick around his mouth and on his cheeks - Sarah's lipstick.

"What were you doing in there with my wife, Puggy?"

Sarah rushed to him.

"Treat, try to stay calm please, he..."

His forearm caught her just below the rib cage in mid sentence, sending her flying backward into a row of empty flower pots on the garage floor.

"You I'll tend to later," Treat said, not taking his eyes from Puggy. "Right now, it's Mr. Lawson's turn."

Puggy backed away from him.

"Now hold up there, Treat. I don't know what you're thinking, but you got the wrong idea."

Treat didn't hear him. Pamplona's bulls stampeded through him, goring his being in a red-tinged rage. Puggy was 205 pounds of raw meat cast before a jackal.

"So how long has this been going on, Puggy? How long have you been screwing this whore wife of mine? Tell me that, at least, before I kill you."

"Treat, if you'll just listen for a minute, I can explain it all. We've been buddies for a long time. Don't do anything crazy."

Sarah's whimper as she picked herself up out of some of the shattered pots distracted Treat for a second and Puggy saw his slim chance to escape. He tried to bolt down the driveway, but Treat was quicker, grabbing him around the neck from behind.

"You're not going anywhere, Puggy," he snarled. "I'm gonna take my sweet time with you."

Puggy panicked, struggling to free himself. "I didn't mean it, Treat! You have to believe me! I'm sorry!" he blubbered.

Treat tightened his grip like a coiling anaconda.

"Oh you're gonna be sorry, that's for sure, you son of a bitch. Sorry is the last thing you'll ever know."

"No, Treat! God help me!" Puggy sputtered.

"God'll have to wait for me to finish with you!"

Even amid his rage, Treat was enjoying himself now, his helpless prey squirming against him and even making him harden.

"Treat, don't kill him!" Sarah shrieked. "It's all a mistake!"

"I caught y'all red-handed, whore, and you're gonna pray for hell before I'm done with you!"

An unseen feather tickled the length of Treat's left arm and his chest seemingly turned to granite. He tried to catch his breath, but there was no air to be had, his lungs suddenly abandoning him. Spears of pain shot through him and Puggy wriggled free from his weakened embrace, both men falling to the ground. Sarah ran to Treat, who was pale and gasping.

"Oh my God! I think he's having a heart attack!" She placed his head in her lap and for the first time in her life saw fear in his eyes. "Puggy, call 911!"

Travis stood outside Treat's office and checked his watch. The sun was falling and it had been more than an hour since Treat left to retrieve his glasses. He had called Treat's cell phone and home number, but there had not been an answer and his impatience was mounting by the second.

In the distance he heard a siren's wail, not realizing that at that moment an ambulance was hurrying Treat to Bratton County Hospital.

He called Emily, telling her that he was in Atlanta and that he needed to talk to her when he returned. She was glad to hear from him and told him that she was going to the Cotton Boll with Tif Bryant after work.

"Don't pick up any cute guys," he had tried to joke with her.

"You better hurry home, Travis, that's all I'll promise you," she had replied.

It was almost 6 p.m. when Travis saw a stocky black man with a neck almost the size of Travis' waist huffing across the gin yard toward the office. The man was

McKenzie Lee Ellis, Treat's right hand employee. Sarah had called him from the hospital on his cell phone and now, obviously shaken, Ellis was going to inform Treat's visitor that he would not be back.

Travis met him at the door and was naturally shocked to hear of Treat's misfortune. He gathered up his file on Emily and strode toward his truck, feeling like he had aged a century since dawn.

"So do you think y'all will ever tie the knot?" Tif Bryant eyed Emily across the table. "Now there's a fine looking man," she said before Emily could answer. The Cotton Boll Lounge was alive with a Friday crowd, and the two of them already had been hit on by a pair of young suits looking to score before their night was over.

"I'm not going to rush things, Tif. What happens happens."

"I hear you, girl, but sometimes you got to make your own luck, if you know what I mean."

"Tif, about the only good luck I've had ever was meeting Travis, and I'll thank you for that by putting your next mimosa on my tab." Emily had changed into a sun dress she kept in the deli storage room and hastily dabbed on some makeup before meeting Tif. She wouldn't dare walk into the Cotton Boll in her work jeans and looking like she had just stepped out of the kitchen. The watering hole wasn't the Ritz, but it was high end for Savannah.

"Now I'll take that offer all night, Em," Tif said. "Unless I get a better one from that tall chocolate number who works at City Hall. He's sitting at a table on the other side of the bar with some of his office buddies."

"Let me know when you get ready to make your move, honey, and I'll make myself scarce as hen's teeth."

"You keep feeding me mimosas and I'll rock his Casbah tonight, baby doll." They laughed and drank and surveyed the late happy hour crowd.

Tif was Emily's best girlfriend by far in Savannah. They were about the same age, although Tif could never be pinned down on her birth date, and each sought the other for advice and company and comfort when only another woman would understand. In their over-cocktails gabfests, Emily had confided that she had left an abusive relationship in Pierpont to come to Savannah and told Tif about some of Lyle's brutality. But never - not even with an alcohol-loosened tongue - had she mentioned her own bloody hands. Tif had been battered herself and their ties of suffering had made them hard and fast friends who could laugh at their pasts even while awful memories lurked.

"Anyway, Travis will be home from Atlanta tomorrow. I can't wait to see him."

"So he's writing a book?"

"Yeah, but he won't let me read any of it until he's done. I guess a lot of writers are like that."

"You got me, Em. The closest thing to a writer I ever dated was that guy who bounced all the checks, remember him? Man could he dribble paper."

"Hey, not to change the subject, but is George Wallace due for any shots? He's been twitching his tail a lot lately. Are y'all supposed to send me a reminder card? Not that I can afford it."

"Em, your cat ain't due for nothing but the oil change they have to have once they get neutered or spayed."

"Huh?"

"It's just a joke of mine I tell these folks after they've had their animals fixed. Thirty weight for cats and forty weight for dogs. I had one old white lady take it hook, line and sinker. She wanted to set up an appointment."

An hour later, Tif indeed had connected with the handsome guy from City Hall and Emily found herself walking home alone. She could have grabbed a taxi, but she needed to save her money for other things. Besides, it was a sultry evening, the kind of Savannah spring night when time itself slowed to a drawl and a dragon's breath breeze was an inhaled potion for sweaty dancing or fucking like porn stars - often both.

Emily had no inclination for either, unless it was with Travis, and so she took her time strolling the streets savoring the sounds of faint guitars and Rebel yells. Saturday was her Friday and Travis would be home and all would be right with her world.

Travis was so incensed about the day that he drove non-stop into the night to reach his farm. He arrived near midnight and, despite having been behind the wheel for more than six hundred miles, he was wired by all that had occurred. Pouring a tall bourbon and firing up a cigar, he settled wearily into his rocking chair on the porch, listening to the night. Perhaps a shooting star over the lazy Ogeechee or the katydids' sonata would give him a sign as to how he could wriggle out of the quicksand into which reality had lured him.

Of course he already knew the simplest out for everyone involved and had to suppress a wish that Treat would not live. Indeed, he shuddered at the thought that he could hope for anyone's death, even someone as despicable as Treat.

Travis had told foreman Ellis that he would call in a few days to check on Treat's condition and he would do so. Right now, however, his twirling mind came to rest on Emily, which prompted a cyclone of thoughts and emotions unto itself.

Never before had he questioned his professional actions, but his feelings for Emily, love or not, had him second guessing his every move since meeting her, analyzing and re-analyzing everything, even his sexual prowess. Despite merely doing his job, he felt he was a betrayer who had bedded her in what was at least innocent infatuation, yet at the same time had been a creaking-springs shortcut toward proving her guilt.

Travis still had every intention of honoring the contract, despite the stunning curve ball Treat had pitched to him before leaving to find his glasses. If Treat survived, Travis would bring Emily to face him, no matter if Treat was on life support, no matter how much it butchered his soul to do it.

The tears welled again, but amid his woe, Travis remembered the most important piece of his murder jigsaw - Emily's tape. It had been in Treat's pocket when he left and it was unaccounted for now and the foundation of Emily's prison cell would be all the more fragile without it.

In his raging wrestle with Puggy, Treat's body finally rebelled. Ten thousand drumsticks, a galleon's hold of tobacco and enough fast food grease to lube a Buick had finally taken their toll, and he had been reduced to writhing for his life in his driveway while the adulterers escaped his avenging hand.

He had suffered a massive stroke that the Pierpont hospital was not remotely prepared to handle and within ninety minutes of the attack had been transferred by emergency helicopter to Carver Memorial Hospital in Atlanta. There, in the cardiac intensive care unit, he bit into survival like an angry bulldog, refusing to let go, literally too mean to die. Sarah was at his bedside as much as she was allowed, and cards poured in, flowers not being allowed in the ICU. In the unit's waiting room where she spent most of her time, she was consoled and cheered by a steady flow of friends who made the hour-long drive from Pierpont. Among the visitors were Randall Herman and Terry Donelson and their wives, but the third member of Treat's golfing Stooges was understandably absent.

On the day of the incident, Puggy Lawson had been rattled and sputtering to catch his breath when he called 911 from the Gillons' kitchen phone to summon aid for Treat.

Paramedics and police had arrived at the house in minutes and Sarah had disappeared into the back of the ambulance to ride with Treat to the hospital, leaving Puggy to answer questions from a rookie patrolman of Pierpont's finest. The kid was surprisingly thorough, much to Puggy's dismay.

"Now Mr. Lawson, a couple of neighbors I've just talked to state that they heard some shouting and what sounded like a scuffle here in the yard," the cop had asked, intent on his notes. "What can you tell me about what happened?"

Puggy was in a bind, not knowing what Sarah - or Treat, if he lived - would tell the police. His unholy illusion of making Sarah his sex kitten had exploded in his face in the worst possible way and if he was fortunate that Treat had not killed him, his luck was not among his panicky thoughts as the policeman waited for his response.

"We had a disagreement, officer. That's all there was too it. We've been friends for a long time. Play golf together just about every weekend."

"A disagreement. So what were y'all arguing about, sir?"

"Now I wouldn't exactly call it an argument, son. It was more of a misunderstanding that got out of hand and then Mr. Gillon became suddenly ill. Is he going to be okay?"

The cop did not look up from writing in his notebook.

"I'd say it's too early to tell. Can you be a little more specific about the nature of your disagreement, Mr. Lawson?"

"He thought I was messing around with his wife."

"I see. Were you, sir?"

"No. Yes. I mean, I was trying, but I hadn't gotten anywhere."

The cop was impassive, scribbling rapidly in his book. He wrote for a full minute before looking up at Puggy with a slight, sideways grin, shaking his head slowly.

"Got caught with your pants down, didn't you, Mr. Lawson."

As ever, Sarah was not wasting her thoughts on Puggy. He was just a stupid, gutless sap who had found a spine for one foolish mission and gone down in flames. If Treat had been able to get to the pistol in his glove compartment, he would have landscaped the yard with Puggy's brains, few as they might be. She had no sympathy that the scuffle made a three-paragraph mention in the Pierpont newspaper, even though no charges were filed, and that Puggy's new life's work was trying to explain to his wife what happened.

Treat's prognosis was not good even if he lived. The heart specialists told Sarah that he was unable to speak and had paralysis along the right side of his body. They were unsure whether either would be short term or permanent, but Treat was in for a long, slow rehabilitation regardless.

Occasionally, late at night in the waiting room or back at her hotel a few blocks from the hospital, Sarah broke into sobs that rattled her body. Sure Treat was a pointy-tailed bastard from hell's basement, but she had been his wife for almost three decades and there were a half-handful of good memories, all revolving around the births of Lyle and Brandon.

The crying always passed quickly. She had been a faithful spouse and a God-fearing Southern Methodist, but there was a line between anything Christian and the iron maiden in which Treat had encased her for all these years.

Sitting by his hospital bed and watching the fluids eke into him from intravenous tubes, she thought of how she had bought this moment - all the cigarettes, alcohol and deep-fried everything had toppled the emperor of pain. And now she stood over him, relishing the right time when no one else was around, when she could work up a good mouthful of saliva and spit in his face.

Travis kept in touch with McKenzie Ellis, who was running the gin in Treat's absence, to monitor Treat's condition. Ellis called Sarah daily at 5:30 p.m. for an update on Treat and she appreciated his kind words and what she knew was his genuine concern. Ellis had worked for Treat almost twenty years and next to Sarah, could read him better than anybody.

Over time, she had grown to rely on his quiet dependability as much as Treat did, but was always taken aback on the few occasions that she had gone to Treat's office and encountered the foreman. He never stared at her - even in this age most black men in small Southern towns knew their place - yet when their eyes locked for the briefest second, she read a look of pity for her from him. It was always unspoken, but was as if Ellis realized what Treat did to her, knowing also that he was helpless to do anything about it.

In his calls, Ellis told Sarah that one of Treat's out of town business associates, Travis Hawthorne, was keeping close tabs on Treat's health. She had never heard of Travis, but Treat worked with a lot of people across the state and she didn't object to Ellis telling him about her husband.

"He's welcome to come visit us if he's up in the Atlanta area," Sarah told Ellis to relay to Travis. "I've got a feeling we might be here for a while."

For Travis, the days that Treat lay in the ICU with his life teetering in the balance were a personal purgatory. Treat's death would mean all his work would be for nothing, the investigation would go to the grave with him and his agency would never see the $30,500 Treat owed them.

On the Saturday morning after his return from Pierpont, he had driven to Savannah, still punchy and frustrated by all that had occurred the previous day. It was May 1 and Emily was glad to see him, affectionate as always when he picked her up after she got off. But Travis already was adding bricks to the emotional barrier he had erected to keep from becoming closer to her. They had gone out for dinner and a few drinks and then back to her apartment to snuggle.

He spent that night with her and on Sunday they had driven out to Tybee Island for deviled crab cakes and a stroll on the long municipal pier jutting out into the glistening Atlantic. They talked, but it was of nothing, both avoiding matters of substance. Emily stifled urges to ask him why he seemed preoccupied and distant; Travis was merely marking time before he, Treat or a hanging judge lit the match to burn her at the stake.

On Monday they picnicked in Forsyth Park, spreading their blanket in the oak shade near the grand fountain and watching acorn-wired squirrels dart after bits of bread like furry lunatics. He kissed Emily good-bye that night and drove back to his farm with Emily's whispered "I love you" resounding in his head. He called McKenzie Ellis from the road, but Treat remained in intensive care.

Emily had watched Travis go, waving to him as he pulled out of the lane behind her apartment. Had she spooked him with her blossoming love for him? Maybe he wasn't ready for commitment or maybe she had moved too quickly. For whatever reason, he was acting differently toward her. The sex was good as ever, but he didn't seem as enthusiastic or happy to be with her, and at times seemed to avoid her eye. Still, she wasn't overly concerned about matters; having survived Lyle, anything else was a cakewalk, at least to her thinking.

She decided that she would talk to Travis the next time they were together and try to determine if anything was wrong. For now, however, she settled into her favorite chair to watch "Jeopardy," with George Wallace making a nest in her lap. She and her mother had watched the game show together when she was a child and she continued to enjoy it.

As Emily relaxed, Travis stared at the white lines disappearing under his truck on the interstate west of the city. Maybe they would give him a clue as to what happened to the tape of Emily's confession.

Travis was up early on Tuesday and put in a call to Elton Livingston, having the good fortune to actually catch the district attorney in his office. He told Livingston about the cassette and how he had his files on the Gillon case ready to turn over to him, but needed final approval from Treat before he could make another move. The D.A. listened intently, saying only that Treat had mentioned hiring a private investigator to reopen the case.

Travis then came to the real crux of his reason for calling Livingston: had the Pierpont police found the tape? Perhaps it was in the yard or in the ambulance or was in Treat's personal effects removed from his clothing at the county hospital before he was airlifted to Atlanta. Travis asked if Livingston would find out for him and the D.A. agreed to the favor. He knew Travis did solid detective work and was a likeable sort. Besides, to reopen an old, supposed suicide case and put away a killer couldn't hurt him at reelection time, although some would ask why it hadn't been done in the first place.

Livingston called him back within the hour. The cops had not removed any physical evidence from the Gillons' yard and nothing had been reported found in the ambulance that carried Treat to the hospital. The officer who handled the 911 call took custody of Treat's wallet, keys and pocket change at the hospital before Treat was flown to Carver Memorial. These possessions had been turned over to Mrs. Gillon that same day before a sheriff's deputy drove her to Atlanta to be with her husband.

There was no sign of any tape.

Travis thanked Livingston for his efforts and told him he would be in touch. Twenty minutes later he was back on the road to Pierpont. His best guess was that the cassette had fallen out of Treat's pocket during the fracas and must be somewhere in the yard; that or it could still be in Treat's pickup that he had driven home from the gin. He believed he could find it, and spent the trip cursing himself for not making a duplicate. Never would he make such an obvious mistake again.

Arriving in Pierpont about mid afternoon, Travis stopped at a convenience store to ask directions to LaCourt Street. Less than ten minutes later, he stopped at the curb in front of the Gillon home. He had the address in his case records. A few gray-white clouds blotted the sky and it was muggy as he sat in his truck for a minute surveying the neighborhood. There was no one else to be seen, everyone probably at work or perched inside under their air conditioners.

Climbing out of the pickup, he walked slowly down the paved driveway, scanning the grass on each side of it. The garage door was closed and the house seemed closed tight, but even if Mrs. Gillon emerged to ask what he was doing, Travis was prepared to tell her the whole story. If Treat died, she was the only hope to retrieve the money for his work.

Squatting, he peered under azalea bushes next to the house and used a downed tree limb to poke into some new rose of Sharon shrubs that looked to have been recently planted. Just to the left of the garage entrance was a small, mulched and bordered rock and fern garden. The lawn along the driveway was golf-course-neat, as was the rest of the yard, and Travis could see that it would be hard for anyone to have missed a cassette tape in a white case amid the greenery. His half-hour search yielded nothing.

Treat's truck was likely parked in the garage and for

a second Travis considered trying to find a way in so that he could search the cab. He quickly nixed the idea; the house probably had a fancy alarm system and if Pierpont's Andy Griffith cops nailed him for breaking and entering or burglary, it would be a terrible blow to his credibility if and when he had to testify against Emily.

He had to remain patient and hope that Treat recovered. If not, he would spill everything to Sarah Gillon and get permission to look for the tape in Treat's truck. Once she heard all the facts, surely she would be eager to have Emily prosecuted and release the check.

Disheartened and simmering, Travis slowly drove away from the big house, Treat's jeering laughter at his plight seemingly echoing out of every window. He stopped in at the gin to see McKenzie Ellis, but the foreman was busy and didn't have time to talk, telling Travis that there was no change in Treat's condition. He considered going by Livingston's office for an impromptu meeting with the D.A., but realized he had nothing more to discuss with him until he had Treat's approval to proceed.

Before leaving town Travis stopped at a public telephone and called the two landscaping services in the Pierpont phone book. Locating the one that worked for the Gillons, he told the manager that he was Treat's life insurance agent and that he had lost a sales motivation tape, possibly in the Gillons' yard. After some initial reluctance, the manager told him that a crew had spruced up the place earlier that day and had not found anything to mention.

One of the neighbors drawn to the disturbance possibly could have picked up the tape. Going door-to-door in the neighborhood was a desperate measure that he would leave as a last-ditch effort.

Out of ideas, at least for the moment, Travis bought some beer and cheap cigars and checked in to the Harbor Sunset Motel, unaware that the room where Emily had honeymooned with Lyle seven years earlier was only two doors down.

He called Emily on his cell phone. She was tired from work and the heat and was going home to take a long, cool shower and relax. Life for her at this hour on this day was simple, uncomplicated - deciding whether to dip the cat's litter box today or wait until tomorrow and worrying if the tip jar ever would be filled with more folding money than nickels.

Travis lit a stogie, cracked open a beer and walked out to the pool, where a white-haired woman was doing exercises in the water. An older man, apparently her husband, was snoring loudly on a lounge chair, his back a boiling-lobster red. Other than the three of them, the motel was empty, as far as Travis could tell.

He decided to relax for a few minutes and then head over to the Pizza Hut to grab some dinner. Maybe if he just settled down, he could think more rationally and determine some way to find and retrieve the tape.

The object of his hunt was enticingly close and had been even closer when he was poking among the Gillons' bushes. The tape and a note to Sarah lay on the counter in the Gillons' kitchen.

Chapter 11

The next two days were a waiting game for all. Treat was improving, but still in intensive care, Sarah by his side. Travis hung around Pierpont until Thursday, combing the driveway and yard again without results. His boss basically told him that he was on his own, but that he needed to put as much pressure as possible on the Gillons to release the check. Travis went back to his farm to try to be patient and to think things out, calling McKenzie Ellis about Treat's health.

D.A. Livingston was anxious to hear back from Travis, even though his heavy caseload did not permit him the luxury of sitting by the telephone.

Even Puggy Lawson was waiting. His wife had been tremendously embarrassed by the hoopla surrounding his run-in with Treat. Tongues were wagging in high gear from the beauty parlors to the churches' front pews to Brattonwood's preppie inner circle, but Marie was certainly more incensed by Puggy's intentions. In his daily groveling since the incident, he had only told her that he had had a "schoolboy crush" on Sarah and had gone to her house simply to talk to her. Their marriage had been severely damaged and Puggy expected to be served with divorce papers at any time. Perhaps the young age of their children could save their relationship, but the thin ice under him was melting.

By the eighth day, a Saturday, Treat was out of immediate danger and was moved from ICU to a regular room on the cardiac wing. His vital signs had strengthened, but there still was no progress with the paralysis or his speech loss.

Sarah fed him the chicken bouillon, apple sauce and gelatin that were his staples, and watched the drip of the IV bags the nurses and aides regularly replaced. His communication was simply one blink for yes and two blinks for no, the face that had snarled and twisted into a grotesque mask over her beaten body now bearing the look of a trapped, helpless animal.

With the doctors' assurances that Treat's condition had stabilized and likely would not change in the immediate future, Sarah decided to go home for a few hours the next day for the first time since everything happened. She told Treat of her decision just before she left him after supper that night.

There was no goodbye kiss - even the thought of it would have made her shudder - but she hesitated at the room door, her Christian compassion making her turn to look at him.

I love you.

Maybe if she said the words they would bring some comfort to this suddenly shriveled man to whom she had pledged her love and life "in sickness and in health" what seemed eons before.

In sickness and in health.

In health, which he had been for most of the twenty-eight years, Treat had robbed her of her dignity, self-esteem, blood, buckets of tears and, several times, almost her life.

In sickness, she had been there for him eight solid days, trembling as she swallowed mouthfuls of spit and recoiling from her most primitive urge to clench hands - strengthened by her backhand grip - around his neck and finish the job God and nature and an orgy of vices had started.

I love you.

The words dissipated like sun-scorched fog before they reached her lips. She had not uttered them to Treat since he slid that big diamond on her finger on June 17, 1971, and nothing that had happened in the interim had rekindled the spark that had been slapped out of her heart. Only fantasy or insanity or long-dead wifely concern or pity would have brought them out of her mouth now and none were present. Sarah spun away from him, the click-clack of her sandals fading down the hospital corridor.

The hour drive to Pierpont seemed like an instant as Sarah was immersed in her thoughts and the tense fatigue wearing on her. It would be good to see the house again, check the mail she knew would be piled up and sink down into her favorite chair for some quiet relaxation and reflection. She would turn off her cell phone, take the other phone off its hook and pick out some more clothes to carry back to Atlanta with her.

She stopped in the driveway, not wanting to open the garage and see Treat's pickup inside.

Everything looked to be neat as a pin, just the way Sarah liked it. Terry Wyatt was reliable as usual. Sarah couldn't believe that Terry would be a high school senior in the fall. The Wyatts lived on the next block and it seemed like only last year that she had co-hosted a baby shower for Catherine Wyatt when she was plump with Terry. For the past two years, Terry had looked after the house on occasions when she and Treat were away, and they had entrusted her with keys and the security alarm code. Sarah had called Terry the day after Treat was taken to Atlanta, telling her to put his truck in the garage, clean up the yard mess, get the mail and newspapers and generally keep an eye on the place.

Sarah unlocked the front door, noting that the landscapers had made their weekly cutting and trimming call. The bill would probably be among her mail. The house was oddly still, as if afraid to even make a settling creak that would spring the infirmed master from his bed and send him plummeting home like a bullet intent on more mayhem.

Sarah knew these walls had absorbed her screams and that the sharp dust of shattered china, glasses, bottles and everything else breakable lived in the floor creases and baseboard crannies, along with minuscule blood stains of hers too small to clean. Such was the history of her life with Treat, the sound of body blows mingling with Perry Como, and for a second as she stood in the front foyer she considered rushing into the den and smashing every record in Treat's collection. For now, however, she had business to take care of; the pleasure of album obliteration would come later.

Terry had stacked the mail on the kitchen counter as she always did, and Sarah sat down at the breakfast table to sort through it. There was so much junk, almost as bad as what she got on the Internet. Then there was one of Treat's golf magazines, electric, water, and cable TV bills, the monthly statement from the club - she would have to write a few checks.

Sarah stood up to get her check book from her purse when she noticed something else on the counter that had been obscured by her fat fox ceramic cookie jar when she first entered the kitchen. A white cassette tape case was atop a note with Terry's familiar handwriting on it. Sarah picked up the paper and read aloud.

"Mrs. Gillon, This tape was in the yard near the driveway. I found it and thought you might want it. - Terry."

She then opened the case, which contained a tape and a business card, which she held to the light of a window. "Travis L. Hawthorne. Private Investigator. Pinnacle Investigations, Atlanta, Georgia." The card also had telephone numbers and web site information.

A label on the tape itself was more startling – "Emily Gillon Confession, 1999 - Lyle Gillon Murder, 1997."

Sarah went to one of the kitchen cabinets and, reaching far in the back, pulled out a dusty bottle of brandy someone had given them some forgotten holiday ago. Pouring an inch into a juice glass, she downed it, the liquid flame searing her throat and misting her eyes, the alcohol burn mixing with her tears.

Treat had one foot in a grave next to Lyle and Brandon, but Lyle had taken a step out of his, kicking aside all the flowers and knickknacks that the red ants stormed before thieves took them. She sat back down, putting her head on the kitchen table, her wails echoing through the house again, as they had so many other times. Resurrecting the events of Lyle's death would only push her closer to her own end.

Somewhere in town a church bell was tolling slowly as if in mournful accompaniment to her mood. Probably the Baptist, Sarah thought. In the next instant she was wondering whether Treat had a cassette player anywhere in the house so that she could play the tape.

Even as Sarah found an old cassette deck in Treat's workshop, inserted the tape and hit the play button, Emily and Travis were window shopping on Broughton Street. Like any late Sunday afternoon, downtown was almost abandoned, only a few stores open and the early summer heat draining Savannah to molasses slowness.

Emily had decided not to rock the boat by approaching Travis about his change of demeanor. She would take everything day by day and, whatever else life cast at her, would meet it face first. The sidewalk cement baked through her $2 flip-flops, burning her feet, but she barely noticed as they walked, making their way toward City Market, a mall of shops and restaurants. There was always a live band performing in the market's open courtyard on weekends and they would have a few drinks there and maybe some supper.

Travis was continuing to mentally distance himself from Emily even if he still was with her on her days off. He didn't want to spook her in any way before he closed the deal. He had tried to call McKenzie Ellis that morning, but couldn't reach him, so he was unaware that Treat was out of the ICU.

"So how's the book coming, Travis?"

Emily's question broke through his wall.

"It's been kinda slow lately, I'm at a point where the story has sort of bogged down on me. I guess it's writer's block."

"Why don't you tell me about it and maybe I can help you. My mama used to read to me a lot when I was a kid."

"You're a sly one, Em. You'll be the first one to read it when I'm done, but you're outta luck until then."

"Okay, okay, just be a stubborn old mule about it," she teased, wanting their relationship to return to how it had been in the weeks after they first met. "When it's finally a big bestseller, you can buy me a fur coat or a crown or something else fancy like that."

"That's a deal, Em. You'd look great in a tiara and flip-flops."

From two blocks away, they heard the courtyard band playing a Jimmy Buffett song and headed in that direction. A crowd of about a hundred people were relaxing under umbrella tables and watching the musicians, who were on an elevated, open stage in the brick courtyard. By now the sun had slipped behind a big oak in Franklin Square at the west end of the market, bringing some additional welcome shade.

Emily and Travis found a table and settled in, ordering plastic cups of almost-cool draft beer. The group, Fire-breathing Poodles, was local and did covers of songs by artists like Buffett, New Riders of the Purple Sage, and John Prine. They were regulars on the courtyard stage.

"I asked that lead singer last week to play an old Ozark Mountain Daredevils song," but I don't think they ever did," Emily said, cupping her hands at Travis' ear to be heard.

"Maybe you should have smiled a little sweeter or left a bigger tip in their jar up there."

Emily shook him playfully by the shoulders.

"Honey, you sling pita sandwiches for a living for a week and then you tell me who deserves a bigger tip - me or these Hawaiian-shirted bozos who are getting paid to play music somebody else wrote."

"Guess you're right. Grab the waitress next time she comes by, will you?"

On the table, Travis' cell phone rang.

"Em, order us another round while I get this, please."

"No arm twisting needed here."

Travis flicked open the phone.

"Hello?"

Sarah Gillon was calling.

In the solitude of her kitchen, Sarah's cries seemed to pierce all. The cheery yellow tiles, her collection of bottled spices in the rack over the range and the redwood bowl of French ceramic fruit on the breakfast table all now held dashes of her new grief, pinches of salt multiplied in a terrible recipe of old wounds reopened.

The tape, about fifteen minutes long, had been muffled and hard to understand in spots. Still, there was no doubt that it was Emily's voice talking about trying to find The Hootch.

Then had come the words that had branded Sarah's brain, and she had rewound and listened to them again and again and again to make sure she wasn't engulfed in a deja vu nightmare.

I killed him, Travis.

I staged his suicide and he deserved what he got.

Old Lucy was his favorite shotgun. I used it on him.

Even on tape and in what appeared to be a rattled, panicky tone, the words were Emily's, the voice the same that had joined Sarah in celebrating Brandon's all too brief stay among them an eternity ago.

Sarah had stumbled to her feet and into the den, staring up at the shotgun mounted there, a twisted trophy of the Gillons' darkest secret. Old Lucy was wickedly silent and still on its wall, the big black maw the last thing her son had seen in his face before a white blast from it returned him to his Maker. And now Sarah was plunged back into the heart-ripping agony of Lyle's death, the tape like a weight around her ankles, sinking her into an unfathomable sea of despair.

She knew as sure as a sunrise that Lyle had been Treat's master apprentice. Some fathers passed on tips for curve balls, baiting a hook, or igniting campfires with rubbed sticks; Treat's son had learned the violent perversion of his dad and ancestors, and Emily had been a breathing target just as she had been for all the years.

Still, Lyle was her son, whom she had joined in creating and suckled and raised and whose life had careened out of control until his collision with death. The baby booties, birth certificate, blue ribbons and other mementos in one of her closet drawers were all she had left of his innocence. Old Lucy was a monument to his downfall.

With an angry scream, Sarah snatched the shotgun from its mounts, no Treat to hammer her to the floor for her insolence. Lurching across the den with it, she ripped open the doors to Treat's stereo, using her free arm to rake his records onto the carpet.

A Perry Como album skidded in front of her, the singer smiling at her from the cover with his clean-cut, Pepsodent pizzazz. Grabbing the gun barrel, she drove the butt into the face, the vinyl inside cracking like a bug under a shoe. Working Old Lucy like an old-fashioned butter churn, she methodically crushed all of the albums, whipping one Beach Boys record against the wall and sending the Grateful Dead's "Terrapin Station" whirling into the front foyer to crash against an antique hat stand.

It was at this point that she stumbled back into the kitchen, gulped another hair-straightening brandy and, taking a minute to catch her breath and thoughts, called Travis on his cell phone, his business card in front of her.

The Fire-breathing Poodles' music was too loud for Travis to immediately hear who was calling.

"I'm sorry, who is this again?"

"Sarah Gillon in Pierpont, Georgia. Treat Gillon's wife."

This time he heard and if there was nothing he could do about the blood leaving his face, he had to maintain his composure in front of Emily.

"I see. So what can I do for you?"

"I think you know damn well what you can do for me."

Travis cut her off before she could continue.

"Ma'am, this connection, at least on my end, is really bad, can I call you back in about two minutes?"

"If you don't, I'll be calling you back in three minutes."

"Yes, fine, goodbye."

Travis closed his phone, Emily still watching the band.

"So who was that, your other girlfriend?" she teased.

"Not exactly." He had to come up with an instant lie. "Somebody maybe interested in buying the farm."

"I didn't know you had it up for sale, Travis. You didn't tell me that."

"It's not for sale, Em, it's just that it's prime property on the river and people are always asking me if I want to part with it. I think this lady is a realtor. I promised to call her back, do you mind?"

"Do what you need to do, Travis. Are you getting

hungry?"

"I'll return this call and we'll talk about supper, okay? Might as well hear her out."

Emily nodded in reply, moving to the music.

Travis walked some distance down the courtyard away from the band and pulled a piece of paper with Treat's home number on it out of his wallet. He could see the back of Emily's head in the crowd as he made the call. Sarah picked up immediately after the first ring.

"Hello?"

"Mrs. Gillon? This is Travis Hawthorne, again. Sorry I couldn't talk earlier."

"So you're a private investigator, Mr. Hawthorne? That's what it says on your card. I guess Treat hired you."

"Yes ma'am, that's right." Travis was banking on his politeness to try to dampen the tension. "Your husband contacted my firm a few months back. How is Mr. Gillon, by the way?"

"We'll get to that, Mr. Hawthorne, but right now I want some answers as to what's going on."

Travis anxiously wanted to know how she had tracked him down, but realized he would have to wait to ask any questions. Sarah Gillon sounded like she was in no mood to tolerate any bullshit and he would not offer any. It was time to come clean with her.

"Ma'am, Treat contracted me, that is, my firm, to look into the death of your son Lyle." He waited for a reaction but there was silence in his ear. "I have been working the case since January and just recently wrapped things up. In fact, I met with Treat the afternoon of his stroke and was going to let him read through my case file. He went home to get his glasses and, well, you know what happened from there."

"And what did you discover, Mr. Hawthorne?"

"Please call me Travis, Mrs. Gillon." He was trying everything to thaw the conversation, but it didn't seem to be working. "I'm sure Treat didn't tell you about all of this because he didn't want to upset you, and I'm sorry that we have to discuss it under these circumstances."

Silence again was his reply. He took a deep breath and

continued.

"What I found, Mrs. Gillon, was that your son's death wasn't a suicide at all as the authorities ruled." The Poodles seemed to be playing louder all of a sudden and he had to raise his voice. "He was murdered."

Travis stepped further away from the bandstand, listening for Sarah's response, but there was none.

"Did you hear what I said, ma'am? It's painful, I know."

"I heard you, Mr. Hawthorne." Her voice was an icy monotone and Travis thought to himself that she was likely in shock or denial or that the few seconds were not enough time for the realization to sink in.

"Who killed my son?"

"Mrs. Gillon, before I go any further, how is your husband? I know he's been in intensive care. I've been checking on him by calling McKenzie Ellis, his foreman. I never intended to deceive you, and I haven't..."

"Who killed my son?" Sarah's voice, stronger now, interrupted him.

"Ma'am, I sure wish we could talk to Treat about this before I give you any more details. At the very least why don't you and I arrange a face-to-face meeting. It's tough and awkward talking about things like this on the phone."

"Mr. Hawthorne, I'll ask you for the last time. Who killed my son?"

Travis was backed into a corner. Treat's check to Pinnacle was from a joint account with her name on it and he couldn't risk her canceling payment on it. He had to tell her the rest of it.

"It was Emily. Your former daughter-in-law, Emily, shot Lyle, Mrs. Gillon. I'm sorry I have to be the one to break it to you."

Again there was no immediate reaction to his revelation.

"Are you still there, Mrs. Gillon?"

"Oh, I'm very much here. Where is Emily?"

"She's living and working in Savannah. That's where I found her after she left Pierpont. She's a waitress in a little delicatessen there downtown."

"And you think she murdered Lyle?"

"Mrs. Gillon, she confessed to me. She staged the

suicide and killed Lyle with his own shotgun, the one he called Old Lucy."

Sarah sat at the kitchen table, hugging the shotgun with her thighs and peering into the barrel as she listened to Travis. She was considering turning Old Lucy on herself. Surely she could find a box of shells in Treat's gun cabinet. The gun's first lethal belch since wallpapering Lyle's brains in The Hootch could end her suffering as well. Someone else could mop up and scrub away the hideous kaleidoscope and she would be forever beyond Treat's reach.

Then she thought better of it. The instant the shotgun pellets tore away her life, he would have defeated her and she wasn't about to let that happen, especially now when she finally was winning in the survival of the fittest. She propped the gun against the wall.

"Mrs. Gillon?"

"So what do we do now, Mr. Hawthorne?"

"That's where things get a little more delicate, ma'am. You see I had a tape of Emily's confession to me, but Treat took it with him when he went for his glasses and I haven't seen it since. Nobody mentioned anything to you about finding a tape, did they? It could still be in his truck."

"I have your tape. Someone found it and left it for me."

Her words were better than heaven's manna to Travis.

"Wow, you have just made my day, Mrs. Gillon." He didn't dare ask if she had listened to it, at least not now; no need to press his luck. "I guess that's how you were able to trace me, am I right?"

"Your business card."

"I can't tell you how important that tape is to my case, even though it would be strong without it. So how is Treat doing?"

"He got out of the ICU yesterday, but is still on the cardiac floor and will be for some time. There isn't any good news yet about his speech returning and his right side is still paralyzed. I know McKenzie told you all about that."

"Yes ma'am he did. He seems like a kind and caring soul."

"He is, Mr. Hawthorne. He told me that you were calling daily about Treat, but I just thought you were some business associate from the gin who was just real concerned."

"I never mentioned my line of work to McKenzie Ellis, Mrs. Gillon. "He didn't ask and I didn't say, not that I would have anyway."

"So what are you going to do with your tape and your other evidence, Mr. Hawthorne?"

"Now that's where we get into the touchy part that I mentioned earlier."

"I'm listening."

"Here's my situation, ma'am. Treat put me between a rock and a hard place, but I've gotta deal with it. He wrote a check to my company in payment for my work and based on the contract that he signed, but then he threw me a ringer. On the day of his stroke he told me that he had cut a deal with my boss and paid extra for a luxury item."

"A luxury item?"

"That's my description of it and it is, to my thinking. He wants to see Emily's face when I tell her I am a private investigator and have built a case against her in Lyle's murder. He's put a hold on the check until that happens."

Emily looked over her shoulder at him and he returned her wave as the band launched into another number.

"I see. Now I have a question for you, Mr. Hawthorne."

"Anything, ma'am."

"You say that Emily killed my Lyle. Did she tell you why she did it? I have my own theory, but that's another story."

"Mrs. Gillon, you are putting me in a predicament. Treat hasn't even asked me that question."

"Oh, I suspect he knows."

"Maybe he does, but that's not the issue here. I'm working for your husband and I've already divulged too much about what I've uncovered without getting his permission, even though you are his wife."

"And as his wife, if my name is on that check to your company, I will void it in a New York minute if you don't tell me what I want to know. I can seek power of attorney status due to Treat's bad health and I have a few judge and lawyer friends in Pierpont. So why don't you just talk to me and save us all some time and trouble."

"I guess you're bound to find out soon enough, especially if the case goes to a jury trial." Emily was dancing with some guy in front of the stage, oblivious to the weighty conversation taking place about her.

"This is very difficult for me to relate, Mrs. Gillon, but Emily shot Lyle because he was extremely abusive to her, mentally and physically. It was ongoing their whole married life together and she was afraid that eventually he would kill her.

"It finally was more than she could endure and so she went to his deer stand that morning, used his prize shotgun on him and passed it off as a suicide. Unfortunately, she got away with it for about a year and a half, but I've spoken to D.A. Livingston and with the evidence I've uncovered, he's ready to reopen the case."

"Do you believe what she said about her reason?"

"I do, I absolutely do. I got to know Emily pretty well over a number of weeks and there really was no other motive that I could come up with. She wasn't unfaithful, and excuse me, ma'am, but you know as well as I do that they weren't the richest folks in Bratton County, far from it, so she didn't do it for money.

"I hate to say it, Mrs. Gillon, but your son just beat the pure hell out of her for more than five years and, in the end, he paid for it. Frankly, I think she's a good girl who just snapped. Now some defense lawyer will twist it into a sob story on Emily's behalf, but there is rarely an excuse for taking the law into your own hands and this ain't one of them. As far as I know, it wasn't self defense, and while there was a pattern of abuse, we should still be able to get a murder conviction with the right jury. Please excuse my blunt honesty."

"I'm a real direct person myself, if you haven't already noticed, Mr. Hawthorne. Were you intimate with Emily?"

"Ma'am?"

"Don't play virgin angel with me. Did you sleep with her to get your coveted confession?"

"Mrs. Gillon, we're on the same side here. Why would you ask me such a question? I am not going to discuss my investigative techniques with you. The thing to remember in all of this craziness is that I'm trying to bag Lyle's murderer and end the stigma to your family that he killed himself."

Exhaustion suddenly swept over Sarah like she had been blind-sided by a high-tide wave at the beach. Too much had happened in too short a time and her world had broken apart like a plastic Easter egg in the hands of a second grade bully.

"I'm sorry about that outburst, Mr. Hawthorne," she said wearily. "It's been a very trying eight or ten days for me and I am not myself. I'm sitting here with a brandy bottle in front of me, something I never do. That wasn't the real me talking."

"I understand, Mrs. Gillon and I wouldn't do anything imaginable to add to your worries. Your husband's health is the main thing right now. Everything else can come later." Travis voiced the sentiment, but he wasn't sincere. He wanted to bring Emily and Treat together as quickly as he could.

"When would you like to see Treat. I can't imagine when I'll be able to bring him home from the hospital, but I'll be going back to Atlanta early in the morning."

Travis didn't hesitate.

"Well if you believe he's up to it, Mrs. Gillon, I can probably be up there with Emily tomorrow afternoon, say around 3:30 or maybe even earlier."

"So she has no idea that you are a private detective and have had her under investigation?"

"No ma'am, not that I know of."

"Then she obviously will have no idea why you are bringing her to Atlanta."

"That's right."

"I certainly am not going to mention anything to Treat before you arrive with her unless you think the shock of seeing her might cause him a setback. Maybe I should talk to his doctors about it."

Even as she spoke, Sarah could envision the sudden

sight of Emily sending Treat and his short-circuited, fat-filled heart over the last horizon.

Happy trails, Treat, until we never meet again.

"I'll tell her that we are going to visit one of my friends in the hospital and when we get to the room, I'll come in first to prepare him," Travis said. "She won't know anything until she walks in and sees Treat."

"You call me on my cell phone, if you can, before you get to the hospital, and I'll make sure we don't have any other visitors. My phone might be off because we're in the cardiac area, but I always check my messages regularly."

"That sounds like a plan, Mrs. Gillon. I look forward to meeting you in person."

"It should be a right interesting little reunion, Mr. Hawthorne. Y'all have a safe trip."

By the time Travis finally clicked off with Sarah, Emily was back at their table and was turned in her chair, looking at him inquiringly. He threw his hands in the air in a seemingly perplexed manner and smiled as he strode back to her.

"What was that all about?" she said as he sat down, kissing her on the forehead. "I'm sure your beer is probably warm by now." She studied him. "Well you're certainly looking real pleased about something all of a sudden. Somebody call to say you won the Georgia lottery?"

"No, no, nothing like that."

"Was that the realtor?"

"Yeah, I told her I wasn't selling the place unless they gave me the keys to Fort Knox."

"I think you'd be crazy to sell it, Travis. It's really beautiful in there with the river and the woods and all. Savannah can get loud and obnoxious just like any other city, I don't care how laid back they say it is."

"You're right, Em." He took a sip from his beer. "Whew, that did heat up quick."

"The band will be back from break in a few minutes. Do you want to get a menu or head back to my place or what?"

"Let me think about it a minute."

"Did you see me dancing with that guy? He was drunk as a lord and all hands, but he was harmless. I told him I had a big-muscled boyfriend who was real jealous and he tamed down his act."

"Hey Em, I've got some business to take care of in Atlanta and thought we might make a little trip out of it, if you can get Tuesday off. We could leave in the morning."

"It shouldn't be a problem, Travis. I haven't asked for an extra day off since I started there. Nick is good about stuff like that. He can get one of the college girls to fill in for me. Let's do it. So what's cooking in Atlanta?"

"Oh just some loose ends to tie up with an estate lawyer about my parents' will. Shouldn't take too long, but I gotta go in and sign a couple of documents, I guess."

"That's fine. Maybe we can hit a couple of hot spots out in Buckhead. That's where all the hipsters are, I hear."

"Yeah, maybe, Em, but there's one other thing I got to do. I got a buddy that's in the hospital up there and I promised I'd drop by to see him if I could. Do you mind?"

"Of course not, Travis. You wouldn't be much of a friend if you didn't. Who is he?"

"Really, we're not that close, but he's older and had a heart attack and I'm sure he'd like to see me."

"What, is he a friend of the family or something?"

"You could say that, Em. My daddy used to have some dealings with him." Travis was lying on the fly now and carelessly grabbed a name out of the air. "Name's McKenzie Ellis."

"Now why does that sound so familiar to me? McKenzie Ellis."

Travis realized he had made a mistake. Pierpont was tiny and Emily certainly could have known Ellis. To his chagrin, she quickly made the connection.

"Oh, I know. McKenzie Ellis worked for my ex-father-in-law at the cotton gin in Pierpont - a kind of big black guy, is that him?"

"No, no, not at all. This guy's white as a marshmallow. I think he grew up in New Jersey or somewhere else up north and might even be Jewish. Funny how they would have the same name though."

As if it hadn't been swishing its tail in her face for weeks, Emily was finally sniffing a rat, if ever so slightly. She was certainly intelligent and there was no naivete left from the Lyle years, but her craving for love had made her place blind faith in Travis. She wanted nothing more than the undiluted happiness and romance see saw in other people and had never known, the couples necking on benches in the squares or walking hand in hand or gazing in adoration at each other. She had wanted it all with Travis, but that dream seemed to be vanishing like smoke from a dwindling fire, and now she was not only questioning his love - doubting it, really - but was wondering if he had some ulterior motive.

She was repulsed by the idea that he would lie to her, but the mention of McKenzie Ellis had sown the notion. Still, maybe it was just a wild coincidence that his friend had the same name as the Pierpont cotton ginner and she could certainly wait until the next day when they walked into the man's hospital room and met him in person. This realization quieted her doubts, although deeply rooted in her sensibilities was a fear of losing Travis and a commitment to crawl over burning coals rather than threaten their relationship.

It was an attitude born of desperation and longtime hurt by a cruel keeper and the feelings nurtured in her by Travis' sweet elixir. She only hoped she hadn't been thriving on snake oil.

They ordered cheeseburgers and listened to the Fire-breathing Poodles' last set before walking back to Emily's apartment. She phoned Nick and, as predicted, he gave her Tuesday off without any questions.

She and Travis made plans to hit the road for Atlanta about mid morning on Monday. They would visit his friend and then Travis would fit in a brief appointment with his family's estate lawyer. Emily was getting excited about an overnight trip to the big city.

As they made love that night, Travis knew this would be the last time he would experience these sensations with this woman.

In a few hours it would be a day of reckoning, and both of them would stand before a bedridden grand inquisitor who still wielded great power, a power that had caused Travis to forsake the friend and lover bucking atop him in the silver shadows.

Chapter 12

In the house on LaCourt Street, Sarah would spend the night curled in a fetal ball, her face to the wall, just as she did when Treat was snoring away beside her in his nightly drunken comas. The fact that he wasn't there and was immobilized in cardiac care fifty-something miles away couldn't begin to change her years of habits.

The alarm on her night stand clock was eternally set for 6 a.m. and she would be up in her routine scurry to cook breakfast for a man who, this day, would not stumble down the stairs to harass her about everything, starting with any traces of pulp in his orange juice.

The brandy already had given her a headache and she had gulped two Tylenol before climbing into the big four-poster bed about 9 p.m.

A mental concoction of the liquor, Treat's absence and Travis Hawthorne's revelations made this the most bizarre of the many bizarre evenings Sarah had suffered under this roof. Reaching across Treat's space in the bed felt like a criminal act and this was magnified when she picked up the TV remote that she was never allowed to touch, the buttons sticky from Treat's tar and nicotine fingers. Flicking through the channels without really seeing what was on, she impatiently clicked off the television, leaving her in darkness cut only by a street light's glow. Earlier, she had thrown some fresh clothes into her suitcase for her return to Atlanta.

Monday would be a defining moment in several lives, including hers, it appeared, but if Sarah was supposed to burn with a raging vengeance after hearing Emily's confession, she was yet to be consumed. She had seen Treat's desire for revenge eat away at him like a terrible parasite, and while it seemed that he finally would get his wish, the bounty hunt for Emily was at least partially responsible for his body's implosion.

More than a year had passed since she had seen

Emily, and Sarah wondered if and how she had changed since moving to Savannah. Tomorrow would not be an occasion to judge a new hairstyle or pounds gained or lost or to replay the few good family memories they shared. In all likelihood it would be an ugly, life-shattering encounter when Hawthorne walked into that hospital room with Emily and ripped her heart out for Treat's avenging pleasure.

She knew why Treat wanted to see Emily; he wanted to absorb the hurt and anguished surprise on her face when she found out about what was happening to her. He had always seemed to enjoy the pain and fear that laced her features, like a cat pawing at a wounded sparrow in no particular hurry, and Emily was a long-sought prey finally run to ground. Sarah thought about getting up and listening to the tape again; maybe that would pump her up for Emily's sacrifice. She thought about calling Puggy Lawson's house, just to say hi, and if Marie answered the phone, well, that would just be too damned bad. She thought about calling Travis again to see what other bloody details he had unearthed about her son's death. She thought about calling their church's pastor, even though she and Treat rarely darkened the door most Sundays. Then she decided that it would be best to do nothing and try to get some rest.

Sarah had never believed Lyle would turn a gun on himself - the way he drank, following in his father's cups, certainly could have resulted in an accidental shooting, but never suicide. Lyle didn't have the temperament for it. Conversely, she never believed that Emily had the spine, gumption or inclination to kill a housefly, much less create and carry out a deadly plot against Lyle. They had never been close, but Sarah had noted her daughter-in-law's caring nature with Brandon and in his brief existence had felt comfortable and secure in Emily's motherhood of her grandson.

In Sarah's mind, only a life so unimaginably awful, like she suffered with Treat, could have driven Emily to take a gun to Lyle.

A thousand times she had wished for the courage to do the same to Treat. A thousand times she had not found the backbone to make it more than a gruesome fantasy with no real happy ending.

If Emily indeed had killed Lyle, would God forgive her or would she roast on a spit in perdition for eternity? Sarah had no answer.

On her side, she stared at the slow-moving blades of a ceiling fan, imagining, as she had on so many other nights, that they were Treat's hands coming at her. In minutes she was beyond his reach again, sleep carrying her to a rarely visited nether world where violence slapped her only in nightmares.

Many miles of baked Georgia asphalt separated the players in Emily's fate with the sun's rise on Monday, but, other than Treat, all were soon making a beeline for Atlanta.

The epicenter of it all was Room 322 of Carver Memorial Hospital's cardiac wing where Treat lay, a tough but injured spider waiting for the fly to be delivered to his web. A nurse's aide spoon-fed him cubes of cantaloupe, three orange slices and a slice of toast with margarine. He had passed on the mushy grits.

While he couldn't raise a victorious shout, Treat's eyes were sashaying with pleasure, and it wasn't about his breakfast. Sarah had called him early, an orderly holding the phone to his ear while he listened to her grand news. Travis Hawthorne was bringing Emily to him today, sometime in the afternoon. The investigator would confront her with the evidence and the facts and Treat would watch her squirm and melt into submission. He damned himself for not being able to leap out of bed and pummel her senseless at the very instant that she realized she had been busted. Still, he was forking out big money for this sick sort of pay-per-view event and he planned to savor every millisecond of it.

Emily the fly and Travis lolled in bed until mid morning, Travis trying to keep cool, but watching the clock like an impatient Amtrak conductor. Emily had dreamed of roses, sweeter and brighter than ever before, and royally plump enough for garden club blue ribbons if they had been real.

The rose dreams were frequent, she guessed because of her love for them and the hours she spent on her collages cut from the seed and home and garden catalogs. Still, it seemed they were most vivid before some major event in her life, like her wedding, Brandon's birth or Lyle's death. She did not know what to expect today, hoping that it was merely a fun trip to Atlanta. The nocturnal visions of the roses always soothed her no matter what happened afterward, and she awoke this Monday in a tranquility that ignored or transcended the banshees swirling around her.

Finally they were up and showered and hurriedly packed an overnight bag, Travis relaxing when his truck accelerated onto the interstate access ramp about 11 a.m.

Sarah was on the road as well. When her alarm clock clanged, she had showered quickly and bolted downstairs, Treat still as much in her head as if he was drooling on his down pillow while she slipped on her bathrobe.

Her quick, bare feet met with an unpleasant surprise at the bottom of the stairs, black shards and bits of some of the fractured records spearing into her soles like she had blundered into a patch of sand spurs. She collapsed on the carpet, holding her feet and cursing Treat and Perry Como. After quick first aid, she was back at her immediate chore with the precision of a mess hall sergeant, preparing the coffee, pancakes and sausages and carefully folding the newspaper beside his plate.

She had called Treat while sitting at the kitchen table, staring at his cooling breakfast and listening to the tick-tock of the nineteenth century grandfather clock in the front hallway. She could sense his glee over the phone even if he couldn't talk, and anything, other than baby Brandon, that gave Treat happiness turned her stomach. All of the food would go down the garbage disposal before Sarah checked all the door locks, switched on the security system and limped out to her car.

Emily's peace from her dream roses did not last, and less than hour into their ride she was brimming with questions for Travis.

"So this friend of yours in the hospital, McKenzie Ellis, right? He did business with your dad?"

"Yeah, he sold farm equipment or something in Statesboro. I never knew him that well, but it's only right for me to drop by and see him."

"Sure it is." Emily watched as they passed a tractor trailer loaded with crates of live chickens. "Want me to grab us a few drumsticks for the trip? Based on last night, I think you're more of a breast man."

"Bingo, Em."

"I wonder how a Jewish guy from New Jersey ended up selling farm equipment in a little Georgia town? I'll bet there's a pretty interesting story there." She was probing him now.

"Far as I know, Em, he had Southern relatives. His family must have moved down here when he was a kid, who's to say?"

"Pretty amazing that he has the same name as the man who worked for my father-in-law. Anyway, I think it's real thoughtful of you to go visit him. I'll probably wait outside or in the lobby."

"Oh no, Em, he'd enjoy meeting you, I think. The sight of a pretty girl will perk him up, I'm sure."

"Did you set up an appointment with your lawyers about your folks' will?"

Travis was beginning to feel like he was being quizzed by a savvy defense attorney.

"No, I just have to drop by their office and sign a document or something; it's no big deal."

"You'd think that all that will stuff would already be wrapped up since your parents have been gone for awhile."

"Well I guess they found something in the fine print that they need me to look at. I'll find out soon enough."

As Emily grilled Travis in the witness stand that his pickup seat had become, Sarah was emerging from the elevator onto the cardiac floor after navigating metro Atlanta's concrete mazes to reach the downtown hospital.

Down the shiny corridor she saw a head nurse she knew

only as Mattie checking some charts or other paperwork in the nurses' station near Treat's room. A dark-skinned black woman in starched white, Mattie seemed to be equal parts Marine drill instructor and angel of mercy, every situation dictating which half surfaced. Seeing Sarah, she stepped out into the hallway and greeted her with a warm smile and a quick but genuine hug.

"Your husband seems mighty perky today, Mrs. Gillon. Don't expect any quick miracles, but he's coming along real good. Doctor Sikorsky was in to see him this morning."

"Y'all have done wonders for him and I'm real grateful for that," Sarah replied. "Mattie, I've got a couple of visitors coming to see him this afternoon, will that be okay?"

The nurse hesitated, grimacing.

"I guess so, Sarah. He doesn't need any big surprises or anything, but if it's a relative..."

"It is, it's his former daughter-in-law and we're a real close family. It'll be her and her boyfriend, and I think they might be able to cheer him up."

"We can't let them stay very long, but if you promise to make it a short visit, I'll allow it."

"Oh, they won't stay very long, I can guarantee that."

Walking back into Treat's room after a night's respite was a return to old ways and bad times despite his helplessness. His eyes met hers at the door, emotionless and unfeeling, and Sarah drew into her memories to a long-ago pond bank where her father had hooked a bass and left it flapping out its life in the leathery weeds, the unseeing eyes flecked with dirt.

Treat had no more use for her than she had for him, even in his debilitation, and for a second she contemplated pulling the confession tape from her purse and snapping it in half in front of him. Instead, she plopped into the cushioned, Naugahyde chair a few feet from the foot of his bed and began whipping through her dog-eared magazines that she had almost memorized during the previous week.

Treat's personal circus would arrive in a few hours if Travis Hawthorne was reliable, and she sensed that he would be. Skimming an article about an Italian designer's new line of mascaras, Sarah contemplated how she would react to the private investigator and the sight of Emily's soul disintegrating before them.

Emily's seemingly endless questions and his own jumpiness were getting to Travis by the time he steered onto an exit just west of Macon to find some lunch. His wristwatch was pushing 1 p.m. and with this stop and getting through Atlanta, it might be about 3 p.m. before he reached Carver Memorial.

Standing in a Wendy's parking lot, he called Sarah while Emily was inside ordering their food. He didn't expect to reach her and didn't, but he left a message saying that they were past Macon and should be at the hospital around mid afternoon. Emily watched him through the window, smiling at him when he came in and sat down at the table with her.

"Did you get your lawyer?"

"No, he was out, but his secretary hooked me in to his voice mail. I told him I'd drop by his office sometime in the morning."

"Where should we stay tonight?" she said biting into her burger. Atlanta's your town, not mine, but I'd sure like to party tonight in Buckhead."

"We can do that, Em. We'll get a motel somewhere off the 285 loop. Nothing fancy, mind you."

"As long as there's no silverfish in the bathtub or cooties in the sheets, I'm okay. Honey, you know I'm not the fancy type, at least you should by now."

"I do know that, Em. Hey listen, let's finish up here so we can make tracks."

"You're the boss, Travis. Did you call your friend and tell him you were coming to see him today or are you going to surprise him?"

"It's going to be a big surprise, Em."

Today of all days, Sarah felt that she needed a cigarette. She had smoked some in high school, mainly because other kids were doing it, and all the movie stars she liked seemed to be bathed in blue smoke on the big screen.

Treat had changed that. All her marriage she had

hated the stench, equating it with his sewer breath, and thoughts about how if he didn't kill her directly, the cancer exhaled from his tobacco-barn lungs would cause her slow death.

Her cut-rope nerves were pleading for some solace and a cigarette might be just the pacifier she needed to calm down. Treat was asleep anyway, resting up for the big moment.

She went outside and bummed a Merit from a man among a small cluster of people gathered in a designated smoking area about thirty yards from the hospital's main entrance. She checked her cell phone and listened to Travis' message. Time was short, her palms damp as if moistened by the dwindling seconds.

Much of the casual chatter among the smokers naturally centered on patients being treated at Carver. Chemotherapy, dialysis, infection, more blood work, carotid artery tests - a dozen medical procedures or conditions were encapsulated in their conversations.

As she took a long drag on the cigarette, making herself dizzy in the process, Sarah realized that all of the innocent talk around her was bound by one unbreakable thread, the devotion to and care of loved ones. It was a thread that did not bind Sarah.

The General Johnston Hotel on Peachtree Street, where she and Treat honeymooned, was only blocks away, but no sentimentality moved her and she dreaded going back up to that hospital room where he lay getting better by the instant. She ground the cigarette out with her heel and headed back to wait for their visitors.

The first glimpse of the Atlanta skyline thrusting through the haze excited Emily. She had only been to the city twice in her life, so this was an event.

"I always wanted to come up here and go to a Braves game but I never did," she said, watching the skyscrapers grow slowly. "My mama and me would watch some of the games on TV or listen on the radio and I used to know all the players' names and positions."

"Yeah, I've always liked the Braves too," Travis

answered, watching the increasingly heavy traffic. "I think they're playing the Dodgers or Padres out west starting tonight. If they were at home, maybe we would have gone to see them."

"Maybe next trip. Tonight it's Buckhead."

Travis stayed on I-75 before taking the Georgia Dome exit to reach the hospital. At 3:10 p.m. he drove into the Carver parking deck and found a space on the fourth level. It had been a long, inwardly tense trip for him and even though the main part of his mission was still before him, he was relieved that they had come this far.

"Oh man, does that feel good," he said, getting out of the cab and stretching, his arms over his head.

"Do you know your friend's room number?" Emily said, climbing out of the truck.

"Yeah, I called patient information when we stopped in Macon. He's up on the third floor."

Travis had no definite plans about what to do with Emily after he broke the news to her. She wasn't wanted on criminal charges, at least not yet, so he had no grounds, or even authority, to hold her. Obviously she would not want to stay with him and there was a very real possibility that in her expected anger she would attack him or one of the Gillons. Travis was almost hoping for that scenario - the Atlanta police would become involved then and she could be held on assault charges until D.A. Livingston decided how to proceed.

"Are you sure you don't want me to wait out here, Travis? I could stroll around and chill out for about thirty minutes or whatever time you need."

"No, Em. I want you to come with me. It'll be cooler inside."

"I never liked hospitals. I guess there's no real reason to, unless you're having a baby or getting cured of something."

"Sounds reasonable to me, Em."

Minutes later they were on the elevator to the third floor. Emerging on the cardiac wing, they followed signs toward Treat's lair. Near the nurses' station, Travis stopped, taking her gently by the arm.

"I'll tell you what, Em. You wait right here and I'll go down and make sure he's awake before we go in. I don't just want to barge in, you know?"

"Sure Travis."

The door to Cardiac Room 322 was ajar about two feet and Travis stuck his head in. His first mental image was of Treat lying awake in the bed and an attractive woman reading a magazine in a chair. The television high on its wall mount was tuned to one of the news channels, but the volume was low. A side table and windowsill were crowded with get-well cards, flower arrangements, potted plants and shimmery balloons tethered on ribbons.

Sarah did not initially notice him; someone was always popping in to check Treat's blood pressure or bring in or take away a food tray. When she looked up and saw him, she thought Travis was another nurse or orderly.

"Mrs. Gillon?"

"Yes."

"I'm Travis Hawthorne. Do you mind if I come in?"

Sarah glanced at Treat before replying and saw the wide-eyed excitement in his eyes.

"I'd say my husband is glad to see you, Mr. Hawthorne. He's got the look of a Pekingese in heat. I just hope his eyes don't pop out of his skull."

She rose, walked over and shook hands with Travis.

"It's good to meet you in person, ma'am. How is our patient here? Treat, how you doing?"

Treat blinked once for yes and raised his left arm slightly to give a thumbs up. It was basically a win-one-for-the-Gipper movie moment, but both Travis and Sarah knew that in real life Treat would never pass for a Jimmy Stewart good guy.

Even now he was in more comfortable company with a Hitler or Attila the Hun or Pol Pot, the only glitch on his resume of misery being that he was responsible for the torture and death sentence of only one instead of hundreds of thousands. Sarah firmly believed that if cruel opportunity had knocked for Treat he would have answered with a body count of innocents and paved their driveway with a paste of skulls and cement to match humanity's vilest.

"Are you alone, Mr. Hawthorne?"

"No ma'am, I didn't come all this way for nothing. This is going to be difficult for all of us, but we'll get through it."

"Where is my daughter-in-law? Let's get this awful ordeal over with."

"I asked her to wait out in the hall, ma'am. Now you realize this is going to be a huge shock to her when she sees y'all, so be prepared for anything."

"So she has no clue about all this?"

"She might have a clue, but that's about it. She was asking me a bunch of questions on the way up here, so I'm guessing that she has got wind something's going on."

Treat's eyes were bouncing between them as if watching a tennis match, his face the color of Thanksgiving cranberries. He hated that she, or anyone else, was in control of any situation, and this was the one instance that he craved power more than ever. It was as if he had a football stadium seat on the fifty-yard line, but was sitting behind Marge Simpson.

Still, his long-awaited prey was merely a few feet away and if his anger toward Sarah didn't detonate his heart he could savor one of his greatest victories with the first step of Emily's downfall.

"I'll call her in," Travis said, and he stepped out into the hallway and motioned for Emily. She appeared in the doorway with a cheerful smile meant for McKenzie Ellis, and to the end of her days Sarah would never forget how her bright countenance clouded in confusion and fear when she saw them.

"What, what is this?" she stammered. "Travis?"

Travis was all business now.

"Emily, you certainly know the Gillons."

"Of course. They were my in-laws. Why are we here?"

"It's real simple why we're here, Em. I'm sorry I had to mislead you, but I'm a private investigator hired by Mr. Gillon to look into the death of your husband Lyle. I've been gathering evidence over the past few months."

"What are you talking about? How could you do this to me?"

Emily felt faint and slumped against the wall, tears filling her eyes. Treat's demented grin as he watched her told her that this was not some cruel joke. Her mind raced back through her time with Travis, the things they had done together, their intimacy, all faked.

Anger, hurt and bewildered shock vied for control of her.

"Now you just stay calm, Emily, there's no need for any trouble. You know as well as I do that you confessed to killing Lyle. What we intend to do is turn over my evidence to the Bratton County district attorney so that he can begin criminal proceedings against you on a possible murder charge."

Emily glared at Travis, who was standing a few feet away from her.

"Now I don't have the legal authority to hold you and you haven't officially been charged with anything, but I'd advise you not to flee or try to leave the state. That could result in additional charges…"

"How could you do this to me, Travis? How could you lure me in like you truly cared for me?" Her voice was shaky but rising. "Private investigator? Do you screw all the people you're investigating and tell them how you love them? Buy them roses and try to make them feel like your princess, or was that all just reserved for me?"

"It was a job, Em. Maybe I made some mistakes and maybe I told you some half-truths, but the bottom line is that if you hadn't murdered your husband, none of this would have happened."

Emily snapped.

"Fuck you and your bottom line!" she screamed. "I did what I did to survive!" She covered her face with her hands and sobbed, watery mascara stinging her eyes.

"I think I've seen and heard enough about all this, Mr. Hawthorne," Sarah spoke up. "Did I mention that I called this morning and cancelled the check my husband wrote to Pinnacle Investigations?"

"Ma'am?" Travis' face twisted in a frown. "You can't do that, Mrs. Gillon."

"I can and did. It was from a joint account and the

check is no more. You're not getting paid for doing nothing."

Treat's facial color had gone from cranberries to cherry-bomb red now and he had the look of one of the frogs to which he had force-fed lit firecrackers as a kid.

"Doing nothing, Mrs. Gillon?" Travis' anger was mounting. "How can you say such a stupid thing when you have a tape of this woman admitting that she blew your son away with his best shotgun?"

"I don't know what you're talking about, Mr. Hawthorne. My son unfortunately committed suicide and that was the ruling by all involved - the sheriff, the coroner and everyone else - when it happened. I suggest you let him, and all of us, rest in peace."

Travis cocked his head and studied Sarah through narrowed eyes.

"I've put together a strong case that Emily killed Lyle. Doesn't that mean anything to you?"

"You evidently didn't hear me, Mr. Hawthorne. I appreciate your concern, but there really is nothing left to be said. You fight me on this and I'll chew you up and spit you out."

Sarah blew a slow, seductive kiss to her husband.

"Good-bye, Treat. I sincerely hope that's the kiss of death for you. God knows you deserve it."

She then walked over and embraced Emily.

"Come on, sweetie, dry your eyes and let's get out of here. We've got a lot of catching up to do."

Emily didn't hear her, watching Treat with the eyes of a cheetah intent on a deathly wounded wildebeest. He and his seed had lorded over her for all these years and she could almost feel her press-on nails embedding and breaking off in his flesh as she gripped his crimson throat.

"Mrs. Gillon, can I see you out in the hallway for just a second?" Travis said. "I think we can clear all this up."

Sarah shrugged. "Not that it's going to have any bearing on my decision, but sure." She clutched Emily by the shoulders and looked into her face, but Emily averted her gaze.

"I'll be right outside here if anybody needs me," Travis said. "Mr. Gillon? Em?" Neither acknowledged that he was even in the room. "I'll take that as a no or a not right now."

He wheeled and disappeared out the door, Sarah following.

With their departure, Emily and Treat knew their own stare-down was over, hatred crackling over the few feet between them like a telegraph line to and from insanity.

The steady beep of a medical monitor and the measured drip of an IV were the last hourglass grains to finality, and Emily did not hesitate, the raised voices of Sarah and Travis swizzling her mind as she grabbed a spare pillow from a chair and nimbly moved to the bedside.

The wildness in Treat's eyes before the pillow covered her face reminded Emily of Lyle's expression when the shotgun barrel filled his mouth. Like father, like son, it had always been, and so it seemed fitting to Emily, her rationale woven amid her anger, that this piece of white trash could be taken out like his spawn, both by her hand.

His right arm flailed toward her in a punching motion like Sarah had seen many times, but Emily used her body weight to hold it down, her leverage enough to overpower. The pillow was made of light, cheap foam and its linen case was white and sterile smelling with the Carver Memorial logo on it and beneath it Treat sucked frantically for any oxygen amid the threads.

Emily shoved downward as hard as she could, one of the bedside machines bleating the alarm of failing vital signs. She knew she had only moments before nurses and others rushed in to try to revive Treat. The thought added power to her hands, and she tried to push his face through the bed, to the floor and into hell itself.

All of Treat's monitors were going crazy now, like cuckoo clocks chirping for death, and the energy and motion under the pillow and starched sheet suddenly ceased.

From the hallway, Emily could hear a nearing commotion, the controlled alarm of hospital personnel trained to save life, but able to shrug off a flat line by coffee break. The punching arm lay outstretched and motionless now, never to strike again and Emily eased her pressure on the pillow as Nurse Mattie burst into Room 322, followed by two cardiac techs.

"Oh, my dear Lord!" one of them blurted as they surrounded and tried to resuscitate Treat, Maggie flinging the pillow from his face.

Sarah and Travis stared in from the doorway, their faces masks of horror and astonishment.

Emily saw none of it. Her attention was on a spectacular arrangement of pink Gallicas in a green-glass vase on the windowsill – a get-well-soon bouquet for Treat from someone in Pierpont.

Amid the turmoil in the room, the roses basked in their own royalty, and she gingerly pulled one of the long stems from the vase, closing her eyes and savoring the aroma of its elegance.

About the Author

Derek is from South Carolina and began writing in the newspaper business. And grew from that. Today he has 14 published books! *Glory Yards* - Rutledge Hill Press, 1993 Chronicles the football rivalry between the Universities of Georgia and Florida, year by year since 1904. *Civil War Savannah* - Frederic Beil, Publisher. 1997. A history of that Southern seaport and her people during the conflict.

The Sentinels - Frederic Beil, Publisher. 2001. My first novel explores a ghostly Civil War submarine traveling through time. Lee's Last Stand - Sailor's Creek, Virginia, 1865 - White Mane Publishing, 2004. A nonfiction looks at the Confederate Army of Northern Virginia's final battle before Robert E. Lee's Appomattox surrender.

The Gallant Dead - Stackpole Books, 2005. Nominated for the 2006 Lincoln Prize, this book focuses on the 123 Union and Confederate generals killed in combat and the circumstances of their deaths.*In The Lion's Mouth* - Hood's Tragic Retreat from Nashville, 1864 - Stackpole Books, 2011. An examination of the last act in the Confederacy's ill-starred Tennessee campaign. *Sumter After the First Shots* – The Untold Story of America's Most Famous Fort until the End of the Civil War – Stackpole Books, 2015. Selection of the History Book Club. *Kamallah's Bracelet* – Frederic Beil, Publisher, 2015. Novel set in Georgia in the 1960s. *Gettysburg: South Carolinians in Battle* – McFarland Publishing, 2021. Nonfiction account of some 5,000 Carolinians in the three-day battle. *Bloody Savannah* – The City's Most Violent Era as Seen by a Crime Reporter – Exposit (an imprint of McFarland Publishing), 2023. A true-crime memoir of my police-beat-decade or so in Savannah, Georgia. *Revolutionary War Camden* was recently released. Derek is also an artist.

9 781963 661439